MW00745521

CARRY
ME
BACK

CARRY

ME

BACK

Laura Watt

ST. MARTIN'S PRESS
NEW YORK

Library of Congress Cataloging-in-Publication Data

Watt, Laura.
    Carry me back : a novel / by Laura Watt.
      p. cm.
    ISBN 0-312-15075-X
    I. Title.
    PS3573.A8587C37   1997
    813'.54—dc20   96-30674
                                         CIP

First Edition: February 1997

10 9 8 7 6 5 4 3 2 1

For Joe

1

The Greyhound bus terminal in downtown Tulsa smelled of diesel fumes, cigarette smoke, and slightly rank bodies. Not a whiff of Dial soap anywhere. Hair pomade, the kind old black men favor, and sour apple jawbreakers, maybe, and a hint of dirty diaper coming off the kid down at the end of the row.

It smelled like freedom to me. New odors, not prison odors. I was fresh out of the state penitentiary down at McAlester. About six hours since I walked out the front gate. Four years inside. I did what they said I did, but I was justified. You've heard of justifiable homicide. This was justifiable kneecap shattering. I'm still glad I did it, but sorry the law doesn't pin a medal on a man for protecting what's his.

My name's Webb Allen Pritchard. What happened was, this guy came to steal my tools. So I shot him in the leg with my deer rifle. I wasn't trying to kill him. And he didn't die, he just lay there, screaming and bleeding all over the AstroTurf beneath my carport. I'm the one who called police. I didn't run. I sat there in my La-Z-Boy outside my home at the lovely Shang-Grah-Lah Trailer Park in east Tulsa, with a bottle of Budweiser and the rifle across my lap and watched that asshole roll around. Man, he bled. Steal my tools, will you? You won't be stealing much from your wheelchair, friend.

I represented myself in court. The public defender's office told me not to do it, but you know how it is. I felt I could tell this story better than anyone else. Those tools were my livelihood. I worked construction. This jerk came around breaking into my place after dark. I was out, but I came home early. Caught him red-handed. He had a record, of course. Breaking and entering. What a surprise.

They tried to make me the bad guy. Dug up my past. That's how it works these days. But my record's nothing next to his. I'm a Boy Scout compared to him. A couple of DUIs, one misdemeanor disturbing the peace, and that time they pulled me over and found one joint in the ashtray. Now this guy, he was in the state reformatory as a kid, in and out, in and out, then one long half-assed crime spree after he graduated from the juvie program. He was pretty stupid, too; he kept getting caught.

He rolled into court, Mr. Ironside, and because he's a crip they just fell all over themselves, made him out to be some kind of disabled saint, his life's ruined, blah blah blah. He winked at me when he took the stand. Winked at me! You sonofabitch, I'll blow away your other worthless kneecap.

Well, they didn't see things my way. I got eight years for attempted murder and served half of it. My tools got stolen anyway, while I was awaiting trial, and my good neighbors at the Shang-Grah-Lah carted off my beloved La-Z-Boy.

The crip, he went straight for a while, conned himself into some bullshit program where they make crocheted keychains, but his true nature got the better of him and he tried to rob a 7-Eleven. Got his wheelchair stuck in the door. Cry me a river. I wished they would've sent him down to McAlester, where I headed the welcome committee, but he wound up in some facility for other criminal crips. I wonder if they put little speed bumps out in the yard, you know, to prevent escapes. Anyway, he's still in there, Mr. Ironside, and I'm Mr. Outside, breathing free.

Here's what I have with me: one suitcase, appropriately cheap and battered and covered with duct tape, as no one ever comes out of the joint with matching leather monogrammed Gucci luggage; a Sony Walkman; and this new banjo, Lil Darlin'. Only she isn't exactly new.

I found her in a pawnshop down on Greenwood. Went there as soon as I hit Tulsa a couple hours ago. Guy in the joint told me about this place where they have nice instruments cheap. I went in there, past an old sign at the door that said NO LIQUOR SERVED TO INDIANS, and asked the guy if he had any banjos. Well, he had all kinds: cheap little Japanese models all the way up to some vintage Mastertones.

How about something in between, I said. How much you got to spend, he asked. When I told him, he said hold on. He went down some stairs, and came back up carrying a really beat-up banjo case. Didn't look too promising.

Here's one you might like, he said. Got some history to it. He opened it up and there she was, the love of my life. An old Gibson, but not a Mastertone. Kind of cobbled together, you could tell. Somebody had built and rebuilt her over the years. Mahogany neck and resonator, rubbed to a satin finish. Strange kind of flower inlay on the fingerboard. And the head was made of hide, not plastic, and real old, probably the original, all yellowed and stained. Written on it in a kind of old-fashioned script were these words: *Doc Mullican's Traveling Hayride & Medicine Show.*

This banjo had character. She had a story to tell, and I wanted to hear it. I lifted her out of the case and cradled her in my arms. You're my Lil Darlin', I said. We belonged together. Her strings were shot but I could hear—no, feel—her mellow tone.

Where'd you get this, I asked the guy.

Old guy brought that in about three years ago, he said. Told us it'd belonged to a friend of his who died. That's all I know.

I paid cash for it and walked on over to the bus station.

She weighed almost fifteen pounds—more—when she was in the case. I just love to hand banjos to people who don't know anything about banjos, which is practically anybody. Just casually say, Here, and watch them try to handle it. It's like dropping a bowling ball in their palm. There was one time, pretty recently, where a man killed his wife by smacking her in the head with his banjo. People laughed about it, and it sounds funny, but if you got hit with a true banjo, a bowling ball on a stick, it would not be funny. It would be, well, homicide. Maybe I should've hit the crip with Lil Darlin', if I'd had her then. No, come to think of it, she might have been damaged.

This banjo was going to be my ticket to a new life. Yeah, I know, I've heard all the reasons why this is stupid from my sister, Dot Pritchard McGee. But she's wrong as rain. It's going to work. I trust myself. I think.

When I worked construction, I also played in a bar band at night, the Wiley Coyotes. Country-rock. I played rhythm guitar. We'd do covers of "Born to Be Wild" and "Sweet Home Alabama," stuff like that. Eagles tunes. Lynyrd Skynyrd. Hank Williams, Jr. Good stuff,

3

but not what I was putting on the tape deck when I was alone. What I like is what I call real country music. They don't play it on the radio anymore. Haven't for decades. Wait, that's not quite true; there's an all-night trucker show you can pick up all across America, and on Saturday nights in the real wee hours, around three A.M., this guy plays Gid Tanner & the Skillet Lickers, Uncle Dave Macon, the Carter Family, Jimmie Rodgers. String band music. Early Grand Ole Opry. Then he'll move up a bit and get into Webb Pierce and Kitty Wells and Ernest Tubb and Hank Williams without the Junior.

That's the kind of music that speaks to me. Not the soulless, computerized shit that passes for country these days. When Ole Hank sings about that lonesome whippoorwill, I hear it, and I get lonesome, and when Bill Monroe gets to chopping on that old mandolin of his, I am truly moved. There's a lot of the blues in bluegrass. Of course, being a banjo player, it's Earl Scruggs who gives me a reason to live. Thank you, Earl.

I was born in 1953. The same year Hank Williams died. When I was a kid, all I listened to was rock 'n' roll. Country to me was something hokey to make fun of, like Porter Wagoner's Nudie suits. He was on TV on Saturday afternoons. He'd step out from behind some hay bales with this fantastic blond pompadour about four inches high, his sequined suit just about blinding you, and launch into some serious nasality. I couldn't stand it. But it was fascinating. He had Dolly Parton with him then; she was just a little ol' country gal with blond hair even bigger than his. That's probably why they parted ways. Battle of the Big-Haired Blondes.

Anyway, when I was in high school, I had this friend who was a bit progressive. He would listen to all kinds of music, not just Top Forty. One day I was over at his house and we were playing records. After we heard some Jimi Hendrix, he pulled out another album and said, Here, listen to this guy, he's a real original. And he put on a Doc Watson album. I was blown away. I had no idea anybody could play guitar like that. Notes flying out like a flock of sparrows. You could hear his fingers sliding over the strings to reach the chord, and he'd just nail it. And his voice . . . mountain minor . . . it gave me the shivers and I didn't know exactly why.

Now, I was vaguely aware of folk music. I had the obligatory Peter, Paul & Mary album, and I had an old cheap guitar and I'd play along. I was so stupid I thought Peter, Paul & Mary wrote "Blowin' in the

4

Wind" and "The Times They Are A'Changin'." Who read the fine print? I was just a kid. So when Doc came into my life, he changed it. I began to haunt used-record stores and explore the unknown world of old-time country music. A rough, dark, inviting world full of cheatin' and drinkin' and bar fights and death, but also a place where God and redemption and Mama and home were held in high esteem. You could sing a song about a man who drowned his girl and used her finger bones and hair to make a fiddle, and follow it up with a sweet little hymn. There was lots to learn from. Bluegrass. Old-timey. Cowboy songs. Bob Wills and western swing. Mountain music. I loved it all.

None of this obsession helped my love life. Linda Townsend, head cheerleader, she of the long chestnut hair and deep green eyes and rich daddy, just didn't understand what I saw in Gid Tanner & the Skillet Lickers. I quickly learned not to bring up my musical tastes too early in any relationship.

My sister, Dot, kept my record collection safe while I was in prison. She understood what it meant to me. She put it in a downstairs closet instead of the garage because I told her heat and cold would warp the vinyl.

All the time I was inside the joint, I kept my chops up on a crappy old banjo they had down there. Just to entertain myself, mainly, but then I started having ideas. They kept it locked up with a couple of other instruments in a cabinet in the library. I'd go get it every evening after supper, and pick away.

Soon, a couple of other guys joined me on guitar and fiddle, and we had a regular little prison string band going. For them, it was just a way to pass the time and forget what a shithole we were in; for me, it was part of my grand plan.

I wasn't going back into construction. Nossir. And I wasn't going back to the Wiley Coyotes, either, or any other bar band. I was going to go it alone playing the kind of music I loved. Hit the road with a fine new instrument and play the festival circuit. Ladies and gentlemen, put your hands together for Webb Pritchard.

"Are you nuts?" Dot said when I informed her of this career move via prison telephone. It was obvious she didn't see the potential. "You can't make enough money to eat that way. Nobody listens to that kind of music except you. It's a stupid idea."

"Thanks for your support," I said. "I'll send you free tickets to the

Opry when I'm on. Maybe I'll introduce you to Reba."

"You'd better go talk to Mr. Shively." My ex-foreman.

"Nope. When I get out, I'm coming by your place, and you'd better have some decent food on the table." Dot was a great cook. "I'm dying on this shit in here."

"OK. How about some turkey roll and Jell-O?"

"Forget it. How about some real roast beef and mashed potatoes and gravy and strawberry rhubarb pie?"

"What happened to the vegetarian phase?"

"Uh, I'll get back on it. It was too hard to maintain in here."

"I could make you a nice nut loaf. Or tofu bake."

"Roast beef, woman. Rare. And pie."

That was a couple of months ago. Now I was on my way to Dot's. It's a long way from Tulsa to Montrose, Colorado. But I don't mind buses. Most people hate 'em. Me, I like sitting up high and watching the world roll by through tinted windows. I hate to fly. The way I see it, if the bus breaks down, you sit by the side of the road till the mechanic or the tow truck shows up. If the plane breaks down, you're basically dead.

"Hey, mister, what's in there?"

I looked up. I must have dozed off. A little kid was standing in front of me, pointing at the black banjo case patched with duct tape.

"It's a banjo."

"What's that?"

So I showed him. I snapped the locks and lifted the lid and let that wonderful smell seep out; pressed velvet and light oil and wood. Lil Darlin' gleamed softly.

"Wow. What's it sound like?"

"Like rippling lightning, son. Go get yourself some Earl Scruggs records and you'll find out." I snapped the lid shut.

He trotted back to his people. They eyed me suspiciously. They didn't know from Earl Scruggs. But I probably looked like a convict. Or a pervert or something.

Suddenly my back hurt from the hard plastic chair. One of the wonderful side effects of working construction. Just then, the P.A. system crackled to life.

"The 2:40 bus to Denver is now departing from door four."

I grabbed my suitcase and picked up Lil Darlin'. She felt light as a feather.

* * *

Did I say I liked buses? Hmmm. Sixteen hours to Denver, and we must
have stopped at every wide spot in the road across Kansas. All the way
I sat next to this old black man on his way to Las Vegas. He wore red
head to toe—even his shoes were red. Boy, where do you find red
shoes? He kept flashing his wad at me, probably a couple of hundred
dollars, all small bills, winking and saying how after he won at the
blackjack tables he was gonna go spend his winnings on a fine woman.
And he knew just where to get one, too. Did I want to come along?
I let him yammer.

A slight layover in the Mile High City, and then another bus
through the mountains and down to Montrose. Dot met me at the station.

She looked great. Dot was always kind of heavy, but she was one
of those women who really couldn't look any other way, and she carried it well. She was three years older than me. Married, two kids in
high school. Her husband, Vern, was a salesman at the local John
Deere dealership. He'd always said he would've blown away the guy's
kneecap, too. Didn't hold my prison time against me.

"Where's that roast beef?" I squeezed her tight and kissed her neck.
Tabu talcum powder, like always.

"In the oven. Come on."

They lived outside of town, in a big frame house on eleven acres.
I'd been there many times. Dot's vegetable garden was the stuff of
dreams. It's hard growing things in Colorado; rocky soil, wind, dry air
and the cold make it so. But Dot managed to bring forth the kind of
goodies I only used to see in the Miracle Gro ads on TV.

I stood out in the garden and surveyed her handiwork. I like gardens.

"We having corn?"

"On the cob. You've lost weight. You look like shit, by the way."

"Thanks. So do you."

"Grandma left you some money."

Out of the blue. Just like that. I pondered.

"Yeah? How much?"

"Fifteen thousand."

I swallowed. A dozen crazy things flashed through my mind, but
I knew instantly what I would spend it on.

7

"If I were you, I'd put it away and watch it grow," she said, lighting up a Merit. "We put our share toward the kids' college."

"Yeah, well, I'm not you. I have to think about this." Her smoke bothered me. "Can you please hold that thing downwind, for Chrissakes?"

She grinned and switched it to the other hand. We stood there awhile in silence, watching the corn plants bob in the breeze. Then we went inside to eat.

One day a week, Dot put in a half day at the *Carbon Copy*, the little newspaper in the even littler town of Carbon. Her title was Food Editor, but what she really did was type in a couple of recipes and sort the mail. The *Carbon Copy* laid claim to one distinction: It had a famous movie critic. Ed Dittmer was a fraud. He was just a guy from the county who ran a few head of cattle and sometimes plowed his neighbors' roads for a few dollars. He liked to think he held some sort of official status because of this, and acted like he did, but actually he just had a blade on the front of his truck. Ed fancied himself a movie expert because he'd seen an awful lot of movies and read a whole raft of movie trivia books. Who was Alan Ladd's stand-in in *Shane*, and shit like that. I used to quiz him, and he'd never slip up.

"Ed," I'd say, perusing the trivia book, "who played the sheriff in *Psycho?*" Practically a bit part. "John McIntire," he'd reply in about two seconds flat. Looking nonchalant. Ed hated Woody Allen movies. "Only New York Jews can understand 'em," he'd say. "If there are any New York Jews here in Carbon, I haven't met 'em."

So he had this bogus column in the *Carbon Copy*. One day, he gave a rave review to the truly wretched *Howard the Duck*, a film not widely considered one of Hollywood's strongest moments. "One of the Year's Ten Best!" he wrote. And somebody somewhere must have seen this issue of the *Carbon Copy*, because those very words soon turned up in ads for the movie.

"One of the Year's Ten Best!"—Ed Dittmer, *Carbon Copy*. It ran in *The New York Times*.

Ed quickly realized he was on to something. So he began to sell his favorable opinion. No matter how bad the film, Ed Dittmer would find something to like about it—for a price. Of course, all this was under the table, so to speak. Give him a movie like *Ninja Androids from Hoboken* and Ed would write, "Better than *Star Wars*!" Now, part of the review might not be quite so glowing, but he'd put the good stuff up front. In the ads, the rave part would be in huge type, and his name, Ed Dittmer, would be in type so small you'd need a magnifying glass to read it.

According to Dot, these mysterious envelopes would arrive at the paper pretty regularly from California, addressed to Ed, and soon after each one appeared there'd be a review that just couldn't be true. Before too long Ed added a carport onto his place, and nobody could figure out how he paid for it. The owner of the paper, Riley Skidmore, didn't care because Ed plowed his road for free. And Riley had a bad road.

Dot and I went into town together a few days after I arrived. I had to go to the bank and she had to type in recipes at the paper. We went to the paper first.

Carbon lay a few miles from Montrose. One street, basically. The paper's office was on that street, in a little storefront. Venetian blinds covering the windows. Not miniblinds, but those wide, dusty ones. I guess Carbon was stuck in a time warp. Ed was the only one there, busy typing in a review.

"Whatcha writing, Ed?" I asked him.

He looked up. "When did you get out?" No howdy do, nothing.

"A few days ago. Don't worry, I'm not armed."

I swung around behind him and leaned over his shoulder. The top of the page read TRUCK MANIA. Below that: "There hasn't been a better road picture since Hope and Crosby."

"Really, Ed? Who's in it?"

He looked defensive. "Tab Hunter and Gloria Loring."

"Wow. That oughta be good for a new driveway," I said. "Or maybe new drapes. Doesn't your wife have a hankering for new drapes?"

He flinched. "It happens to be a pretty decent movie. But you wouldn't know, would you, having been locked up for so long."

"No, I wouldn't know. All they let us watch was Robert Schuller's *Hour of Power* on Sunday morning. But I don't think I've seen Tab Hunter on the cover of *People* magazine lately."

I waited around while Dot typed in her Apple Crumb Delight. I could vouch for it; we'd had some the night before. She took care of

9

some of Riley's paperwork, and we were off to the Montrose Bank.

"I really wish you wouldn't spend Grandma's money this way," she said as she swung the ancient Buick onto the county road. She swerved to avoid a rabbit.

"It's not Grandma's money, it's mine. If you think about it, it makes sense. I'm buying my independence."

"You're buying a foolish dream."

"I won't be in your hair anymore."

"You don't have to do this to be out of my hair. And you're not in my hair. A little underfoot, maybe."

It didn't take long to withdraw the fifteen thousand. It made a huge wad that made my wallet as fat as a stuffed catfish.

Next, we drove over to Wally's, the biggest used-car dealer in six counties. Wally had everything from old VW bugs to pickups to a $45,000 Range Rover somebody lost in a divorce. That wasn't what I was after. Dot and I prowled the lot, looking. I finally found it: a little motor home, kinda road battered but not too bad. Nine years old, 82,400 miles on it. Basic tan. It had a stove, a sink, a fridge, a bunk, a fold-out table, and a toilet. No shower. Orange shag carpeting halfway up the walls. Cigarette burns on the paneling. Of course, the main thing was, it had a tape deck that actually worked. A real rarity. I sat up front in the captain's chair and spun that big ol' wheel around and looked out through that great wide windshield. America, here I come. Wally was asking $16,000. Gimme a break. With the cash in hand, I dickered him down to $12,750.

It was like driving a houseboat. I had to take the corners pretty slow. I followed Dot back to the house, doing about twenty-five. It felt strange, driving. I hadn't driven in four years. As a younger man, I might've felt like jumping on a motorcycle or buying a hot little Camaro, but now, commandeering a widebody felt just right. I had a home. It was mine. I was free.

At four in the morning, I woke up and pulled on some jeans. I made the bed real neat, and slipped downstairs in the dark. The house was completely quiet. I pulled a hundred-dollar bill out of my wallet and left it on the dining room table where she'd see it.

The RV was chilly inside, and stale. I stowed Lil Darlin' where she wouldn't fly around, settled a box of tapes on the console next to me and started the engine. I backed out and slowly rolled down the long dirt driveway. Turned south onto the county road. I looked back. The house hadn't stirred. I dug for a tape and found what I needed. It might as well be Doc.

The first notes filled the cab. "Highway of Sorrow." Jesus, I hope not, I thought, and headed for Telluride.

2

I tried to stay focused on the music as I headed down to the San Juans, but my thoughts kept staying to women.

I'd had my share. You might think they were all honky-tonk angels with press-on nails and sweet little heart tattoos between their shoulder blades, graduates of the local beauty college, and you'd be wrong. Well, OK, there were a few of those. But the ones I loved were not like that. They weren't lady lawyer types, either. No, the ones I loved were soft and gentle but smart and sassy, and of course they understood about the music. And there was one serious lapse in judgment. I'll get to her in a minute.

I married Lynn when we were both about twenty-five. She had light brown hair and this unbelievably terrific smile. We met in the downtown Tulsa library. The big main branch. I had developed a taste for Raymond Chandler mysteries. She was sitting at a table, poring over a book on the history of magic. I slunk around the stacks, keeping my eye on her for at least twenty minutes before I screwed up enough courage to go sit down across from her.

God, she was pretty. At first I was casual, glued to my Philip Marlowe. But then I inquired about the book she was looking at (boy, I'm a clever one sometimes), and we took off from there.

Suffice it to say we had four good years. Then it started to fall apart, as these things are apt to do. I went one way and she went another.

We never had kids. She kept saying she wasn't ready yet, and that was fine with me.

Last I heard, Lynn was living somewhere in the Pacific Northwest. Running a quilt store.

After that, I ran through a string of women who weren't good for me. The fun ones. Dot always knew right off the bat. She'd meet them once and make the dead-on prediction. Fortunately, I didn't marry any of them.

Then I met Sandy.

She was a barmaid working on a degree in computer something-or-other. She wanted to get out of the bar business and start up a desktop publishing company. Funniest woman I ever met. Made me laugh so hard I'd blow the beer right out my nose. We moved in together and she taught me how to cook. To this day I make four dishes I'd be proud to serve anybody: vegetarian chili (mine's not sweet like some—it has a kick to it), cheese enchiladas with bitter minced onion, roasted Cornish game hens stuffed with wild rice dressing, and pizza made from scratch. The dough and everything. Beyond that, hand me the Lean Cuisine.

I taught her to play the fiddle. Kind of a joke, really, because I don't exactly play the fiddle. No instrument sounds worse in unsure hands. You can strum a guitar, hold down a simple chord and make it sound nice. You can pick a banjo without knowing anything and it won't be too bad because it's tuned to an open chord. You can put two fingers down on a mandolin neck and brush the strings and no one will leave the room. But a clueless fiddle player has got to be the worst. The sound can only be compared, unfavorably, to a cat being run over by a front-end loader. "Twinkle, Twinkle, Little Star" is probably about six weeks down the road for the beginning fiddler. That's how hard it is. So together, Sandy and I struggled with it. She got better quicker. The pupil outran the teacher. We did duets, me on banjo and her on fiddle.

And we did get married. By this time, I was thirty-two. Ready again. We bought a little house in Tulsa and settled down. For some reason, four years seems to be the limit with me and women. I don't know, things start out great, then move into a kind of smooth routine, then the rocks appear, then bigger rocks and bigger rocks and finally the crash. In this case, it was another man. Sandy had finished her degree, quit the bar business and gone into desktop publishing, like she'd hoped. She took on a partner, this guy who also worked out of his home. They put out business brochures, annual reports and newsletters, things like that. Not being a computer nerd myself, I didn't know about E-mail. Their little electronic romance was hotter than a pistol before I even had a clue. It was well beyond the screen by the time I found out.

I was so pissed I didn't even want to try to patch things up. Fuck it. I moved out, and into the trailer at the Shang-Grah-Lah. She served me with divorce papers five months later. She served me! I didn't contest it, and that was that.

About two weeks after I moved into the Shang-Grah-Lah, bad news moved in next door. It was one of those things you look back on and decide it was a "learning experience." Her name was Rhonda. Big boobs, tight tank tops and a foul mouth. A winning combination.

She kept eyeballing me as I went about my business. I knew she'd come over eventually. Sure enough, one Saturday afternoon I was out in the La-Z-Boy, having an afternoon nap. Something nudged my foot. I came to, and there she was, standing there smiling at me. Holding out a Budweiser.

"Hi."

"Hi."

"What's your name?"

"Webb. What's yours?"

"Rhonda. Rhonda Harlan. Webb your first name?"

She was just twenty-three, a dangerous age. Already divorced twice, with two little kids. They lived with their grandma, because Rhonda really couldn't be bothered. Her life was already so full of excitement and tragedy, children would have pushed things over the brink.

"See here?" She pulled the side of her mouth out, pointing to a gap in her teeth. "That's where that fuckin' asshole Eugene hit me so hard he knocked my tooth right out. The dentist is building me a fake tooth. Then the hole won't show no more."

"That's wonderful. Where's Eugene now?"

"In the county lockup. Fucker can't make his bail."

"Glad to hear it."

"Hey, wanna go dancing tonight? I know a place. You ever go to Wild Willie's?"

Warning bells were going off absolutely everywhere. I should have said no thank you, pretty gap-toothed lady, and turned her around in the direction of her trailer and gone inside my own and locked the door and drawn the shades and settled in for an afternoon of Andy Griffith reruns.

"Sure. Eight o'clock?"

She twirled around in my tiny yard. Such a kid. "All right! I gotta go do my hair. See you at eight."

She hopped off like some hyperactive rabbit, and I was left to ponder the supreme stupidity of my decision.

I knew Wild Willie's. I'd been thrown out of Wild Willie's before. Not for anything bad. They just weren't too tolerant of fistfights on the dance floor.

I behaved myself that night, and the second night, too, but the third night the bad karma that swirled around Rhonda Harlan came home to roost at Wild Willie's. We were only on our third or fourth beers when you-know-who showed up. I wasn't about to let him do any dental work on me, so I swung first. Eugene was a crazy little fucker, all right, kicking me with his pointy-toed cowboy boots. Ouch. After about two seconds of that, I couldn't take it any longer, and I kneed him in the groin. Down he went. Out the door I went.

I watched for him around the Shang-Grah-Lah for days afterward, but he never showed up. Rhonda avoided me. Finally one day, these two boys came around. Big boys. Mean-looking boys. One of them was swinging a piece of pipe. I thought I'd fallen into a bad biker movie.

"What can I do for you?" I asked, wishing my deer rifle was at hand.

The bigger one spat in the dust. "We hear you been messin' with a friend of ours, and his lady."

"Well, where's he? Why doesn't he take care of his own problems instead of sending the goon squad?"

"Stay away from him, asshole. Stay away from his lady. Don't show your face anymore at Wild Willie's."

"Will do. Fine by me. No hard feelings." I wasn't about to start something with a lead pipe.

"We know where you live," said the smaller of the two. The bright one.

"Yes, I see that. You certainly do."

The guy with the pipe seemed disappointed I wasn't willing to get into it, but I had long since decided Rhonda Harlan wasn't worth it. Eugene was welcome to her. Hell, she wasn't even a good dancer.

They turned to go. I thought I had gotten off easy but then the big one let fly with the pipe at the dinky aluminum pole holding up one side of my awning. The flimsy metal crumpled like a toothpick and the green-striped canvas collapsed onto my La-Z-Boy. Knocked over my barbecue, too, dammit. They were laughing. I went out to straighten up the mess. After that, things were peaceful around the Shang-Grah-Lah until I caught the crip stealing my tools.

What I needed now was to meet a woman not like Rhonda. A sweet little bluegrass woman to share my RV. We'd put one of those bumper stickers on the back that reads, "If this old trailer's rockin', don't come a'knockin'." I'd cook her some enchiladas and we'd share hot onion breath the rest of the day. I'd serenade her on Lil Darlin', impressing her with a slow waltz instead of a breakdown. She would like Raymond Chandler, too.

I was horny.

Telluride is at the end of the road, nestled into a box canyon in the heart of the San Juans. The Switzerland of America, some real original thinkers call it. I was headed for one of the biggest bluegrass festivals in the country. Big names. Little names. No-names, like me. I figured if I wanted to start a career in banjo music, it'd be a natural place to jump off.

I was in high spirits as I wound down the curving road into the valley. Beautiful day. Wildflowers exploding everywhere. Temperature around sixty-five in the high-altitude sunshine. My juices were flowing.

I slowed as I rolled into the edge of town. A man in a high-visibility orange vest stepped in front of the RV and held up a big stop sign on a stick. He was not smiling.

"Hold up there."

I stuck out my head. "What's the problem?"

"Do you have a permit?"

"A permit? For what?"

"A camping permit. Can't bring that RV in without one." He was chewing a big wad of gum.

"Well, no. Where do I get one?"

He moved the wad to the other cheek. "If you don't have one by now, you ain't gonna get one, mister. You had to mail away for it months ago. Sorry. You'll have to turn back."

My happy mood was draining away fast. "Now look here," I said, "I drove all the way from McAlester, Oklahoma. You're telling me this festival is locked up tight? You can't just show up and have a good time?"

Cars were stacking up behind me. Mr. Orange Vest pressed his lips together tight. "You can't bring in that RV without a permit. Period. You might find a place over in Naturita."

"How far is that?"

"Forty miles."

I could have run him down, but instead I backed up ten feet, cut the wheel and made a squealing U-turn. I was grinding my teeth. So this was what it had all come down to. Country music, which started out being played on porches and at pie suppers a d grange halls, music of the down-home folks, had been taken over _ , a bunch of overor-ganized suits who issued permits. What would Hank Williams think?

I drove about two miles back up the valley and pulled off a little dirt road to assess the situation. I could look down on the festival from here. I could even sort of hear it. It was big. Big enough for me and my RV to get lost in.

I waited a long time, like maybe five hours. My plan required it. Just before dark, I started the engine and rolled back down toward town.

As I had hoped, Mr. Orange Vest had been replaced. Lucky me. It was Ms. Orange Vest. This time, I didn't wait for her to step out. I flagged her down. I wore a big shit-eating grin.

"Hey there, darlin'. Which way to the performers' tent?"

She was cute, and very young. Maybe sixteen. I must've looked like Pops to her. She eyed the RV.

"You in one of the bands?"

I winked at her. "That's right, hon. Pop Go The Weasels. We go on at nine. I'm the banjo picker." I had Lil Darlin' up front with me now, propped up in the passenger seat where she could see it.

She pointed down the road. "Go as far as the church, hang a right and follow that. It'll take you right to the stage area."

"Thanks." I put it in gear and got past Checkpoint Charlie. Now all I had to do was find a place to park this whale.

As I had feared, the town was locked up tight. The campground was full. All the legal parking places were gone and all the illegal ones roped off or taken by sheriff's vehicles. As I nosed the RV through the crowds, it occurred to me that the people didn't look right. They were too well dressed for a bluegrass festival, with Day-Glo fanny packs

17

and cycling clothes, skier-type sunglasses and perfect teeth. Weight-room bodies. Tanning salon tans. Guy with dreadlocks on the corner selling falafel sandwiches. And everywhere, muscular young goons in skintight T-shirts: FESTIVAL SECURITY.

This was a bluegrass hoedown?

In the beginning, back in the forties and on into the fifties, blue-grass music catered to a country crowd, but over the years its fans have evolved into a mostly urban mix. People searching for roots music, people drawn by the haunting melodies and simple lyrics. People sick of digitalized, oversampled, overmixed synthesizer tracks. I liked it be-cause it was music stripped bare to its soul.

But this scene looked straight out of MTV.

I swung the RV off the main drag and headed up a side street. Vic-torian houses. Little gardens. Porch swings. The hill climbed sharply. Toward the top, a few blocks on, the houses began to peter out. Tel-luride is not a very big town. The next-to-last house on the right was a run-down affair. Somebody had once painted it purple, but that had faded to a washed-out lavender. No one was parked in front. On im-pulse, I cut the wheel and pulled the RV up against the curb.

I didn't see her till she was standing at the driver's window. I had reached down to grab something, straightened up, and there she was.

"Are you thinking of parking here?"

She was about thirty-five, wearing a denim shirt and blue jeans. Laughing gray eyes and dark blond hair starting to go gray. She was smiling. Somehow, I wasn't too worried.

I grinned, not the kind of grin I'd given the girl in the orange vest.

"Yes, ma'am, I'd hoped to. Couldn't find anywhere down there."

"Where you from?"

Gee whiz, I'm fresh out of the Oklahoma State Penitentiary, where I did four years for gunning down a dirtbag in my front yard. But he deserved it.

"Just over from Montrose."

She was eyeing Lil Darlin'. "You play that thing?"

"Like lightning." I can be so corny sometimes. Like when I'm ner-vous.

"What's your name?"

"Webb. Webb Pritchard."

She paused for the slightest second, weighing things, I guess, then said, "Well, Webb, I guess you can park here. I'll tell the sheriff you're a guest. Just don't be noisy. My little girl goes to bed about nine, and I'm not far after that."

I reached out and we shook hands. I asked her name.

"Marie. Marie Cook."

"What do you do in Telluride, Marie Cook?"

"I own a quilt store. It's called Crazy Quilt."

I thought of Lynn, my ex, and shook my head.

"What's the matter?"

"Nothing. I knew somebody ran a quilt store one time."

"It's a wonderful art form. You'd be surprised how popular quilts are."

I had something to ask her, but I was embarrassed. I got out of the cab now and stretched. Thinking. Finally, I said, "If I gave you, say, twenty dollars, would you possibly allow me to shower here for the next couple of days? My RV has limited restroom facilities. I know it's a lot to ask."

She nodded. "OK. But make it around six in the evening. That'll be the best time."

I peeled off a twenty and handed it to her. "Thanks. When I pulled into town, I didn't think I would even get to see this festival. Security goons everywhere, no camping left. I'm expecting to see yellow police tape wrapped around the stage."

She smiled. "You know, it started out as a real small festival, just a bunch of hippies camping. But it's got out of hand. Last year they had twenty-five thousand people show up. The sheriff's had to crack down. It's too bad."

"You like bluegrass?" I asked her.

She shrugged. "Some of it. But you knew this isn't really a bluegrass festival, didn't you?"

"I started wondering when I saw the crowds. They don't look like bluegrassers."

"There's a few diehards every year. But the bands keep moving farther and farther away from it. The promoters want to appeal to, whatever, a wider audience, I guess. You'll see."

"Any room for an old unplugged banjo picker?"

"Go on down there and find out," she said, turning to go.

I watched her slender figure disappear inside the lavender house. Nice woman. I grabbed Lil Darlin' and locked up the RV. Headed on down the hill toward the music.

Showtime.

3

I wandered down the hill to the main stage area, where I could make out some mandolin sounds but not much else that sounded good to my ear. Long before I got close enough to see the band, I could hear they were plugged in. Electric bass, electric lead guitar. Sounded like their name ought to be My Amps Are Bigger Than Yours. The singer was some guy with long blond hair and black leather britches, shaking the microphone as he wailed through "Don't This Road Look Rough and Rocky." An old bluegrass tune, to be sure, but what they were playing wasn't bluegrass. The crowd, of course, didn't know any better.

I got in a short line and found out it was going to cost me $35 to get in for one night. For that, they'd clamp a plastic wristband on me, funnel me into a dirt corral, and herd me to the back right next to a stack of speakers. Blow my eardrums out. Screw that. I knew that for free, Lil Darlin' and me could pick the night away over at the campground.

I said no, thanks, bought a small Coke for $2.75 and headed for the trees at the far side of the festival. If there were any real bluegrassers at this shindig, that's where they'd be.

It was dark and cool and the dust kicked up little swirls under my boots. I walked among the Day-Gloers feeling alone. They wore their spandex with ignorant pride, lost in a culture of noise and TV and lousy values. I was above all that, of course—a mostly broke middle-aged unemployed ex-con who hadn't been laid in four years. Yeah, my prospects were bright. I was a man among boys. Make way for the king.

Suddenly I heard it. It cut through the night like a razor. Somebody was playing a banjo, playing "Rawhide" and playing it right. I stopped, frozen in the middle of the road. He hit all his licks, and then a sweet fiddle came right over the top. Did I hear a mandolin underneath? Hot shit, my people were here, after all.

The Day-Gloers melted into the shadows as I hurried toward the sound. These boys were into it now, with the bass thumping harder. I heard the guitar, a big-ass dreadnought, a Martin most probably, had to be, the way he was hitting it. Boom-chucka, boom-chucka, boom. The banjo player was laying back like he was supposed to, chunking chords, biding his time. I realized I was holding my breath, waiting for him to come back in. I got to the edge of the campground and still couldn't see them.

Tents and RVs were scattered among the trees. I dodged some laundry lines and stepped in somebody's cold fire. No one was around. I guess most people had gone over to the stage area. But pickers always lurk in the woods.

The music was louder now but still off somewhere beyond the campsites. My foot landed on something soft and squishy in a sleeping bag, oh shit, but it was only a pillow. At least nobody hollered. The forest grew denser and the campsites fewer. I picked my way through some chokecherry bushes and caught a glimpse of a campfire up ahead. Figures in silhouette.

Me and Lil Darlin' stepped into the circle of light. The song ended. There were five of them, the right number. Guitar, bass, banjo, mandolin and fiddle. They didn't need two banjos, but jamming etiquette dictated that I'd get my turn.

They all nodded at me, the fiddle player dipping his bow, and I took a seat over on a stump. The woods beyond the light of the fire were utterly black. I wasn't even sure now what direction I'd come from. The guitar player, a big, bearded fellow, said two words—"John Hardy"—and they were off and running again, ripping through the tune as fast as I'd ever heard it played. And it's a very fast tune.

Who were these guys? And what were they doing at the Day-Glo festival? A bunch of renegade bluegrassers down from Naturita, escaping their wives? The one traditional band in the lineup, getting in some practice time away from the Big Amps? Whoever they were, they were good.

They burned up two more tunes and then the banjo player stepped aside to light a cigarette. He motioned me to step in. By now, I had unsnapped the case and taken out Lil Darlin', but she wasn't tuned. I took a moment to do that, and jammed my fingerpicks down a little tighter. I didn't need them flying off in the middle of my break.

The guitar player nodded at me. "What's your pleasure?"

"How about a little 'Theme Time'?"

I kicked it off. My fingers flew over the fretboard so fast I could barely feel the strings. My chops were up, way up, but it had been so long since I had played with good musicians that it took a minute to get in the groove. God, it felt good. For a second I thought of Ernie— Ernie Blankenship, my prison playing partner. He'd tried to keep up. Tried like hell, bless him. But I'd be pushing the time, and he'd be dragging it, and that's awful hard on a banjo player.

These guys were pushing me. And still playing relaxed. I got through my first break and laid back, hitting rhythm and letting the music carry me along. The sound of the five acoustic instruments, what steel strings and wood can do, filled my head and traveled down my body and shot out my feet. I wanted to dance.

The song traveled the circle several times, each time different, each man weaving his solo, the devil's music burning hot, and the fire played off our faces like the cinders of hell.

How much time passed? A minute? An hour? At long last, my fingers told me it was time to wrap it up, so I stuck my boot out, a universal signal. At the last nanosecond I decided not to try my tricky new tag lick and went with the safe ending. But I played it clean. It was good.

The woods fell silent. My fingers were tingling. "All right," said the guitar player, smiling. "Nicely done, son. Let's slow it down, boys. Any ideas?"

"A waltz," said the fiddle.

" 'Wildwood Flower,' " said the mandolin.

"That's not a waltz," said the bass.

"Yeah, but it's sweet," said the guitar player. "Let's do it."

He hoisted the big Martin higher on his broad chest and kicked off the old Carter Family chestnut. Key of C, of course.

The other banjo player had slipped back in behind me. He started playing a duet line above mine. Real natural. Not flashy. Talk about sweet!

The slow song was as magical as the fast one, banjo notes spilling out like liquid mercury while the other instruments built a lilting, solid base around it. It was almost spooky, but I felt Mother Maybelle Carter there, and half expected her to step out of the shadows and come in on the Autoharp as her sister, Sara, sang:

"I'll think of him never, I'll be wildly gay,
I'll charm every heart and the crowd I will sway.
I'll live yet to see him regret the dark hour
When he won, then neglected, his frail wildwood flower."

Her plain, keening voice would have melted a stone.

We were halfway through the old song when I felt something different. A slight change in tempo? No, something else. A feeling. Strange. I looked down at Lil Darlin' and she was vibrating, like she had hit a high frequency. She was just humming in my hands, from her neck to her tailpiece. Holy shit.

I stopped playing, but my fingers were welded to the strings. Lil Darlin' had grabbed hold of me and wouldn't let go. The humming ratcheted up into a whine. I couldn't hear anything else anymore. My eyes rolled back in my head as the single note wound around me and cranked higher, higher. My eardrums threatened to shatter. The note became a very bright white light, and just when it couldn't get any brighter, it exploded into darkness.

"Son? You gonna play?"

The voice seemed to come from a long way off. Deep and twangy.

"Son? You all right?"

"He's all right."

Lil Darlin' let go. My arms dropped like lead. My hands were numb.

Slowly I raised my head, like I was under water or something, and looked around the circle. Hank Williams was standing there.

"Son? You with us?" He placed a hand on my shoulder. I felt it. It was real.

"I—"

"He's had a little too much moonshine, is all," said the fiddle player, who wasn't the same fiddle player I'd been playing with moments ago. The other men laughed.

None of them were the same. They were different guys and they wore different clothes—baggy checked shirts and baggier, high-waisted trousers. One was wearing a cowboy hat. And Hank was there. No mistaking who he was. Wearing a western-cut suit in the middle of the woods. Extra-pointy-toed cowboy boots. A string tie. His anteater face was very pale. He was smoking a cigarette with one hand and holding a bottle with the other. I smelled whiskey on him.

What the hell—? I whirled around and looked behind me. There were the woods, the ones I'd come through. I whirled back around. The fire looked the same. One of the ends of the logs had burnt into a flaming slingshot, which I'd noticed before, and it was still there. I checked my watch. Close to nine-thirty, same as before. Then I saw I was wearing different clothes, too, clothes like the other men wore. A rough green plaid shirt I'd never seen. Chinos like my dad used to knock around in. Big brogans of a kind they don't even make anymore.

"Here, son, have a snort." Hank was holding out the bottle. What could I do? I took it. The fiery liquid raced down my throat and it was no hallucination. It hit my gut and poured down to my toes and slithered back up. I laughed with pleasure.

"That's better." Hank took another long swig and drained the bottle. "Well, boys, I don't know about you, but I'm goin' into town to find me a little poon. It's been too long. At least two hours." He threw back his head and honked like a donkey. The men joined in. Hank threw his empty bottle into the fire.

I was just standing there, trying not to freak out completely, wondering what kind of acid they'd slipped into my Coke back at the festival, when Hank slung a skinny arm over my shoulder and said, "Come on. I need some company." He swung me around and he started leading me off into the woods.

"Wait. Lemme take off my banjo." I slipped Lil Darlin' over my head and gently placed her in the velvet-lined case. I stroked her wood and wondered what had possessed her. She gleamed at me in the fire-light, not giving up a clue.

I was following Hank Williams through the woods. He died in 1953, the year I was born. Passed out in the back seat of a Cadillac on the way to a gig and never woke up. Didn't make thirty. Lived fast, died young, didn't leave a good-looking corpse. Pills and alcohol do a mean job on you in a hurry. In pictures, he always looked so thin, but in person, he was positively skeletal. His face below his cheekbones sucked into big hollows, and his eyes were sunken, too. But they burned with a crazy light.

I didn't know what to do other than follow him. It was Alice through the looking glass. Hank cut a path through the trees, his lanky legs making time. I had no idea where we were headed; didn't know what had happened to the Telluride Bluegrass Festival. For all I knew, we were still there.

Up ahead, a large clearing appeared. I hadn't seen that before. There were cars parked there, forties and fifties models, Fords and Dodges and Chevys. Those big fat jobs with all the heavy chrome and teeny windshields and running boards. I checked out a license plate: 1951.

"Hey, Hank," I said. It was the first time I had spoken directly to the ghost, or whatever he was. Maybe I had died and gone to heaven. Some people would agree that hanging out with Hank Williams would be heavenly. He stopped and turned around. "Yeah, son?"

"What year is it? And where are we?" Why not get right to the point?

He started laughing. "Man, you are fucked up! You don't really know, do you?"

"No."

"I'm gonna teach you to drink good whiskey, son, not that mule piss those other jokers drink. It's June 12, it's 1951, and we're standing in the state of Colorado somewhere in the beautiful Rocky Mountains. That answer your question?"

"Not all of them. Who am I?"

"Winston Churchill!"

I frowned at him.

"Hell, son, if you don't know who you are we'd better get you to a doctor." He read my face. "Aw, you're Webb Pritchard, far as I know. Look, you want a doctor?"

"And you're really Hank Williams? The Hank Williams? This isn't a joke?"

His sharp brown eyes flickered with interest. He dropped the country-boy act. "You been taking pills, too? What you got on you, boy?"

"Nothing. If I told you what's going on, you wouldn't believe me."

"Try me."

"Shake my hand, Hank."

"Why?"

"Just shake my hand."

He held out his hand and I took it. It was warm and solid. Real. As real as me.

He pulled it away and stared hard at me. He didn't say a word. We stood there in the deep ruts of the clearing, listening to crickets. At last, he said, "I've heard of some special kind of tequila they give you down in Mexico will do this to you. That, or peyote. You ever hear of peyote?"

"It's not peyote, Hank. It's not even LSD."

"LSD?"

"Something happened back there at the campfire I can't explain. I can tell you what happened, but I can't tell you how or why."

He reached in his pocket and pulled out a set of keys. He walked over to a banana yellow Cadillac and slid behind the wheel. I got in on the other side.

"Tell me about it while we ride into town," he said, guiding the big car smoothly over the rough dirt. I settled back into the cream-colored upholstery and marveled that there were no seat belts.

He pulled out onto what looked like a county road, a two-lane blacktop. Now that we were out of the trees, I recognized the valley. I was still in Telluride. The festival was gone. I looked down at my brogans and saw where someone had rubbed polish into the shoelace holes by mistake. The polish was splotchy in places.

Hank lit a cigarette and dangled it outside the window, trailing smoke. He shot a sidelong glance at me. He said nothing.

I started worrying that if I told him, something might go wrong. The time-travel gods might not like it and have me die. Or time might warp around like a boomerang and hit me from behind, sending me into some kind of forever limbo. Aw, what the hell.

"I'm time traveling, Hank."

"Yeah?" He didn't bat an eye.

I took a deep breath. "Yeah. When I started picking with you guys back at the campfire, when we started "Wildwood Flower," it was 1994 and I was in town for a bluegrass festival. I heard the music through the trees, and followed it, and found five guys picking around the fire.

I joined them. In the middle of that song, my banjo started freaking out and I kind of blacked out or something. When I came to, I was still standing there with my banjo, only you were there. And I'd gone back in time forty-three years. I'm not even born yet, technically speaking."

Hank just smoked his cigarette. Calm son of a bitch. We were cruising Main Street now. The Victorian mining town looked virtually the same as it had earlier that afternoon when I drove in, only there weren't any Day-Gloers or security goons or guys with dreadlocks hawking falafel. It was just a sleepy little small-town street.

"I know you think I'm bullshitting you, but I'm not." Something occurred to me. "Hey, how old do I look?" I hadn't seen myself yet. I didn't feel different.

"You've got some miles on you. I'd say you were close to forty."

"I am forty. Or, at least I was."

So my body hadn't changed. It might've been fun to be twenty again.

Hank pulled the Caddy over and parked in front of a saloon. He set the brake and turned to look at me.

"Tell me one thing."

"What's that?"

"Am I an old guy? What happened to me?"

It wasn't what I expected him to say. I didn't want to tell him the truth, that he'd be dead in less than two years. I fumbled for an answer.

"Yeah, I thought so," he said before I could think of a reply. "I'd better have fun while I can." He got out of the car and I got out, too, and we headed into the Sluicebox.

The floor was sawdust and the smoke hung thick. I was slightly amazed no one recognized Hank. He got us two bottles of beer and we took a back table, where we could watch the goings-on. I marveled at the people. So this was what it was like after the war. The women: print dresses and dark lipstick, seamed stockings and bulletproof bras. The men: short, oiled hair and wide lapels. Like an old newsreel come to life. God, even Elvis hadn't happened yet. The jukebox was playing some big-band number. Not country.

In that era, bluegrass hadn't really broken out as a separate entity. It was all country, whether it was hillbilly jug band music or Hank's hard twang or Earl Scruggs and his banjo instrumentals. You'd find all of them on the same bill, traveling in tent shows or working the Opry or the Louisiana Hayride.

"What are you doing in Telluride?" I asked Hank.

"Penance."

I laughed. "You on a tour?"

"Yeah, we're on a tour, Mr. Peyote-head."

"Who's on the bill?" I had my hopes up.

He scratched his nose. "Let's see. Me and my boys. Daniel Eberhardt. Perry Weems. Kit and the Kaboodles. The Taggart Family. And Lula Mae Loudermilk. That's it."

I'd heard of all of them, seen their old black-and-white publicity stills. Heard most of them on old recordings. Even caught a kinescope of Kit and the Kaboodles on some late-night nostalgia channel. Kit Morrison's band, based around Kit's barrelhouse piano, was a cross between a straight country act and a comedy routine, which was fairly common in those days. Daniel Eberhardt was going to switch to rock 'n' roll in ten years, but he didn't know it yet. Right now he fronted a hard-driving, hard-country band. Perry Weems was a crooner. The Taggart Family was old-timey, like the Carters; they dressed up in gingham and straw hats and did audience singalongs. Lula Mae Loudermilk was a country comedienne, and by God, she was still around in my time, occasionally playing the Opry, though she was older than dirt.

"You're the headliner?"

"Of course. Who else." It wasn't a question.

"And I'm in your band?"

"Christ, Webb. Cut it out."

"But I told you, I'm time traveling. In a sense, I just got here."

"Yeah, yeah. Whatever."

"Now you don't believe me?"

"I never believed you. I believed the whiskey."

"How long you known me? Where'd I come from?"

"We picked you up at Cain's Ballroom in Tulsa, 'bout a month ago. You'd been fired from Wayne Webster's band for being drunk onstage. But I liked your guitar pickin'."

"I'm a banjo player."

"You play guitar for me, son. Banjo got no place in my band."

I looked down at my beer. I knew it wasn't the whiskey.

"What's the name of this collection of all-stars?"

"They call it Doc Mullican's Traveling Hayride and Medicine Show."

I blinked. Lil Darlin'. She'd come home.

"All right, Hank. I'm along for the ride."

He shot me a grin and settled back in his chair. "What you need is a good steak and a good woman and a good night's sleep. That'll set you right. And quit drinkin' that mule piss. I don't want you puking all over my car seat. We got us a long drive tomorrow."

"Where we going?"

"Denver."

Somebody put a jitterbug on the jukebox and a couple got up to dance. Hank ordered us a couple of whiskey chasers. Johnnie Walker Black, not mule piss. The last thing I remember was swallowing the booze and watching the woman, her yellow print dress blurring across the sawdust floor at the Sluicebox Saloon.

4

I could smell the inside of the camper before I opened my eyes, a stale aroma of old shag carpeting permeated with cigarette smoke. My mouth held a strange metallic taste. I lay there on my bunk for many seconds, and I knew that it had not been a dream.

I sat up, narrowly missing the edge of the kitchen cabinet with my head. Morning light sifted dimly through the curtains. I looked down at myself, and saw I was wearing briefs, my usual bedtime attire. My Levi's were folded over the back of a chair, my boots kicked over on the floor. No sign of the big leather brogans or the checked green shirt.

Lil Darlin'! Where was she? For a panicked moment I thought she was gone forever, but no, there she was, the banjo case lying on the floor. Nothing seemed different, but everything was.

Someone knocked lightly on the camper door.

"Webb? Webb, you awake?"

It was Marie's voice.

"Hold on, I'm not decent." I grabbed my Levi's and yanked them on. Stretched to get the kinks out. Took two steps and opened the door.

She was standing there smiling, holding out a mug of steaming coffee and a blueberry muffin. "Thought you might need this."

Paranoid, I wondered if she knew anything was amiss. I took the coffee and the muffin. "Well, thanks. Thanks a lot. I could use it."

She looked wonderful in the sunlight, standing there in faded denim, an old blue bandanna wrapped around her head, a splotch of grape jelly dribbled down the front of her work shirt. She squinted up at me, grinning.

"You must've had quite a night."

"You have no idea." I took a sip of the coffee and it seemed to wash away the metallic taste and bring me back to the present. It was hot and sweetened with honey.

"I'd invite you in, but it's a bit cramped," I said, turning to grab my shirt. "And I haven't had a chance to clean up yet."

"Meet you on the porch," she said.

I got my boots on, combed my hair and sneaked a look in the mirror. Same old me. Where are you, Hank?

The porch wrapped around the old lavender house, with a view of the town and the valley. We sat in white wicker chairs at a small table. She had set out a pot of coffee and more muffins, and there was a sliced peach on a plate in front of me.

I was embarrassed. "Uh, you don't have to feed me," I began, but she hushed me up with a wave of her hand.

"I know," she said, "but I'm curious about you. It's not often I get a visitor from another time."

I was biting into a muffin. I stopped in midbite.

"Huh?"

"Last night. You don't remember?"

I wasn't sure how to proceed. "Remember what?"

She drew herself up in her chair. "I was out here on the porch last night, about midnight, sitting in the swing, when you came back. You were in some kind of a daze. I thought you were drunk, frankly, but then I realized you were just . . . confused. You were babbling on about Hank Williams. You told me you'd just seen him. You asked me what year it was."

"I did?"

"You did. You seemed quite convinced you had just jumped back in time. I steered you into your camper and I guess you fell asleep. How do you feel?"

I didn't answer her. I began rubbing my eyes very hard. I stared off toward the town. "Well." That's all I said. I can be brilliant when the situation calls for it.

"Well?" She reached for her coffee.

"Well. They must've slipped me some very bad acid down there."

"Yeah, they were warning people about that over the sound system," she said dryly. "And don't eat the magic mushrooms."

We sat for a while without saying anything, and it was nice, because you can't usually do that with people you've just met. You're trying to think of something clever to say, but with her, it felt natural and easy.

"I don't remember coming back here," I finally said. "And I wasn't drunk. All I had last night was a Coke. For two seventy-five." She cocked her head, and the breeze caught her hair and lifted it back, exposing her long, fine neck. She took a muffin and started eating it.

"Well, you weren't yourself, that's all I can say. And I don't even know you," she said, laughing.

I took a chance. "Wanna know what happened? At least, what I remember happened? You'll think I'm crazy. You'll never give me another muffin."

She waved me away. "I know all about it. You were time traveling with Hank Williams."

I nodded, knowing this conversation was twice as bizarre as any I'd had in prison. And people talk some weird shit in there.

"He was as real as you are. He put his hand on my shoulder. We shook hands. I can describe him down to the last detail, Marie, I really can. And the town was gone, I mean, it wasn't like this," I said, pointing down the hill. "It was 1951. Just a little worn-out mining town. The festival wasn't here at all. I was even wearing different clothes."

"How'd all this start?" She kept munching on the muffin. She must've thought I was nuts.

I told her about finding the bluegrass pickers in the woods, and Lil Darlin' going crazy on me. She listened without laughing, without smirking, without a trace of scorn, God bless her. I told her everything I could recall, and how the last thing I knew I was sitting in the Sluicebox Saloon with Hank. When I finished the story, we just sat there. The sounds of the festival cranking up began to drift over the town. They were testing the P.A. system.

"Look," I said, "you don't know me from Adam. You must think you've got a nut case parked in your front yard. If you want me to leave, just say so."

"No. Don't go. Maybe I believe you."

"You do? Then you're the nut case," I said, smiling. "I'm just worried what Lil Darlin' might do the next time I pick her up."

"Maybe I don't believe you," she said, popping the last of the muffin into her mouth and licking her fingers.

The screen door banged open and a little girl came out. She looked to be about seven or eight. Blond hair. She resembled her mother. She was wearing a nightgown decorated with dinosaurs.

"Well, Sleeping Beauty," Marie said, reaching out to stroke her daughter's hair. "You certainly slept late. I'd like you to meet a friend. This is Mr. Webb Pritchard. Webb, this is Carla."

The child stuck out her tiny hand and pumped mine vigorously. I liked this kid. She had brass.

"Very pleased to meet you, Carla," I said.

"Hi, mister. Is that your RV?"

"Sure is. Your mother was kind enough to let me park it during the festival."

"Are you a musician?"

I smiled. "That's debatable. I play the banjo, but I'm not in a band. At least right now. I'm just here to soak up the atmosphere and hear a little music. Pick a few tunes. You like the banjo?"

"I don't know."

"Would you like to find out?" I was curious myself if Lil Darlin' was going to freak out on me again.

"Yes!" The child ran down to the RV and yanked open the door.

"Carla!" her mother called. "Stop right there! That's Mr. Pritchard's home. We don't go around just waltzing into people's homes, do we? Especially in our nightgowns! Go get some clothes on."

Carla bounded back up the yard and into the house, blond hair flying. Marie stood up and began to clear the table. I thanked her again, went down to the camper and climbed inside. Lil Darlin' lay in the corner in her black case. I was afraid to touch her. My heart raced. What if she took me back again? Did I really want to go back? I stood there for a full ten seconds, then impulsively squatted down and unsnapped the brass locks. Slowly, I lifted the lid.

My truest love was gone.

The case was empty.

I couldn't breathe. I couldn't think.

"You coming, son?"

It was Hank.

His head bumped the top of the camper. Christ, he was back, and he was inside my goddamned camper.

"Jesus, it's you!"

"You coming?" he repeated.

"Do I have a choice?"

"Sure. You like that pretty lady, don't you? Want to see where that leads instead?"

I stared up at him. I couldn't believe he was actually here. "Well, yeah, wouldn't you? I've been in the joint for four years, man. Besides, aren't you coming around at a bad time? I'm about to start my new career."

He jerked a thumb toward the town. "You call that music? You know what the real music is, Webb. That's why I'm here. I'm offering you a chance to go on the road with me. Hank Fucking Williams. The real thing."

"Why'd you bullshit me last night about the time traveling? You knew all along. This is your doing."

He smiled in the dim light. "Just checking you out. I had to know how you'd handle it. Some folks might go off the deep end."

"Well, I am off the deep end, dammit." My head started to hurt and I shut my eyes.

The screen door slammed. Carla's voice called out from the porch. I looked up and Hank was gone. I looked down and Lil Darlin' was back in her case. He was yanking my chain.

The camper door flew open and Carla poked her head in. "Hey, Mister Webb, are you gonna play your banjo?"

"Just call me Webb, hon. Sure, I'm gonna play it. Gimme a sec." I hefted Lil Darlin' over my shoulder and stepped out into the sunlight. Things were out of my control. I got up to the porch, got settled on the railing and put on my fingerpicks. Tuned up. Carla sat right in front of me. Marie leaned against the wall, sipping another cup of coffee. I had no idea what might happen once I started to play.

"Here's a little ditty called 'Groundhog,' " I said, and launched into it with the feeling I might pitch off the porch and land in a tent show somewhere in the past.

But nothing of the sort happened. I just played "Groundhog."

"That was *great!*" Carla yelled when I finished. "Can you play the Lion King?"

"Afraid that's not in my repertoire, but I do know this one," I said, and began to pick an old Jimmie Rodgers tune, "Waiting for a Train." I sang along, something I do a lot of in private but not much of around other people. The sound of my own voice pleases me, but I'm never sure if others feel the same way. I sang a mournful song about trying to get home. Marie smiled and watched. I gave them a few more, then I set the banjo down and said, "Listen. I've got to get down to the festival. How about you two joining me? Think your mom'd like that?" I looked right at Carla.

"Can we, Mommy? Can we?"

And that's how we ended up spending the day like a little family, even though I didn't have the nerve to ask Marie what happened to Carla's dad. It was obvious there was no man around. Just the girls in the faded lavender house on the hill. I was careful not to push it. I offered to pay their way in, but Marie insisted otherwise, and that was better for several reasons, one of them being I hardly had any money left. I was down to a few hundred dollars and I had no idea where the next hundred was coming from. It was also better because that way she didn't feel she owed me anything.

We sat in the hot, high mountain sun and ate too much junk food, listened to the music, people-watched and wandered amid the food and craft booths. I decided it was good that people who didn't have a clue about bluegrass were at least exposed to a tiny bit of it, but it still was no bluegrass festival to me. That high lonesome sound was missing. That is, until . . .

We were sitting smack in the middle of the audience. We'd heard four or five acts, and Carla was getting cranky, the way little kids do. The last band had failed to impress me. Hell, the last several bands. Pastor Mustard, the emcee, stepped onstage and surveyed the sun-drenched crowd.

"That was great, wasn't it?" he asked, and the masses responded with cheers. I didn't clap.

"If you thought you came up here into the San Juans, way out in the middle of nowhere, down this box canyon into a dead end, and weren't gonna hear any *blue*grass, you're dead wrong, my friend," Mustard said. "We've been featuring acts that show you where the music's going. Now we'd like to show you where it's been. These guys have only been together for a couple of years but they sound like they been doin' it since Bill Monroe invented it. Here they are, ladies and gentlemen, all the way from Barns Gap, Kentucky . . . Rawhide!"

It was the band in the woods. The guys I'd played with. Suddenly I sat up like I'd been hit with a cattle prod, straining to see and hear better. I poked Marie in the ribs.

"It's them! Those're the guys!"

"What guys?" Carla said.

"Friends of Webb's," Marie said. "You're sure?" she said to me.

"Yes."

There was the big burly guitar player, thumping on the Martin, the skinny fiddle player, and the rest. Yep, it was them. They got through their set and then we hurried around to the side of the stage area. I intercepted the guitar player as he came out of the secured Artists Only corral, or whatever they called it.

"Hey! Enjoyed your set," I said, looking him right in the eye.

He pulled up short. "Well! The hot picker! How ya doin', Webb?"

So he knew me.

"Fine." I had to be careful because Carla was there. "You guys are the best thing I've heard. Not a whole lot of bluegrass at the old Telluride Bluegrass Festival."

"That's true." He chuckled and turned to Marie, bowing slightly. "Howdy, ma'am. I'm Bill Pierce. Webb here was jamming with us last night, and he just about blew us out of the water."

"Pleased to meet you, Mr. Pierce. I'm Marie Cook. This is my daughter, Carla."

Pierce winked at Carla. "How do ya do?"

"Fine, thank you." Carla made a sort of curtsy motion.

We stood there and made small talk about the festival, about the weather, about everything in general, and then Pierce said to me, "Why don't you come jam with us again tonight, Webb? We'll be in the same spot, about nine o'clock."

"Maybe I will," I said, pondering this possibility. We said our good-byes and Marie said we should head home. Carla was tired. And so was I.

To put it in his own tender words, did I want to go out on the road with Hank Fucking Williams? Well . . . yes and no. Yes because, my God, what country musician wouldn't sell his own soul to do that? And no, because what if I couldn't come back? Or what if it screwed up the present? This was my little dilemma.

And there was Marie. She cooked me supper that night, over my feeble protests. She let me buy the groceries. Steaks, fresh corn and green salad. So much for my vegetarian phase, as Dot would say. I had a feeling Dot would approve of Marie.

"Is there a Mister Cook?" I asked when we were done eating and Carla had gone into the parlor to watch television. Marie and I were sitting out on the porch.

"There was," she said.

"I mean, I figured that out."

"We split up last year. He's in Wyoming."

"Divorced?"

"Not yet. I'm working on it. It's such a hassle."

"I'm divorced myself. Twice, in fact. But I'm not such a bad guy."

"I know that."

I didn't know when I'd get around to telling her about the prison thing, if I ever would, but I knew now was too soon. I hoped she wouldn't start asking a lot of detailed questions about my past.

"You going down to jam with those guys?" she asked.

"Well, I'm pretty curious. Probably."

She focused her eyes on mine. She was lovely. Maybe I shouldn't go.

"You should go," she said, as if she'd read my mind. "If it's not too late, I'll wait up for you. We could have a nightcap out here, if you want."

"I'd like that very much. You know what else I'd like!"

"No. What?"

"I'd like to take you and Carla to dinner tomorrow night. Here you keep feeding me, and I'm parked in your front yard, and I'm a total nuisance." The money would be a problem, but I'd deal with that later.

"That would be nice," she said.

"You pick the place. I have no idea where to eat in this town and not get ripped off."

"I know a place."

"I knew you would. Now, I think I'll go down and find the Rawhide boys. Thanks for the steak. It was great."

I grabbed my banjo and headed for the woods. This time I didn't hesitate as I crossed the campgrounds. I knew exactly where I was going.

Sure enough, I saw their campfire up ahead, through the tangle of underbrush. They were talking, not playing. Their low voices drifted through the trees.

Just like the night before, I stepped into the circle of light. Bill Pierce and the others were there. He looked up with a grin.

"Great! I knew you'd come. Glad you made it."

"Oh, I knew he'd make it." It was Hank.

I spun around. There he was. I spun back around, and Pierce and his boys were suddenly gone.

"What's the deal?" I didn't know what to think.

"The deal is, we're heading to Denver with this show, and you're either with us or you ain't," Hank said, lighting up a filterless cigarette and blowing smoke in my face.

"What about . . . Marie?" I said softly.

"You're either with us or you ain't," Hank repeated.

I looked at his narrow face, sharp in the firelight. His cream-colored suit with the wide lapels matched his dust-free cowboy boots, and a diamond pinky ring glittered on his left hand. Forty years after this man died, his influence was heard and felt in every country song. His low-down genius still burned brightly through the dark heart of country music. He *was* the dark heart.

"I'm with you," I said.

"Hot damn!" he said.

And that's how I joined Doc Mullican's Traveling Hayride & Medicine Show and went on the road with Hank Fucking Williams.

5

The back seat of Hank's Cadillac was a fascinating, disgusting place. Empty pill bottles, empty booze bottles, dirty underwear rolled up into moist, smelly balls, well-thumbed girlie magazines, asthma inhalers, cartons of cigarettes, half-opened bags of hard candy, scraps of paper with bits of lyrics scribbled on them, and a case of Dr. Mullican's Pep-M-Up Elixir. The flotsam of a life on the road. Hank could hardly see out the back window. He liked to drive.

"You oughta get yourself an RV, Hank," I said, kicking back in the roomy front seat.

"You oughta get yourself a Cadillac," he shot back.

This was how he traveled. The days of the big customized buses hadn't arrived yet. So many things were in the future. I thought of how much I knew and he didn't, and then had to laugh. He knew it all.

"Who's Dr. Mullican?" I asked.

"Old fart owns this outfit."

"Is he really a doctor?"

"Like I'm a Japanese admiral. Hell, no. He's a quack. But he bankrolls us."

"What's the elixir? Does it work?"

Hank grinned and reached under the front seat. He drew out a flat, dark bottle with a yellow sunburst label. He handed it over. I unscrewed the cap and took a sniff. Pure-D alcohol. A trace of mint, a little camphor.

"I gauge it to be about ninety proof," Hank said. "Terrific stuff, if you can stand it."

"People buy this shit?"

"Do people buy this shit? Little old ladies can't get enough of it. They're throwing their canes away and buck-dancing after a few snorts."

Hank reached in his coat pocket and pulled out a pill bottle. He shook out four brown capsules and swallowed them in a gulp. "Gimme that," he said, reaching for the elixir. He washed down the pills. "God-almighty," he said.

The Caddy rolled on through the dark. I thought about Marie. About how her brown hair looked soft resting along her cheek. Where was she right now? Was she waiting up for me on the porch? More to the point, where was I, really? Marie's world was the real world, not the one I inhabited at the moment. It was real enough to me, but possibly to no one else. Hank was a ghost, I guessed. This banana yellow Cadillac, with its creamy upholstery and no seatbelts, was a phantom, too. And yet, it was absolutely solid beneath me. Hank was solid, too. Thin sonofabitch, but solid.

I thought about my "career." The one that only existed in my head for now, but the one that held a lot of promise for the future. The one my sister held no stock in. Maybe I could base out of Telluride, spend the summers on the festival circuit . . . Hell, it wouldn't be a lot of money, but I knew of others who got away with it. Biggest scam on earth, playing music for a living. "When you gonna get you a real job, boy?" Lots of folks were doing it. Why couldn't I?

Well, for one thing, I was zooming through the mountains toward Denver with Hank Williams in a time warp. A small problem. Sorry, I won't be able to make the Opry this weekend, sir, me and Hank are playing a gig in Colorado. Hank who? Why, Williams, who else? No, not Junior. Nossir. Senior. The real article. What? Am I drunk? Nossir. Well, I've had a little of Dr. Mullican's elixir, but . . .

We drove a long way without saying anything. The big engine hummed. I must've dozed off, because the next thing I knew the sun was coming up. We were on a lonely stretch of highway cutting straight through a long valley. Up ahead, a cafe beckoned. Hank slowed and cut the wheel.

"I'm as hungry as a heifer in a snowstorm." I swear, he said that.

We ordered up big plates of bacon and eggs, biscuits and gravy, and washed it all down with gallons of burning coffee with sugar dumped into it. Not a Sweet'n Low packet in sight. Hank also had a big glass of buttermilk. He was busy sopping up some of his gravy with a bit of biscuit when I said to him, "Wonder how many fat grams are on that plate? Do you know what your cholesterol is?" I was just messing with his head a little. God knows he'd messed with mine.

He swallowed the gravy-soaked gob and winked at me. "It don't really matter because I'll be dead in two years, won't I?"

Well, that shut me right up. How did he know about cholesterol?

I waited till he was through and had lit a cigarette and was blowing smoke rings lazily across the diner before I said what I really needed to say.

"Hank," I said firmly, "I can't be in your band on this tour. I'm a banjo picker, and you said there's no place for a banjo in your band. I've got to play the banjo, man. It's what I set out to do."

"Why don't you just do both, then?"

"Both? What do you mean?"

"You can play guitar for me and do your solo act as well."

I thought about that for a minute.

"Won't that sort of dilute my impact? I mean, a solo performer has to come out and pow! Really sock it to the crowd, you know what I mean? He's got to give them something they haven't seen before. They'll already have seen me if I'm part of your band. I won't be anything special."

"Wear a disguise."

"What?"

"Black out your teeth, wear a wig and a hat and they won't know you."

"Get outta here! You gotta be kidding. I'm gonna ruin my act like that?"

"No, you idiot, you'll do it in my band. We can do a little comedy routine."

"I'm not a comedian, Hank!"

"I need a guitar player, son. You said you'd come along for the ride, remember? Well, this is part of the ride."

"No, I'm afraid it is not part of the ride. When we met, what was I playing? A guitar? No. I was playing Lil Darlin', my beloved five-string."

The man at the next table had turned around and was staring at us now. The waitress, who had heard every last word, was leaning on her elbows on the counter, looking intently at the empty booth to our left.

Hank curled his tongue under his lower lip, pushing it out. He shot a sideways glance at the waitress. "You are on the road with me, Webb," he said evenly. "I'm not on the road with you. I don't need your banjo act. Now, do you want to be part of the show?"

"You're Hank Williams!" the man at the next table suddenly blurted out. "I'd know you anywhere! Hey, folks, it's Hank Williams!"

The few souls who had somehow ended up at this remote diner at this ungodly hour now swiveled about, all focused on us. Hank was pissed.

"Check," he said loudly.

The waitress rushed it over, smoothing her hair and pulling back her shoulders. I was amazed. Two huge breakfasts, $1.65. Wow.

"I can leave you here right here, right now," Hank said calmly as he paid the bill. "Like I said before, you're in or you're out, son." I felt about twelve years old. "I'm in," I said miserably.

Blacked-out teeth?

"Is he funny?" Doc Mullican demanded to know.

"Hell yes, he's funny," Hank was saying.

"Do something funny!" Doc Mullican said to me.

Jesus.

"He's not in costume," Hank said swiftly, "and he's not in makeup and he's not ready, Doc. Just wait'll tonight. You'll see."

"And you do something else?" Doc Mullican looked doubtful.

"Yessir," I replied. "I play the banjo and sing. Straight," I added. "No comedy."

"You don't look funny to me," Doc Mullican said. "He don't look funny to me," he said to Hank.

"He's funny! He's a goddamn riot, OK?" Hank turned on his boot heel and left Doc Mullican's hotel room. We were in Denver, hours away from doing our next—my first—show, and the boss was not impressed with the new arrival.

Mullican, with the bulbous red nose, overhanging gut and general look of dissipation that screamed *alcoholic*, stared hard at me. Too hard.

"Christ, Pritchard, how old are you?"

"Forty."

"For crying out loud. How come I never heard of you?"

"I've been in prison." Shit, what did I really have to lose?

He sighed wearily and rubbed his chin. "OK. Only because you're Hank's problem am I doing this. You go on tonight. Two spots. You're on with Hank, and you're on later as yourself. You get one chance. One chance only. You blow it, you're outta here. I don't stand for any shit around my show. It's a clean, family show, and stay away from the girls. Understand?"

"I understand."

"Have you tried my elixir?" he said, uncapping a bottle.

"Doc," I said, "it's dynamite."

Hank and I had arrived that afternoon, pulling up at a seedy-looking motel on the outskirts of Denver. The others in the show, it turned out, were not far behind. We were playing the Stock Show Arena. The place held forty-four hundred, and Hank would pack them in. The arena didn't have the world's best acoustics, but who was complaining? My first gig out of prison and I was sharing the bill with a legend.

We were unpacking in our room, which had two hard beds, dusty venetian blinds and brown cloudy water running out of the tap.

"How come," I asked him, "you stay in such a rat hole? Aren't you a big star?" I thought he might dislike this avenue of conversation, but no, Hank just pulled out a bottle of Early Times and talked while he poured us both a stiff one.

"Yeah, I guess it looks bad, don't it. Well, it is bad. What happened, I got thrown off the Opry for a while. Man's got to make a living, so I hooked up with Doc Mullican. It's only till the Opry sees the light."

"What'd you do to piss off the Opry?" The Grand Ole Opry was the Holy Grail of country music. The biggest of the bigtime. Especially in 1951.

"Coupla small things. I didn't show up for some shows, and once I did show up I was kinda drunk."

"Yeah, Hank, that's pretty small."

He started laughing. "They need me. I'll be back."

He was right. He'd be welcomed back and thrown out of Ryman Auditorium, home of the Opry, many more times before it was over.

I needed some time to rehearse. I had a repertoire of maybe fifty songs, with fifteen or so down near perfect. I had to whittle this list down to four or five for tonight's performance. Or so I thought.

"What song you gonna do?" Hank asked me.

"Well, these are the ones I was thinking of . . ."

"These? Whaddaya mean, these? How many were you thinkin' of doing?"

"Uh, four or five, I guess. A short set."

He fell back on his bed, laughing. He stared at the ceiling. "Four or five, he says. Just four or five!"

"OK, three or four?"

He sat up. "You people in the future don't know when to get off, do you? You got a lot to learn about show business, son. You'll do one song. That's how the show goes. You're on, and you're off. It's fast-paced. That way we don't lose the audience."

"How many songs do you do?"

"I'm different. I'm the headliner. I do two the first time, then we come back out later and do two more."

"I see. So I'd better pick my best song."

"Nah, I'd pick my worst. Something you'll stumble on."

One song. One lousy song. A slow one wouldn't do. Had to be an up-tempo number. If I had one song to play, I'd play . . . "Cripple Creek." I didn't sing on that one. There were lyrics, but I played it as an instrumental, like most banjoists. It was probably the one song I could do no matter what. Those fingerings were so burned into my brain that I was sure I could carry on even in front of forty-four hundred people, even during an earthquake, even if somebody threw a tomato at me. Which was possible.

"Hey, write me a tune," I said to the master.

"Hey, pay me."

"How about 'Cripple Creek'?"

"Sure. They like that."

There was a knock on the door. Buck Gallagher stuck his head in. He was the fiddle player in Hank's band, the Drifting Cowboys.

"We're here, boss."

Buck nodded at me like he already knew me. I nodded back.

"Little change tonight, Buck," Hank said. "Webb's gonna do a solo number somewhere in the show, so we're gonna hide him out while he's playing with us. A little comedy disguise."

Buck grinned broadly. "Oh, boy."

I smiled weakly. "I've never done comedy before."

"Even better," Buck said, and ducked out.

Hank stood up and stretched his endless praying mantis legs. He checked his watch. "Five o'clock. I'm gonna cruise, son. See you at the arena about six-thirty. Show's at seven."

He headed for the door.

"Hank! Don't we need to figure out this comedy thing? I mean . . ."

But he was gone.

The Stock Show Arena sat smack in the middle of acres of cattle yards, and smelled of cow shit and sawdust. Doc Mullican gave me a ride over after Hank abandoned me, and even bought me a hot dog and a Coke on the way in. I decided he wasn't so bad.

I was dressed for the occasion. When I had checked the little cardboard suitcase that mysteriously materialized in our hotel room, I found a couple of pairs of slacks that fit, fresh underwear, a scarf I took to be a form of neckerchief, and three crisp cowboy shirts with pearl-snap buttons. I chose a red shirt. Freshly showered and shaved, I finished the job by slicking back my hair with some water, a style I had not affected since roughly 1963. But it seemed to fit in here.

Doc guided me through a side door at the arena and back around through some wooden tunnels. I could faintly hear fiddle music coming from somewhere. We kept walking a ways and finally arrived at a plain door.

"In here," he said, and swung it open.

A crush of people filled the room, smoking, drinking, laughing, swearing, waving fiddle bows and tuning guitars. They turned to look when I came in, then turned away just as quickly. I wasn't somebody famous. I wasn't Hank, I guess.

I carried my banjo case in and found a spot against the wall. I was tuning up and trying not to look nervous when a fellow came up to me and stuck out his hand.

"Perry Weems, pleased to meetcha," said this lanky youngster. He was the crooner, an early harbinger of country singers like Jim Reeves. His Adam's apple bobbed up and down quite a bit.

"Webb Pritchard," I said, offering my hand.

"You're Hank's new guitar player."

"That's right. But I have a solo number, too. I'm really a banjo player." I wanted to make that plain to people. It mattered to me.

"Do you play like Earl Scruggs?"

"I try to. By the way," I added, "I've heard you. I like your singing."

"Really?" He grinned eagerly. He had to be all of nineteen or twenty. "Where'd ya hear me?"

Oops. I couldn't exactly tell him I'd bought a retrospective of his greatest hits one day when I saw it in the sale bin at Kmart.

"Uh, it was last year. I'm trying to remember."

"Musta been at Roanoke. I was mostly in that area last year."

"That was it. Roanoke."

A short woman rushed up at that moment and saved me. She was in her mid- to late forties, plumpish, wearing a puff-sleeved dress and a red straw hat, and holding a ridiculous guitar that was way too big for her and painted all over with daisies.

"Honee! I'm Lula Mae Loudermilk and how in hell are ya!" she bellowed at me. "Ya ready for the bigtime?"

I had to laugh. I shook her hand, then shook my head. "I'm not sure, Ms. Loudermilk, but we'll all find out tonight." I suddenly realized I had just called her Ms., then realized just as quickly that it comes out Miz, so I was all right. Living in the past was a tough gig.

"Ya better call me Lula Mae or I'll whack ya," she said. "We're all family here, Mr. . . . ?"

"Pritchard. And ya better call me Webb or I'll whack ya." She liked me for that.

"What tune ya gonna do?"

"Thought I'd do 'Cripple Creek.' "

"That's a good 'un. They like that." Hank's exact words.

For all the backstage banter, I was getting very, very nervous. Where the hell was Hank? I hadn't got my "disguise," and the band hadn't rehearsed.

"Do you drink, Mr. Webb?" Lula Mae was asking me.

I wondered what the correct response was, but went for the truth. "Yes."

"Good! We'll have one after the show. Break a leg." And with that she bustled off through the crowd of country musicians.

Now the door flew open. It was Doc Mullican.

"Right now, everybody. Right now."

46

They began snuffing out cigarettes, slipping flasks out of sight and heading out. Heart pounding, I followed up the rear. Showtime. The bigtime.

I could feel the crowd out there more than I could hear them. Forty-four hundred eager fans, clutching ticket stubs and craning their necks for a glimpse behind the curtain. Why, look, Aunt Mabel! I think I see Hank Williams!

I wished I could see Hank Williams. Please God, I prayed, don't let this be one of those times when he shows up smashed out of his gourd. I was sinking in a sorry reverie when the show began. Doc Mullican went out and delivered a homely monologue.

"Howdy, friends and neighbors, howdy! Welcome to Doc Mullican's Traveling Hayride and Medicine Show. And a fine show it is, ladies and gentlemen."

His voice echoed around the arena, reminding me of the P.A. system at my old high school auditorium. The main microphone seemed more suited for a cattle auction than a music show.

"And now let's welcome the king of the barrelhouse piano, Kit and the Kaboodles!" Now the lights flooded the stage and there was Kit, already seated and already pounding the bejesus out of the keyboard. He was a big, beefy man and he put his weight into it, shoulders dipping and rolling, brow beading up with sweat. Jerry Lee Lewis would borrow some of Kit's moves ten years later.

It was boogie-woogie country, and it was hot. The crowd loved it. I was glad for that; we weren't playing for a bunch of stiffs. I remembered a gig I had once in Oklahoma, where the—

"You ready?" Hank laid his heavy hand on my shoulder. I almost jumped out of my shoes.

"Jesus! Where you been?"

"None of your business, but it had to do with a lady," he leered at me, laughing.

"Where's my disguise?"

"What?"

"My disguise! For the comedy routine!"

"Oh, yeah. Let's get you something. We're almost on." He casually strolled away. I was near apoplectic. My whole body was breaking out in a flop sweat when I turned and found myself face to face with an angel. A perfect angel.

"You must be Webb Pritchard," she said, reaching out and taking my horribly clammy paw between her warm and tender hands. "Welcome to the show. I'm Nancy Taggart. I'm with the Taggart Family?"

"Yes," I said, suddenly dizzy. "And you are . . . ?"

She looked puzzled for an instant, then laughed a beautiful, silvery laugh that warmed me to the toes. "It's Nancy. Nancy Taggart." She patted my hand. "Now don't be nervous, Mr. Pritchard. You're going to be fine." She gave me a reassuring glance and melted into the backstage darkness.

Then I watched the Taggarts go on. They were a family band, playing old-timey, and Nancy played fiddle. She was so graceful in her plain gingham dress and ugly black shoes she looked like a Bolshoi ballerina out there. She was too good for this earth. I wanted her.

"We're on," hissed Hank in my ear. Damn it, he was beginning to grate on my nerves. Interrupting my reverie about Nancy was a capital offense. He handed me a big black pair of eyeglasses and a pointed dunce-type cap. "Put these on."

"Is this it! You're kidding!"

Doc Mullican's voice echoed again.

"You're in for a treat, folks. The biggest star of the Grand Ole Opry . . . Mr. Hank Williams!!!"

The hat slipped down and covered my ears. I couldn't see anything out of those glasses but a big blur. Somebody gave me a shove and I stumbled out onstage. I felt a guitar being pushed into my hands. I was truly about to throw up from fear when the loudest roar I've ever heard washed down from the crowd, from the rafters to the floor, building into a crescendo that rocked my bones. They wouldn't stop. I could barely make out Hank, standing like a steel reed up at the mike, bowing ever so slightly this way and that. So this was what it was like. Finally, when the noise subsided to a deafening level, Hank turned my way and I heard him utter, "Lovesick Blues."

The gods were with me, for I knew this song backwards and forwards. I kicked it off, and suddenly we were a band. God, we were a great band, because we were backing Hank Williams. When he hit the yodel part, my own knees went weak, so I knew the audience was feeling it, too.

Well, it took another three or four minutes for the applause to die down after that one, and when it did, Hank said, "I've got a new band member tonight, folks, want you to meet my cousin Yahooey." And I knew he was indicating me. I couldn't see a frigging thing, just a blur of spotlights and swirls of color.

The crowd laughed. I must've looked like a complete fool. I bowed deeply. What the hell.

"Tell me, Yahooey, what's the difference between a guitar"—he said it *git*-tar—"like that one there you're playing, and an onion?"

I stared in the general direction of his voice.

"Boy, I don't know, Cousin Hank, what *is* the difference between this here guitar I'm playing and an onion?"

"Nobody'd cry if you cut up that guitar!"

The audience roared with laughter.

"Tell me, Yahooey," Hank continued, "how can you tell if the stage is level?"

"Now you got me there, Cousin Hank. How *do* you tell if the stage is level?"

"*Git*-tar picker's drooling out of both sides of his mouth, that's how," Hank said, and began slapping his knees and har-de-har-harring.

I hoped that would be it, and it was. He launched into "Jambalaya" and we were cooking again. It was over so quick. Soon I was being led off the stage and into what seemed like a dark pit. But it was just stairs, once I took off the glasses. Then the dunce hat.

"You did fine, son," Hank was saying, patting me on the shoulder. Doc Mullican came up.

"OK, he's funny," he said, shooting me a wink and hurrying on. It was sort of controlled chaos backstage. I suddenly wondered where Nancy was.

But by then whoever went on after Hank was finishing up, and somebody was calling my name.

"Pritchard! Go! It's you!" a man was saying. I picked up my banjo and took a humongous breath. Time to get nervous all over again, and I was barely recovered from Hank. I walked to the bottom of the stairs and began climbing. Up at the fifth step was the stage. I could see the lights.

"What song are you doing?" Suddenly Nancy was there, at my side.

" 'Cripple Creek.' "

Her eyes widened. "Oh, you can't."

"What? Why not?"

"That's what Lula Mae just did."

"She just did 'Cripple Creek'?"

49

Up on stage, Doc was saying, "And now here's a young man that's going to go real far. A fine banjo picker, a fine singer and a fine Christian—Webb Pritchard!"

Nancy nodded. "Lula Mae just did 'Cripple Creek.' "

Like a condemned man heading for the gallows, I went on up the stairs to face the music.

6

All my life, I'd wanted to hear the cheers. Hear a big crowd go, Yay, Webb, way to go, buddy, we're with ya! Instead, when I was playing bars they'd be drunks, mostly, whoopin' and hollerin'—not because they thought the band was hot, just because they felt like being loud.

Who could blame them? You don't go to a roadhouse to hear the band, you go to get drunk and get laid. Or if things are going real bad, to get drunk and forget. That's the time a little Kitty Wells on the juke-box is like salve on an open wound. Kitty always made me feel better because her own life sounded so damn rotten. Kitty, and of course Merle. Merle Haggard, with a face like a piece of corrugated tin beaten with a ball peen hammer, has been down that road. "She was always there whenever I needed you." Tell it, Merle.

What I'm saying is, I've been down a lot of roads but I wasn't pre-pared for this one. I was scared shitless. I think it's a different kind of scared shitless when you're young and starting out, and you don't know how to act or be but somehow you just know you'll get through to the other side. There's something indestructible there. It's not like that at forty. At forty, a man knows he might not get through to the other side, and brother, that's scary.

My way of dealing with that kind of fear had lately taken a turn for the desperate. Like when a guy in the joint, who was a lot bigger than me, had decided I was a worthless piece of shit and he was going to kill me. This was last year. There I was, on my best behavior in my last few months before getting out, counting every day, and this asshole decided to screw it up.

Well, I knew talking wouldn't do any good. Guy's IQ was about room temperature, you know, and his forehead kind of sloped back at an angle from his eyebrows. Hands the size of goddamned hams. I'm not kidding, he worked in the laundry.

I'd lie awake on my bunk at night, in the wee hours when you hear guys cry out in their sleep and the fluorescent lights that never go out fill the air with a hum you don't notice in the daytime. That's when I'd do my thinking about him.

One day, he came over and set his tray down right across from me in the dining hall, and he just started staring at me. That's all, just staring and chewing. I'm literally about to shit my pants. He could knock my head off with one flick of his wrist.

When I was younger, I know how I would've handled this. I would've stood up, leaned over the table and stuck my face in his face and said, You got a problem? And yes, there would've been a problem, a big problem, in fact, and he would've stood up and it would've come to blows and we would've ended up on the floor and I would've ended up with a fork stuck in the side of my neck.

But at forty, you do things a little differently.

Some kind of mellower survival instinct kicks in, a hormone, who knows. All I know is, as I tried to control the bubble of fear rising in my chest I remembered some old George Raft prison movie from decades ago. I calmly reached over, picked up my spoon and began to whap it loudly on the metal top of the table. Whap. Whap. Whap. Whap. Whap. Whap.

My enemy looked startled. Confused. And then, as I had hoped they would, other guys started banging their spoons in time with mine. They were banging like fools. Just like in the movies.

Whap. Whap. Whap.

I forced myself to stare right back at him, bore a hole in his head. I started grinning. That threw him. He was staring back, but eventually he looked away. That's when I knew I'd won. He never bothered me again.

So as I got to the top of the steps to the stage, I was scared, but in a way I wasn't. I didn't have that indestructible feeling, and I knew I might fuck this up royally, but my life had taken on a what-the-hell quality since I hooked up with Hank. And besides, I knew that George Raft would help me out. Only it wasn't George Raft this time, it was George . . . Jones! Who wasn't even famous yet, technically, but would be, and whose life and work were an inspiration to me.

I came up into the lights to warm applause, and I had no song to do because that bitch Lula Mae had just done a number on me by doing my tune. I would take care of her later, I decided. What a hell of a note. I'd seen her on *Hee Haw* all those years, thinking she was just a sweet old gal, heavy on the cornpone but loaded with talent, and now I find out that behind that big hat and big guitar and big smile lurked a she-devil. All right, I could deal with that. After all, I was George Jones. He'd dealt with a few she-devils in his day.

I strutted up to the mike and took a deep bow, like I deserved it. I did. These folks, forty-four hundred strong at the Stock Show Arena, didn't know they were looking at a man from the future. A man scared shitless.

"Howdy," I said. That's all I said. I couldn't think of anything else. George Jones wasn't coming to my rescue the way George Raft had.

I blinked in the spotlights. My moment in the sun stretched from a nanosecond into a millisecond and strung out to a half second and then dripped over onto a full second. An eternity in show business. Dead air. Somebody coughed.

And then Earl took over. Thank God.

From some buried lint-pocket in my brain, where I'd been stowing all my Earl Scruggs licks, one of them suddenly woke up, realized I was in deep shit, shook the sleep from its eyes and raced down the spinal cord out to my hands. My fingers jumped to life on the fretboard of my banjo and started playing "Ground Speed," one of Earl's best tunes, a fast breakdown full of twists and surprises.

Now I was truly on dangerous ground. Earl Scruggs hadn't written this tune yet! But hell, I'd started it and I had to finish it. I couldn't just veer off into "Wreck of the Old 97." I knew this number in my sleep. Maybe not quite as well as "Cripple Creek," and it was more difficult to play, but it was going to save my ass in front of forty-four hundred country music fans. I hoped Earl wasn't sitting in the audience.

I got to the middle part and started to relax a hair. I looked up. It was blackness past the lights and I was glad to be blinded. I did not want to see beyond the front of the stage, believe me. Because then Earl might desert me and Webb Pritchard would be up there all alone and I would die right there in front of all these good people.

I got into it now, faster and faster, and decided I might as well get really stupid. I threw in a few Bela Fleck licks. Yowee! Got away with it. You won't hear the likes of this for another forty years, friends, I silently told my audience. Listen up.

Well, I ripped that puppy to shreds. My last break was so fast I thought my fingers would catch fire. My fifth string broke as I tore off the last notes. I didn't care.

They roared. They stamped their feet. I couldn't fucking believe it. Where are you guys in the nineties, when I need you . . . I bowed deeply several times and backed away toward the darkness behind me. Now I knew what Hank knew, what it felt like. The drug of adulation. The adoration, like an orgasm from the people . . .

"Jesus, will you get off the frigging stage?"

Hank's hissing voice in my ear and hand on my shoulder told me it was time to, uh, get real. He fairly pushed me down the dark steps. My trick knee cried out.

I got to the bottom and Lula Mae was there. She was beaming.

"You were terrific, Webb! They love you!"

"No thanks to you."

She pouted, and it really didn't work on her fortysomething face. Her stage makeup creased.

"Aw, you know more than one song, kid. I wanted to see if you had what it takes. Well, you did. That's all. We still having a drink after the show?"

I pushed past her without answering. I was looking for Nancy. The banjo picker from the Taggart Family walked up just then. He was shaking his head in disbelief.

"Man, what was that number? I never heard it before. Sounded like your banjo was on fire out there."

Uh-oh. "Thanks. It's just a little tune I picked up somewhere."

"Will you teach it to me?"

"Uh, sure." What could I say? "No, I'm afraid not, you see, Earl Scruggs won't write this tune for another ten years, and Bela Fleck's not even born yet . . ."

We talked banjo for a while, something I always find pleasurable, but I kept watching for Nancy out of the corner of my eye. I finally spied her coming our way, and was about to step over, when Mr. Ubiquitous blocked my path.

"We're on," was all Hank said, and I had to grab that stupid hat and glasses again. My moment in the sun began to fade into a shadow. Hank's shadow. He was starting to piss me off.

Once again, I had to stumble up those steps, not able to see a goddamned thing through those Coke-bottle lenses, and stand near the back of the stage, out of the limelight. I swore to myself I wouldn't do this comedy thing again. Hell, I might not play with Hank again. The crowd had loved me as Webb Pritchard, banjo picker extraordinaire. I wasn't about to make a fool of myself night after night just to make him look good. Fuck him.

He brought down the house all over again. God, he was amazing. So fragile in the flesh, a jackstraw filled with talent. It held him up, made him live. He could project it. It was there, in him, burning, and it made him the greatest country music star there ever was. Damn him. This poor Alabama boy, he wasn't handsome, he wasn't honest, in some ways he wasn't too smart, he was mean and lowdown and two-timing. He could turn his charm on and off like a faucet. But when he sat down in a hotel room or the backseat of a car, pulled out his guitar, licked a pencil and started putting his life down on paper, and strummed a few little licks to get things started, baby, that was it. There was nobody better. Not then, not now. And he could sing! He told his own stories better than anyone, sang 'em in a plain, straight, hard country voice, and when he threw in a little yodel women broke down and strong men felt weak.

Man, he was pissing me off.

We did one encore and the show was over. I suddenly felt tired. All I wanted was to go back to my hotel room and sleep. It was not to be. As soon as we descended into the backstage area, the bottles came out and the party began. Somebody handed me a Lone Star longneck. Somebody else handed me a shot of bourbon. Doc Mullican, already well in his cups, came swerving by and clapped me on the shoulder.

"Well done, my boy, well done," he said, regarding me with a look he might have used at a prize-hog auction. "Fine debut. Never heard that song you played, but it was a corker. Do it tomorrow night, you hear?" And he lurched off.

Great. I would make my mark in country music ripping off Earl Scruggs tunes before they were written. Wonder what Earl would have to say about that.

I'd have to do my own tune. I'd have to write one. Fast. The best songwriter in the world was my roommate at the moment. That couldn't hurt. I was wondering if Hank could think up a number for the banjo when Nancy swam into view, all gingham and clodhoppers. She was beautiful.

"Oh, Webb!" she said, grabbing my elbow. I turned into mush. "That was simply wonderful! Everybody's talking about that song you did. I had no idea you could play that way. What was the name of the song?"

" 'Ground Speed.' "

"Did you write it?"

"No. No, I didn't."

"Who did?"

Now, Earl Scruggs was already quite famous in 1951. He was in his prime, in fact, coming into his own as the "Paganini of the banjo," as *The New York Times* would later put it. He was breaking new ground, turning the instrument on its head and making some of the most influential recordings of his career. A couple years earlier, he and Lester Flatt had left Bill Monroe and the Blue Grass Boys, the seminal band in bluegrass music, and he was a force to be reckoned with. In short, I couldn't fuck with Earl.

"Uh, I forget." Pretty lame, I admit.

"Oh, come on."

"No, really, Nancy, I just heard it somewhere . . . I'm not even sure I could play it again."

"Bullshit!"

I looked at her in shock. I couldn't believe she would say that, this sweet little country gingham gal. Back before women said bullshit. At least, I know my mom wouldn't have said it.

"Bullshit!" she said again, and laughed a tinkly laugh. "I'm going to get a beer. I'll be back."

She was gone before I could react, but then Lula Mae shanghaied me. I was still mad at her.

"You still mad at me?" she asked, draining the last of her Lone Star.

"Hell, yes, I'm still mad. You could've screwed me up bad out there. In front of forty-four hundred people. I've never played in front of that many people before."

"I know. I could tell."

"So why'd you do it?"

She shrugged. "To see what would happen."

"Gee, thanks a lot. Hope you were entertained."

"Well, if you hadn't pulled it off, you don't belong here. But you did, and so it was all right. Right?"

"No, it wasn't all right. It was a shitty thing to do."

"Let me buy you a beer, then."

"We've got plenty of beer here."

Lula Mae eyeballed me. "Get with the program, Webb. I'm asking you out for a beer. Get to know you better. You can get to know me. I can tell you don't know much about this business. I could help you."

I looked down into her homely face, hard with stage makeup, and I saw something tender around the edges. Not attractive, mind you, but tender. A middle-aged woman who'd spent her whole life on the road, playing stock show arenas and county fairs, smelling cow shit and staying in fleabag motels. Dealing with hard men. Men who drank too much and were stupid, besides. She'd carved out a space for herself, by herself, as far as I knew, and that was no easy thing for a woman to do in 1951.

Nancy returned.

"OK."

"We're going out for a beer," I said to her. "Wanna come?"

She looked at Lula Mae and read her face, and shook her head. "No, I think I'm too tired tonight. Dad's not feeling well, either. I should stick around."

I wondered if Nancy, who was probably about twenty-two, would be like Lula Mae when she got older. I tried to remember what had happened to the Taggart Family after Elvis, but I couldn't. That probably meant that rock 'n' roll destroyed them, and they went back to the hills, and obscurity.

"Let's go, then," said Lula Mae.

I followed her out of the arena to her car, a battered old Dodge. A far cry from Hank's creamy Cadillac. It was filled with a woman's things: makeup kits, hatboxes, dresses strung up on hangers. The tattered upholstery smelled of talcum powder and cheap cologne.

"Where to?" I asked.

"I know a place," she said, slipping into gear.

"I bet you do, Lula Mae," I said. "I bet you do."

I was expecting a roadhouse, but she took me to Carmine's, a jazz club downtown. She had wiped off her makeup and had a light wrap thrown over her puff-sleeved dress. She'd slipped out of her black-strapped clodhoppers and put on some flats, and she really looked pretty normal. I wasn't embarrassed to be with her.

We went down some low steps and entered a subterranean space filled with smoke and dim red lights. A three-piece combo—piano, bass, drums—was cooking on a tiny bandstand. "Hey, Carmine!" she called out as we entered the room. A short Italian man appeared out of the dark and welcomed her warmly with a hug.

"Lula Mae. How long has it been?"

"Too long, babe. How about a booth and a couple of beers. This here's my friend Webb."

Carmine bowed to me formally. "Welcome. You're a musician?"

"All my friends are musicians," Lula Mae said. "He plays the banjo. He's new to the Hayride."

"A banjo player. A jazz fan, too, perhaps?"

"I like all kinds of music," I said, "as long as I can hear the melody."

"Melodies we have," Carmine said, sweeping us into a booth. "Two Lone Stars?"

"Two Lone Stars," said Lula Mae, "and two shots."

It was about midnight. The place was a little over half full. Not a Hank crowd, for sure. No sawdust on the floor, no Kitty Wells on the jukebox. No farmers. Nobody who'd been at the Stock Show Arena earlier that evening. We were totally anonymous. I liked the change of scenery.

Carmine brought our drinks. Lula Mae settled back and rolled her shoulders, stretching her neck and jutting her chin.

"Aaaah. Nice to relax, isn't it?" she said. Even in the forgiving light of Carmine's, Lula Mae wasn't young. All her years on the road showed through, and she was comfortable with it. Not like some women, who panic when they hit thirty-five. I thought of her on *Hee Haw*, decades from now, all wrinkled and still perky as hell. What a dame.

"Where'd you come from, Webb?"

"Oklahoma. Tulsa."

"Bob Wills territory."

"Yep."

"You know him?"

"No, but I love his music." That was the truth. I had all his albums.

"I've played Tulsa many times. Cain's Ballroom. Nice town. But not wild enough for me."

"Me, either. That's why I left. Where're you from?"

She smiled. "New York City. Brooklyn, actually."

"You're kidding."

"Nope. My parents were Irish immigrants. They owned a bar. We lived above it."

"But . . . your accent. Your act. Country music."

"I've been gone so long. Wanna hear my life story?"

"Sure. Isn't that what people talk about in bars? What time does Carmine close up?"

"I'll keep it short. Just the highlights."

"OK."

"Like I said, my folks ran this bar in Williamsburg. In Brooklyn. I had six brothers; I was the only girl. My parents let the boys help out in the saloon, but they didn't want me there. Too corrupting. So of course I was there every chance I could get. Mostly, I loved the music. We had Irish music, Irish bands. I knew all the songs by heart.

"I was smart in school. They were going to send me to college, a big deal for an Irish girl from Brooklyn, but when I was seventeen I met this banjo player—"

"Banjo player!"

"In an Irish band. His name was Michael. He was very hand-some."

"Don't tell me. You ran off with him."

"I ran off with him. Indeed. My parents had a heart attack."

"I bet."

"We got married, of course, and we traveled with the band. I got pregnant. We had a little boy. We named him James. Jimmy. I thought my life was set. You know how it is when you're young. You know it all."

I just nodded and sipped my beer. I hadn't touched my shot yet.

"But I didn't know it all. After a couple of years, Michael was cheating on me. Then he ran off with a singer. That bitch. I can still see her. She ended up broke and alcoholic after Michael left her. Served her right.

"Anyway, there I was, barely twenty, with a kid and no husband. No money. The guys in the band were sympathetic, but what could they do? I didn't want to go back to my folks. I'd seen the world and it didn't stop at the Williamsburg Bridge. I couldn't see a life mopping up behind the bar.

"One of the guys in the band had a sister in Nashville. She was married to a musician. She offered to take me in if I'd do her housekeeping. It was just a temporary thing. Till I figured out what to do. So me and Jimmy moved in with this family. We lived above the garage. I started meeting a lot of musicians through the family, and that's how I got into country music. I started singing at parties. Just for fun. I wasn't real pretty, so I'd tell jokes to win people over. I got rid of my Brooklyn accent. I turned myself into a hick. Mary Margaret O'Shaughnessy from Bedford Avenue became Lula Mae Loudermilk from Deep Gap, Tennessee."

Mary Margaret?

"And it worked. I polished the act. Somebody told me I should turn professional. I began playing at little bars around Nashville, and that turned into an offer to go on the road with the Gully Jumpers. You heard of them?"

"Uh, no."

"Most people haven't. Anyway, we played every roadhouse from Wheeling to Mobile. I learned fast what worked and what didn't. It was tough on Jimmy. I worried about how he was growing up. What the road was doing to him. After trying a bunch of times, I was able to get somebody at the Opry to audition me. And I passed. I joined the cast. You know how tough it is, to break into the Opry? And I did it without sleeping with anybody, either.

"That's when I was able to base out of Nashville. Me and Jimmy moved there, and got a little house, and he started going to school regularly."

I looked around the bar. The guy on drums was brushing a single snare with a soft rhythm. The piano player was doing Gershwin. Lula Mae kept talking. I kept listening.

"Then I met Bob. He worked behind the scenes at the Opry, and he became my manager, my husband. My savior. A father to Jimmy. Those were the good years."

She reached for her shot, untouched till now, and drained it. I knew something terrible was coming. She was silent for several moments.

"And?"

She looked away, across the room. "And then he died. Killed in a car accident one Saturday night after the show. He was taking a friend home. I wasn't with him."

"I'm sorry."

"Yeah," she said softly. "We were married fourteen years. Jimmy finished high school, and I kept working. There were other men . . . but nobody important. A lot of drunks."

"What happened to the Opry? How'd you end up on the Hayride?"

She smiled bitterly. "They dropped me two years ago. Said I was too old and not funny anymore. Maybe they're right."

"Too old! How old is Uncle Dave Macon? He's over a hundred." He was actually in his seventies.

"He's a legend, honey. I'm not. I'm a forty-eight-year-old woman with an act that may be passing into history. I can't change now. This is what I do."

I wanted to tell her she'd find a whole new audience in twenty years on *Hee Haw* as a wisecracking granny in a big straw hat and a silly gingham dress. But for now, she was a lonely, middle-aged woman looking into a future of stock show arenas and bad diners.

"Where's Jimmy?"

She brightened. "He's in Nashville. He works for Fred Rose at Acuff-Rose Publishing. He got married three years ago, and they have a baby girl. I'm a grandmother."

"Congratulations."

"Now, Webb. How about you?"

"Oh, it's not very interesting."

"Watch out. Those are the wild ones."

"Well, let's see. Like I said, I'm from Tulsa. Both my parents taught school. My dad taught high school science and my mom taught Spanish. They made us do our homework. We always had a lot of books around the house and we all read a lot. My sister Dot and I, we were real smart kids. But when I got to high school . . ."

Lula Mae nodded knowingly. "You turned wild."

God, if she only knew. I couldn't tell her I'd become a major pothead and totally blown off my education. Turned hippie. Dealing drugs and living in crash pads. Nobody was doing that in the twenties, when I would've been in high school by her calculations.

Instead, I said, "I got in with a wild crowd and dropped out. Broke my parents' heart."

That part was true. Dot was already in college when I quit my junior year and left home. I remember my dad telling me I'd be back. But I never went back. Life just kept pushing me on down the road. I outgrew the hippie phase, but somehow I never got around to finishing my education and taking the path I suppose my parents had wanted me to take.

"I've been knocking around for a while," I said, leaving out the prison part. "I'm trying to get my act established. I used to work construction, but the music was too important. I'm forty years old. Been married a couple times. Didn't work out."

"Kids?"

"No."

"Anybody special in your life?"

I thought of Nancy first. Then Marie.

"I see."

"I didn't say anything!"

She smiled. "You didn't have to."

"I like you, Mary Margaret O'Shaughnessy."

"How about one more beer and we call it a night?"

"That sounds dandy."

We drank a while longer, not talking, just listening to the combo play Gershwin melodies. Around two-thirty, we split the tab and left. I held her arm as we walked out to the Dodge. She drove carefully back to the shabby little motel where we were all staying.

"G'night, Webb."

"G'night, Lula Mae."

I fell asleep that night hearing "Ground Speed" in my head, but it kept getting all mixed up with "Rhapsody in Blue."

7

Living in the past got hard sometimes. No 7-Elevens, no automatic teller machines, no TV. You get used to things like that being around. I could do without a lot, but I really missed eating microwave popcorn and watching the Cowboys on Sunday afternoons. Not that I had a lot of opportunity to do that down at McAlester. I'd pop a tape into the old VCR when things got slow around the Shang-Grah-Lah. Maybe *Top Gun*, or, if I was in one of my occasional sappy moods, some bitch-from-hell tearjerker with Bette Davis. She's my secret vice, Bette is. *Dark Victory. All About Eve. Whatever Happened to Baby Jane?* So here I was, out of prison but still trapped in a world without access to my favorite vices. I'd have to get myself some new vices.

On the other hand, there were some good things, too. Home cooking sure tasted better before everything got reduced to Hamburger Helper and women forgot how to use a stove. The air was mostly clear. Kids minded their parents. Nobody locked their doors at night, at least as far as I could determine. And a man wasn't confused about whatever power trip his woman might be on. They had power trips, all right, but they kept them to themselves and worked on you in subtler ways. And they still won.

Nancy wasn't quite the naive kid I had first made her out to be. Turned out she'd been on the road since she was practically a baby. The Taggart Family band had started with her grandparents before World War I, an Appalachian string band traveling the South in a converted hay wagon. Since then, it had blossomed into a thoroughly professional outfit. Dad Taggart was boss. His name was Chester, but everybody called him Muley for some reason. Muley Taggart was close to fifty. A plain-looking, plainspoken man with five daughters, two sons and a wife who kept things running smoothly backstage.

He knew I had my eye on daughter Nancy. He didn't think much of it.

We were fixing a flat one afternoon on a county road in southern Nebraska. Doc Mullican's show was caravaning from Denver toward Omaha. Hank's Caddy had blown a tire. Hank was too wiped to help. I had to drag him out of the backseat so we could jack the car up. He was standing a ways away, just sort of swaying there in the hot summer wind. Muley was helping me.

"Webb, you're a good man," he said, loosening the lug nuts. He handled that tire iron like it was a toothpick.

I didn't really say anything. I had a feeling what was coming.

"You're a good man but you got no business around my Nancy. She's too young for you, you know what I mean?" Muley squinted up at me.

"We're just friends."

He snorted and spit a bullet of tobacco juice into the dust.

"I don't blame you, son. I'm just tellin' you to keep it light."

"She's a grown woman, Muley."

That made him stand up. He was much taller than I was. His face was hard.

"As long as she's in the Taggart Family, she's under my wing. She wants to head off on her own, that's her decision. Until then, keep clear of her, you understand?"

Well, he was holding the tire iron, not me.

"Don't worry. She's teaching me some fiddle tunes, that's all. We sound good together."

"Yer not gettin' it, are you, son?"

"I guess not."

"Where I come from, a man has intentions, he makes himself plainly understood. He offers something. A farm, a home, a business in town. A future. None of my daughters is going to run off with some two-bit banjo picker without a dollar to his name. You been in prison, I heard. That true?"

"Yeah, it's true. I shot a guy who was stealing my tools."

Muley stared down at me for several moments, his fingers wrapping and unwrapping around the tire iron. Then he squatted back down and resumed his task. He didn't say another word. He didn't have to.

That night, the show was bunked down at the Piney Cone Motor Hotel in tiny Alma, Nebraska. The last several nights, Nancy and I had been meeting after every show, playing little duets off by ourselves. She started it. She had come to me after the second night at the Stock Show Arena in Denver, toting her fiddle.

"Let's play some tunes."

"Right now? Where?"

"I don't know. Anywhere."

We found a quiet corner and tuned up. It was all so innocent. She tapped her foot and kicked off "Old Joe Clark," which I knew, and together we rollicked through dozens of songs. She was a natural. Banjo and fiddle complement each other well, and she and I did, too. She knew far more tunes than I did, and her sources were impeccable. Mine, of course, were well diluted. I learned songs off Greatest Hits albums, out of books on old-timey music, and from archival videos. Sometimes, people taught me tunes. But Nancy knew them from the mountain people themselves, from her grandparents and her father. And you could hear it in the way she played.

I was feeling low that night at the Piney Cone. I had been on the road with the Hayride for about ten days. I didn't know if I'd ever get back home. And now Muley Taggart had told me I couldn't see his daughter anymore, not if I didn't want a tire iron upside the head.

There was a knock at the door. I looked over at Hank. He was snoring on the bed. I got up and went to see who it was.

"Hi! Ready to do some tunes?" It was Nancy.

"Uh, not tonight."

"Oh. Why not?"

"Cause your old man'll kill me."

"Dad? What are you talking about?"

"He told me today I shouldn't see you anymore. He was holding a big steel bar at the time."

She giggled. "I don't care. He doesn't know I'm here."

Women are a powerful thing. When they're standing right in front of you it's awfully hard to worry about fathers with tire irons. I pulled her into the room and shut the door. Hank just kept snoring.

"We can't stay here," I said. "We'll go somewhere."

"How?"

"We'll take the Cadillac."

Hank always kept his car keys in his right front pants pocket. Unfortunately, he was wearing his trousers at the moment. I approached the bed slowly. Nancy was covering her mouth to keep from laughing out loud.

I bent over Hank. His mouth was open. His skinny chest rose and fell, rose and fell. I reached down and slipped my fingers gently into his pocket. He didn't move. My hand slid down. Deeper. I felt something cold and hard. Keys. My fingers closed around them.

"Hey!" Hank jerked awake. "What the hell're you doin'?"

My hand shot back like it had touched a hot iron.

"Uh, stealing your car keys, Hank."

He raised up on his elbows and saw Nancy. He broke into a broad grin.

"Aw, hell. Have a good time. Muley know you're here?"

"No," Nancy said.

"Good. Hey, bring me back a bottle of Johnnie Walker, will you? Black Label." He tossed me the car keys.

Nancy and I slipped out the door and dashed along the side of the motel like thieves, finally reaching the big, gleaming automobile. She crawled in and stayed down low while I put it into gear and rolled out of the parking lot, nice and easy.

We went a couple miles. A thought struck me.

"Hey. I didn't bring my banjo."

"That's all right. I left my fiddle back in your room."

We both laughed like hell.

Now Alma was by a lake, so we drove out there. Seemed like the natural thing to do. We had picked up Hank's booze first, plus a bottle of bourbon for ourselves. We were tooling along in the Caddy, feeling pretty fine. Sharing swigs from the bottle. I saw a dirt road turn off toward the water, into the woods, and I took it. Nancy didn't say anything.

I turned on the radio and there was Hank.

"Goddammit, you can't get rid of the guy," I snarled, and snapped it off.

66

"Let me try," Nancy said, and turned it back on. She found a station playing mellow dance music. We left it there.

The road got bumpier, but you could hardly feel it in the big ol' Caddy. She rode like she had butter in her shocks. I took her down farther, till we reached the shore of Harlan County Lake. It's a big lake. You could barely make out the other side. Just some faraway lights. We were parked under some trees, and a warm breeze blew in the windows.

I took the liberty of sliding the front seat back several inches. Nancy passed me the bottle. I took a good long drink. I handed it back to her, and she took a big swallow.

"What do you think of the Hayride?" she said. Her brown hair cascaded invitingly down her neck.

"It's a nuthouse," I replied. "Where else can you find Hank Williams and me on the same bill?"

She smiled. "Everybody thinks you're really good."

"They've never heard Earl Scruggs."

"Some of us have. I have. You're better."

"Uh-huh. I'm sure Earl would agree."

"You'll get a chance to find out."

"What?"

"I hear Flatt and Scruggs are playing Omaha when we are. With Hank on the bill, they'll come around for a visit."

"Thanks for giving me a reason to be nervous." My God, I was going to get to meet Earl Scruggs in his prime? Hear him play? That's like an artist being invited to watch Michelangelo paint the Sistine Chapel. What would I play? Jesus, I couldn't do any of the famous licks he hadn't invented yet, certainly couldn't do any of his tunes. My entire repertoire was based on Scruggs-style playing! We were due in Omaha in two days. There wasn't any—

"Webb."

"What?"

She flowed into my arms and put her mouth over mine. Oh God in heaven, it had been four years and I just lost it. Her arms wrapped around me and I fell into her sweet warmth. Her smells enveloped me, shampoo and talcum powder and some kind of nice toilet water, made me crazy. Woman smells. I undid her blouse, fumbling like a schoolboy. Her breasts tumbled out and I buried my face in them, kissing her all over. The best part was, she was kissing me back.

67

I pressed her down until she was lying on the seat, and not once did she resist. Her skin was like velvet. I was about to explode. The blouse finally came all the way off, then her skirt. She undid my belt, then the buckle, and unzipped my pants. We were both moaning.

"Not yet, Webb," she whispered.

"Come on," I said, pushing her thighs apart with my knees.

We got closer by inches. I couldn't hold it anymore. I drove home, and she took me, wrapping her legs around my waist, arching her back. Warm, sweet Jesus. We rocked that Caddy like a hobbyhorse, and when we were finished we rested awhile and then did it again.

Afterward, we lay there in the darkness, on the smooth upholstery. I don't know if the GM designers back then knew it—they probably did—but the front seat of a '51 Caddy was just about perfect for making love to your girl. Big enough to get some maneuvering room, but small enough so she couldn't get away. We lay there for what seemed like a long time. Sounds of crickets filled the woods. Just holding her was heavenly. I would've fallen asleep, I think, but she nudged me with her knee. We sat up and arranged ourselves. She began putting her blouse back on.

"You're wonderful," I said.

"So are you."

"It's . . . been a long time, Nancy."

"I could tell."

"Next time I won't be so fast."

"You were fine."

I started the car and she reached over and flipped on the radio. Hank's nasal tones filled the air.

I started my car and she reached over and flipped on the radio. Hank's nasal tones filled the air.

"Our faithful chaperone," Nancy said, laughing. I turned Hank's Caddy for home.

Muley never did catch us, but he must have known something was going on. After our night of love under the trees, Nancy and I managed to get together nearly every night, with a little help from Hank. I'll say this for the guy, he understood about women. Not that he understood women themselves, mind you, hell, he was as mystified as the rest of us, but he understood about them. That's two different things.

Now that my sex life had returned, everything looked better to me. I still thought about Marie, but I'll admit, less and less frequently. As the days passed, I began to fall into the rhythm of the road. We'd play a show, then hit the highway at first light. Ride all day, find a motel, rest, then play a show. There were close to thirty-five of us in the Hayride, counting a few stray spouses, children and yellow dogs. The Taggart Family, Nancy's clan, traveled in a bus. This was way before that became the standard for country music performers. Theirs was an old diesel-belching tin can with about a million miles on it. Musically, they had it together; mechanically speaking, no. The bus was always breaking down. Everybody else traveled in cars. Hank's was the fanciest, though Daniel Eberhardt had a new Buick that he polished almost hourly. It was certainly cleaner than the Caddy.

The show headed on into Omaha for a three-night stand. I smelled the cow shit before we got there: a stockyard town. A brown town with a brown landscape. All the places we hit that smelled like cow manure went for Hank in a big way. I told him this.

"So?"

"Soooo, guess you're just a cowshit kinda guy."

"You ever plow, son?"

"Plow? You mean, like in a field?"

"I mean, plow, behind a mule."

"No, Hank, can't say that I have. That experience somehow escaped me."

He got right up in my face. We were standing in the parking lot of the Plainsman Inn in downtown Omaha. We had just come off the road.

"Too bad. If you had, you might understand what my people are about. Sunup to sundown, workin' that row, workin' the land, smellin' that shit. Farmers, ranchers. Country people. Come Saturday night, they're ready to rip. We give 'em what they want. I give 'em what they want. They know I understand 'em."

"You ever plow, Hank?"

He started laughing. "Hell, no. I'd rather sing and chase women."

The prospect of Omaha did not thrill me. The specter of Earl Scruggs loomed over me like the sword of Damocles. Doc always liked me to play "Ground Speed," but I couldn't get away with that here. In fact, the sooner I got away from playing Scruggs licks and tunes the better. Everybody was talking about how Earl and Lester, Lester Flatt, that is, were going to turn up. They were playing another venue in town. I thought about that: Imagine the good people of Omaha having to choose between Hank Williams and Flatt & Scruggs.

"Feel like going out, Edna?"

"Sure, Lon. What would you like to do?"

"Paper here says Hank Williams's at the Cow Palace."

"Yeah, Lon, but Flatt and Scruggs are over at the VFW hall."

"You got a point there, Edna."

Plus, my nerves were wracked that Earl would see me play, period. I could manage to stay away from his songs, but picking in front of the Pickmeister was going to be a trial by fire. Geez, maybe I should stick to rhythm guitar for the next few nights.

"Got a problem?"

"Hi, Lula Mae."

I had been musing my fate in the lobby of the Plainsman. Hank was entertaining a ladyfriend in our room, so I was temporarily homeless.

"Hank toss you out?"

"Afraid so. I can't figure out what to play tonight."

"What's wrong with what you have been playing?"

How could I explain?

"Well, Earl Scruggs is supposed to show up tonight. I'm nervous, is all."

She laughed. "Earl's just a North Carolina boy. I know him well. He's just folks. You don't have any call to be worried. I'll introduce you!"

I looked glum.

She sat down next to me and patted my knee. "The time for you to be nervous is over and done. I already pushed you over that cliff."

I suddenly needed to be alone. As nice as I could, I got away from Lula Mae. I went back to my room, and knocked softly on the door. No answer. I knocked harder.

From within: "Go away!"

"Hank, it's me."

"I don't care, go away."

"Hank, I just need my banjo. That all right?"

Silence. I heard female giggles. Much shuffling about. In a minute or two, the door opened a tiny crack. Hank's eyeball appeared at the crack.

70

"What do you want, boy? Next time you and Nancy get together, I'm gonna come around and serenade you."

"I need my banjo. It's by the chair."

"Hell." He shut the door. He was back in a second, shoving my banjo case out.

"Now git!"

The door slammed.

I took the banjo around the side of the motel where there was a patch of grass and a shade tree. I took out the banjo, tuned her up, and began doodling, just doing some finger exercises. I had to practice some new shit before tonight. The show was about three hours away.

My fingers gradually limbered up, and I started working on a few tunes I thought might do the trick. They had to be flashy and fast, but nothing Earl would do. I tried five or six before settling on a jazzed-up version of "Cluck Old Hen." You could play it real fast and make it seem wilder than it really was.

Then, just for fun, and because I was loose, I lit into "Ground Speed." I didn't even play the whole thing, just a slice of it, a couple of up-the-neck licks and a shave-and-a-haircut ending.

"That was mighty nice."

I looked up and there was Earl Scruggs.

My heart stopped. God, he was so young. The Earl I'd seen in person at a couple of festivals was well into middle age, a graying eminence.

"You played that real nice. How do you do, I'm Earl Scruggs." And he stepped up and shook my hand.

"I—gosh, I know who you are. I'm pleased to meet you. I'm Webb Pritchard."

"You with the Hayride?"

"Yes, I play in Hank's band right now, but they give me a spot to do one banjo tune."

"You ought to do that one I just heard you play."

"Uh, that's just a couple licks I was working on."

"Do 'em again." He just stood there, grinning at me.

Jesus, what could I do? I played 'em again, but just the few licks I had played before. Not the whole song.

"Yeah, I like that. That all you got?"

I nodded stupidly.

71

"I could see where that might go into a D chord there. Do you mind?" And he took the banjo off my shoulder and hoisted it onto his own. He dug into his pocket and pulled out his fingerpicks and put them on. He played back the licks I'd just played, note for note, then added a couple of his own.

"Yeah, like this," he said, and started improvising like crazy. I was spellbound.

Finally, I said, "Mr. Scruggs, you're my all-time favorite banjo player. You've been a huge influence on me."

"It's Earl. And I don't think you need much help. You sound like you know where you're going with it. Nice banjo." He handed me back Lil Darlin'.

He was such a kind, straightforward guy, I wanted to cry. I wanted to fall down on my knees in the grass beside the Plainsman Inn and tell this man he was the greatest bluegrass musician who ever lived, the man who reinvented banjo playing and inspired generations of pickers and who sometimes had single-handedly kept me going in the joint.

Instead, I said, "Thanks."

"Hey, is Hank around?"

I rolled my eyes. "Well, he's around, but he's tied up at the moment, if you know what I mean. That's why I'm out here."

Earl laughed. "Well, I'll see him tonight after the show, then. Look forward to hearing you play again, Webb. Keep workin' on that tune." And he walked away.

I stood there under the shade tree without moving for a very long time. Then I burst into tears, for no good reason.

8

Hank took a long time. Finally, around half past six, I got back into our room. Hank was sitting cross-legged on his bed, completely naked except for his cowboy boots.

"New image for the Hayride?" I asked, getting ready to shave. "It's gonna go over big with the women, I'll tell you that." I filled the basin with hot water and started jabbing my shaving brush into the mug of soap, stirring up a lather. "Don't know if Doc Mullican'll go for it, though."

"I feel like writing a song," Hank said, and stood up. He went tearing around the room in his milky white birthday suit, looking, I suppose, for a pencil and something to write on. I turned around, my face half lathered.

"Do you always write songs naked?"

"Watch me," he said, and plopped back down on the chenille bedspread. I could count every one of his ribs.

"Don't you want your guitar?"

"Nope." He bent to his task.

Then he looked up. "Wait."

He got up, went tearing around the room again and found what he was looking for: his hat. He settled back down on the bed.

"Mmmmmmm." He was humming.

"Can I watch?"

"What are you, some kind of fairy? Wanna stare at a nekkid man?"

"No, I want to see you write a song."

"Ain't nothin' to see. Awright. You can look but you can't touch."

"I'll try to control myself."

His pencil scratched away at a scrap of paper he'd found. He'd hum a little, and scratch a little.

"Well?" I asked after several minutes of this. I continued shaving.

"Well, what?"

"Well, how's it coming? I mean, what're you writing? Can you hear the song in your head?" The process just didn't look all that enlightening to me.

He frowned. "I need hep."

"You want me, Webb Pritchard, to help you, Hank Williams, write a song?"

"Just a word. If I said to you, 'Take me back,' what do you say?"

" 'To old Virginny.' "

"Yer pullin' Ole Hank's leg, son. If I say, 'Take me back,' I'm gonna follow with something like, 'the way you used to do,' right?"

"How about 'Carry me back.' Not take me, carry me."

"Why would I want my woman to carry me back?"

I shrugged. "Sounds better."

Hank sat there thinking, a naked man chewing on a pencil stub. Then he began writing again.

"Did I help?" I asked, leaning over his shoulder to look at what he was doing. He smelled sweaty. "You stink," I said.

"I been screwin', I ain't gonna smell like no daisy," he replied. He kept writing for maybe fifteen minutes, while I bathed and dressed. The show was barely an hour away.

"C'mon, Hank," I said. "You'll be late."

"I got it! We got it! We got us a song!" He leapt off the bed and waved the piece of paper in my face. "This is it! The song that's gonna put me back on the Opry! Old Hank shall rise again!" And he marched into the bathroom, in his cowboy boots and hat, and slammed the door.

"Hey, Hank," I called out. I could hear him start the tub. "What's it called?"

"What?"

74

"What's it called? The song?"

" 'Carry Me Back.' "

I had a secret plan no one knew about, not Doc Mullican, not Nancy, not Lula Mae, and certainly not Hank.

The Hayride was playing the Cow Palace, another fabulous stock-yard venue. It was near downtown. Hell, back in '51, everything was near downtown. You'd be driving through open fields and bam! there was a town. Not like today, where you sort of creep up on a city bit by bit, past the newly sprung tract homes and the Wal-Marts and the Sirloin Stockades and the Taco Bells and then there's the older suburbs and then finally the city limits and then, buried somewhere in the middle, downtown.

So everything was pretty much within hollering distance. I knew Flatt & Scruggs were playing the VFW hall, and their show started an hour before ours did. I left Hank singing in the bathroom, and left the hotel on foot, setting out to find the VFW hall. If I turned down a chance to see Earl Scruggs in his prime, I might as well hang up my banjo and go be a shoe salesman. And I was not about to do that.

I walked along the streets of Omaha, dressed in my spiffy stage duds, carrying my banjo case. I got a few looks from people. After a few blocks, I came to a little old gas station. That's something they don't have anymore, either, though I'm old enough to remember them. You know, the kind where a guy comes out wearing black-green coveralls with the name *Bob* stitched over the pocket in red thread. And he pumps your gas and cleans your windshield and checks your oil while you shoot the shit with him. That was the kind of gas station this was.

I knew Bob would know where the VFW hall was. Hell, he probably belonged.

Sure enough, he came right out when I wandered up. I looked at the name, stitched in red thread above his breast pocket. *Bob.*

"What can I do for you?" he asked, sticking his grease cloth in his back pocket. He held a wrench in his other hand.

"I'm looking for the VFW hall."

He stared at my banjo case. "You ain't Earl Scruggs, are you?"

"Gosh, no," I said quickly, laughing. "I hope to go see him."

"I really like that Flatt and Scruggs," Bob said. "Boy, he can pick that banjar." That's how he said it.

"That he can," I blandly replied.

"Do you play like him?"

"Well, I try." I couldn't help myself. "Actually, I play with Hank Williams at the moment." At the moment! What a total bullshitter!

Bob looked startled. "No! You don't say!"

Now I was embarrassed. "Uh, well, I play a little backup, that's all."

"You don't say! The missus and me are goin' to that show tonight. Will we see you?"

"You bet."

"If we came around back, do you think you could get us an autograph? Of Hank?"

"Uh, sure. Come around back after the show, uh, Bob."

He stuck out his greasy paw. "It's really Bill." He pumped my hand energetically. When I brought it away, it was streaked with black grease. I gingerly reached for my handkerchief.

"Anyway," I said, "I've really got to be getting to the VFW hall. Where would that be?"

"It's too far to walk. I'll give you a lift. I was about to shut 'er up for the day, anyhow."

Bob, or rather Bill, scurried about shutting 'er up and then backed an ancient Ford truck out of one of his bays. I carefully placed my banjo in the back and climbed into the cab. More grease.

"Hope you don't mind a little dirt," Bill said, clearing away debris so he could sit down. I was getting my stage clothes filthy. Ah, well, Earl, you'll be worth it, I thought.

We bounced along and it seemed like we were heading away from town.

"How far is it?" I asked, after a few minutes.

"VFW hall's a little ways out, maybe five miles."

Holy shit. How would I ever get back to the Hayride? I had a thought.

"Hey, Bob, I mean Bill, would you do me a big favor? I'll get you two Hank autographs."

His eyebrows shot up. "Sure. What?"

"When you and your wife head for the Cow Palace, could you swing back by the VFW and take me back? I can't miss the show."

He nodded instantly, then he frowned. "I'll have to ask Mabel. It's out of our way."

"You do that. She'll understand."

We were silent the rest of the way. I think he was working on how to break the news to Mabel, who, I gathered, was not as big a Hank fan as her husband was.

He swung the old Ford down a side street and there was the hall, with a big crowd out front, edging inside. I opened the truck door and hopped out. I looked at my watch.

"I'll be out here at seven-fifty sharp, Bill. OK?" That, I hoped, would give me enough time to get back to the Cow Palace and be ready a couple minutes before Hank's first number.

He looked worried. "OK."

"Don't be late!" I called, watching him drive off in a cloud of dust. Boy, Hank'd be pissed if he knew where I was.

I pressed into the crowd, trying not to bang my banjo against too many people. It was a real crush of folks, and the hall was packed. Gee, they didn't want to see the Great Hank Williams? I didn't blame them.

It cost me $2 to get in. I was too late to get up front, but I managed to work my way along the side until I got within forty feet of the stage. It was five after seven. Come on, guys, I silently whispered to Lester and Earl. I don't get to see your whole set.

Some of the novelty of being in the past had begun to wear off, I have to be honest, but I admit my adrenaline was pumping. Flatt & Scruggs! Live! In Person! In '51! I mean, for some it would be a chance to see Elvis before he got fat, for others the Beatles at the Cavern Club. Or Sinatra in the fifties. For me, it was Earl Scruggs when he and Lester were just starting out.

They were already seasoned road veterans, having spent the last several years in Bill Monroe's band. But a couple of years ago, they had broken with Bill, and now they had their own band and their own sound.

I was the only person in the room who was aware that Earl was on the verge of greatness. Then I looked around. These people knew how good he was! For crying out loud, I was starting to bullshit even myself.

The room was close. So many people. Women in cotton print

dresses and men in overalls, squirming children on their mamas' laps. Old farmers and their portly wives, holding hands. Fanning themselves with straw hats. A night on the town.

There they were! Lester Flatt, Earl Scruggs and the Foggy Mountain Boys! They stepped out into the lights and the room was pandemonium. People stomping on that old wood floor, whistling, calling. Hey, Earl! Hey, Lester! Play us a tune!

And they did. I was swept away in the very first moments, Earl's flow of notes so clear and clean you could've driven a semi truck between his sixteenth notes. What timing! What tone! How does the man do it? Nobody sounds like him, before or since. There're faster pickers and flashier pickers, but they can't hold a candle to Earl.

Lester Flatt, his low voice so different from Bill Monroe's high tenor but so perfect for bluegrass, keeping that solid rhythm on the guitar. He died in the seventies. It was strange, seeing him now. But of course, Hank was long dead, too.

Did you know the acoustics in an old VFW hall in Omaha are just about perfect? Especially when it's jammed full of people? They ought to build recording studios that way, just get the plans for the VFW hall and round up a bunch of people and let 'er rip.

They played tune after tune. I was in banjo heaven. It was all true what I'd heard about Earl. He was one hell of a genius. He was twenty-seven years old on that summer night in 1951.

Earl Scruggs didn't invent the five-string banjo. It was a popular parlor instrument in the early part of this century, and was used in minstrel shows long before that. Country bands had pretty much always had banjos around, but what Earl did was turn it into a lead instrument. In his hands, it came alive in a whole new way. He dreamed up licks and runs and rolls nobody'd ever heard of, threw in jazz and blues riffs and combined it with a technique so flawless—no, not flawless, *original*—that he blew everybody away when he joined Bill Monroe's band in 1945. People would come for miles around just to hear this kid "play the fancy banjo." People who know say that Monroe's sound only jelled once Earl came aboard. It was the full flowering of a musical style—bluegrass.

I stood there all wrapped up in it, beating time with my foot. The woman next to me, a big ol' gal in a yellow dress, was hopping up and down, trying to clog-dance in a space the size of a postage stamp. She stepped on my foot, hard. I let out a yelp nobody heard, and that some-how woke me up. Shit! What time was it?

I looked at my watch. Eight-oh-five. I was dead meat. I was due on stage at the Cow Palace in five minutes.

Shoving people out of my way, I made a mad dash for the door. The banjo didn't help. I finally cleared the hall and ran outside. Bob, or Bill, or whatever, and his wife weren't anywhere in sight. I was standing in the middle of an empty street. I saw a kid, maybe sixteen years old, having a smoke.

"Hey, boy! Want to make a dollar?"

He eyed me suspiciously. He didn't say anything.

I strolled over, trying not to look quite as desperate as I was.

"You got a car? I'll give you a dollar to take me to the Cow Palace."

He said, "Sure. For two dollars."

"Fine."

"Give it to me."

"Where's the car?"

He turned and walked down the block toward a beat-up old Dodge.

"You in a hurry, mister?"

"You might say so. I'm supposed to be onstage with Hank Williams in about thirty seconds."

"Yeah."

"No kidding, I am. Can you get me there quick?"

"If it'll start."

We got into the Dodge and he got it started, after about six tries. I tried to stay cool. I mean, what could happen to me? I'd get fired? This wasn't even my real life, for crying out loud!

The kid drove like a bat out of hell, squealing his tires on the turns and running a few red lights. I was glad.

"What's yer name, son?"

"Elmer."

"Elmer what?"

"Elmer Doolittle."

"I'm Webb Pritchard."

"Pleased to meetcha."

We shook hands awkwardly. I glanced at my watch: Eight-thirteen. I was even deader meat.

Elmer found the Cow Palace and we jerked to a stop around back, where I had directed him to go. I was fumbling for some bills when he said, "I want to go backstage and meet Hank Williams."

"Look, kid, I'm really sorry, I'm already late and I'm probably fired."

"I want to go backstage and meet Hank Williams. You said you know him."

"Well—"

"And where's my three dollars?"

"It was two. Here. Come on!"

I ran inside with Elmer hot on my heels. I had never been inside the Cow Palace and I had no idea where we were. I could hear the show, of course. It came from somewhere . . . left. I steered left. The two of us hurried down a concrete tunnel that smelled like hay and cow manure. It seemed my whole career was spent in a stockyard. The music got louder. It was Hank, all right. I was not only dead meat, I was pulverized and pressed into an Arby's roast.

We came out at a dead end, some kind of cattle pen. Goddammit. Elmer shot ahead and climbed the white painted gates. He unlocked them and swung them open from the inside.

"What're you doing?" I asked.

"This way!" he said, and ran toward the other end. I followed, huffing, with my banjo banging against my bum knee. Sure enough, at the far end of the cattle pen was an exit. We took it, climbed some stairs and came out under some bleacher seats in the arena. We could see the stage.

Hank was up there. I strained to see who was playing rhythm guitar for him, but I couldn't tell.

"Look, kid, I gotta go. Enjoy the show," and I ducked out on Elmer before he realized I was gone. He was mesmerized by Hank.

I knew what direction I was headed now, and in a minute or two I had found my way backstage. Of course the very first person I ran into was Doc. The last person I wanted to see.

"You're fired, Pritchard." He looked at my clothes. I was a mess.

"Wait," I said. "I can explain."

"No explaining. No second chances," he said, and turned on his heel.

People wouldn't look at me. Perry Weems was shaking his head. Lula Mae mouthed the word later at me. Nancy was in a huddle with her family and didn't come over.

Hank was coming off. He swept down the stairs on a wave of thunderous applause. He saw me.

"Well, the wandering banjo picker, I do declare," he said, not smiling. "Where the hell you been?"

"At Flatt and Scruggs. I lost track of the time. I'm sorry."

He just looked at me with those piercing brown eyes and drew a deep breath.

"Doc fire you?"

"Yeah."

"You're as bad as me. You know you get fired from the Hayride, that's the bottom?"

"So I gather."

"Go on back to the hotel. Doc won't want to see your sorry ass around here tonight."

Shit. I'd really blown it. I trudged back the way I'd come, and there was Elmer, still standing in the same place under the bleachers.

"I'm fired," I said. At the moment, he seemed like my only friend, this pimply-faced kid from Omaha.

"That's tough," he said. "So I won't get to meet Hank Williams?"

"Afraid not, son. But we can watch him."

So we stood there in the dark for another whole hour, craning our necks to see the stars of Doc Mullican's Traveling Hayride & Medi-cine Show. It was a pretty good show; I'd never seen it from out front before. Daryl Taggart, Nancy's brother, was playing rhythm for Hank in my place. He did fine. I woulda done better.

When it was over, I asked Elmer for a ride back to the Plainsman Inn.

"Two dollars."

"Cripes! Can't you do me a favor? I just got fired, for Christ's sake."

"Two dollars."

"Jesus."

"Well, you said I'd get to meet Hank Williams and I didn't get to."

"I got us in free, didn't I?"

"I didn't get to meet Hank Williams."

I sighed and handed over the money. He dropped me at the hotel and roared off, tires squealing in the night. A true friend.

I undressed and got under the covers feeling pretty sorry for myself. What would happen now? Would Hank send me back to the future? Or would he strand me in the past?

I fell asleep. I don't know how long I was out, but it was pretty late when I heard Hank come in. He was whispering to somebody. Great. Now I'd have to pretend I didn't hear all the moaning and groaning going on two feet away in the next bed.

"Webb! Wake up."

I buried my face in the pillow.

"Webb! Got a friend I'd like you to meet."

He must really be drunk, I thought, and I rolled over. The room was still dark.

Hank switched on the bedside lamp. I squinted into the light. The friend was a man, not a woman.

"We've met, I believe."

"Howdy, Earl."

9

So they threw you off the Hayride, I hear," Earl said, parking himself in the one small chair in our hotel room. "That's a shame."

I sat up in bed. "I went to see you," I said, "and I didn't get back in time to make the show."

Hank had cracked a bottle of scotch and was pouring drinks for the three of us. "He done got carried away by your brilliant playing, Earl," he said, handing Earl a glass. "Webb's never seen you before," he added.

"You haven't?" Earl said. "That's mighty hard to believe. Where you from, Webb?"

"Oklahoma."

"Ah, well. We haven't been out that way lately, it's true. Did you like the show?"

I nodded. "Nobody plays quite like you do. You're an inspiration."

Earl looked at Hank. "Your man's no slouch, either. I heard him play this afternoon, out back here at the hotel. He hit a few licks I've never heard."

"And now I'm out of a job," I said.

"Maybe not," Hank drawled. "I had a little chat with Doc."

My hopes rose. "And?"

"I think he'll come around. After he cooled off a little, I told him what had happened, told him you were trying to pick up on some of Earl's showmanship, learn from the master, some bullshit like that, and that some people who promised you a ride never showed up."

"That's not quite how it happened."

"I know. So you'll be beholden to Ole Hank for saving your tail."

"So I'm not fired?"

"I didn't say that. I said I think he'll come around. Right now, you're still fired, far as I know."

We sat there awhile, in room 3C at the Plainsman Inn in downtown Omaha, Hank Williams, Earl Scruggs and I, talking about what we loved best, music. Their two styles were very different, but they had more in common than most musicians. Both were southern boys who knew they were lucky not to be looking at the back end of a mule all day. Or working in a box factory. In spite of their stardom, they kept themselves and their music "low to the ground." Hank may have driven a new Cadillac every year, but he ate cornbread like the rest of us.

As I sat there sipping whiskey with these two legends, I realized what I wanted out of this whole experience was two things: to soak up the old music, and to come out alive on the other side. The first I was sure of, the other I definitely wasn't.

I wanted my music to emerge organically, like theirs did. I could never be reborn as a poor southern boy, growing up in an atmosphere rich in old hillbilly and folk music, but man, I was here now and I could absorb it from the people who played it best. Who else my age could say that?

"Why'd you pick me, Hank?" I asked.

That shook him. It must have been the whiskey that made my tongue so loose. He knew what I meant, too.

"I thought you could pick a mean git-tar, son."

"No, really. Why me?"

Earl looked interested. Hank stared into space.

"Well," he said after a long moment, "I knew you had it in you, Webb. You had the old ways, the old feeling. You've played a lot of crap, been around too much of it, but deep down you're like us here." He indicated Earl. He tapped his chest. "You have an appreciation for this music that goes deeper than just learning the old songs. They live in you. Your head's in the present, but your heart's in the past."

I was about to get all choked up when he said, "Plus, I needed a git-tar picker, even though you keep claiming to play the banjo."

"You want me to bring this music to my people?" I asked, trying to find a way to say it with Earl sitting there.

Hank leaned forward off the bed until the light from the little hotel lamp was sharp on his face. The way the shadows fell, he looked much older than his twenty-seven years. His eyes were feverish.

"Yes, Webb. I want you to be the messenger. Tell them how it was. Tell them how it really was."

"Nobody will believe me."

"Not that. Bring it to them when you play. You're hearing it all now, soaking it all up. Let it soak in good, into your bones. Let it set there awhile. It'll come out in your music. Your people, they've forgotten country music. It's a lost art. It's like those cave drawings nobody even saw those for a million years. They were lost to time. Then when the scientists shone their light in there, and saw those wild animals dancing across those walls, they were struck dumb by the beauty. That never changes. The feeling's there, just waiting to be uncovered. Uncover it, Webb. That's your mission."

The room fell silent. My mouth was hanging open and I closed it. Nobody said anything.

Finally, Earl stood up. "That was quite a speech there, Hank. It wore me out. Thanks for the drink. It's late."

He turned and shook my hand. "Keep playing like you're playing and you'll go a long way."

"I— Thank you, Earl. You don't know what it means to me just to meet you."

He put on his hat and headed for the door. Hank saw him out.

"Cave drawings!" Earl said, chuckling, and disappeared down the walk.

Hank turned to me and winked.

We were having breakfast the next morning in the Plainsman Inn coffee shop, me and Hank. As usual, he was eating enough for three people: big slabs of country ham smothered in red gravy, biscuits, eggs, pancakes with syrup, and a glass of buttermilk. I was having orange juice and a danish. My stomach was unsettled.

"I feel like Mr. Phelps," I said to him, watching him put away the food. Hank probably weighed 130 pounds, dripping wet.

"Who's Mr. Phelps?"

"*Mission Impossible*. Jim Phelps. As in, 'Your mission, Jim, should you decide to accept it . . .' "

"What're you talking about?"

"You wouldn't get it. But this tape may self-destruct in five seconds."

The other Hayride regulars began to straggle in. It was a beautiful summer morning, with sunlight streaming in through the windows, and everyone just looked like hammered shit. Must've been quite a party after the show last night. Hank, of course, was made of sterner stuff. Or sterner drugs.

Lula Mae plopped down next to Hank, across from me. The light was not kind.

"Mornin', Lula Mae."

"Mornin', Lula Mae."

She scowled at us. "Go to hell."

I laughed. "Same to you."

The waitress came by and poured coffee. Lula Mae gulped at her cup like it was some kind of life-giving elixir.

"Christ, you people must've had quite a time last night. Sorry I missed it," I said.

"Don't be," she croaked. "Unless you call watching Doc Mullican puke all over Daniel Eberhardt's new alligator shoes quite a time."

Now I was really sorry I missed it.

"What else happened?"

She raised a hand to shield her eyes from the sun pouring in the window. "Christ, don't they believe in venetian blinds around here? Well, after the show we all met up over at Corky's."

"He don't know Corky's," Hank said.

"Oh. It's a dive. Anyway, we were all there, and everybody got pretty awful drunk, and Perry called Daniel a queer and Daniel hit Perry and then there was a real big bar fight and Doc got in the middle of it. Daniel punched him and that made Doc throw up, right on his new shoes."

"Perry Weems called Daniel a queer?"

"Actually he called him a fruit."

"Just as bad," Hank said darkly.

"I'd say so," I agreed. "What brought that on? Is Daniel, uh, is he homosexual?"

"Shit no, he ain't no faggot," Hank said, diving into his stack of pancakes. "Perry just likes to get to him because he dresses so fine and has the fine car. I think he's jealous."

Lula Mae flagged down the girl and got some more coffee and a danish like mine. "Doc said everybody was fired, and he means everybody."

Hank didn't even look up.

"Everybody's fired?" I asked. This sounded good for me.

She nodded. "Yeah, except he does this about every third city we play in. Don't worry. We'll all be at the Cow Palace again tonight."

I looked up and saw Perry Weems walking in. He looked ill. He sort of oozed onto a stool at the counter and put his head in his hands. Thirty seconds behind him was Daniel Eberhardt, who looked even worse. His skin was positively gray. When Daniel saw Perry at the counter he did a military right turn and bolted for a booth in the back. Perry never saw him.

That's our Hayride. One big happy family.

"You suppose Webb's still fired?" Hank asked Lula Mae.

She pondered. "Now Webb's a different case. He was fired before the fight at Corky's. On the other hand, Doc may not remember he fired him."

"Should I just show up tonight?" I asked.

"Not a bad plan," Hank mused. But then Doc came into the coffee shop. I tried to squeeze back deeper in the booth, but he spotted me instantly.

"Mornin', folks," he said, tipping his hat. He leaned on the back of the seat behind Hank and Lula Mae and addressed me.

"How was Flatt and Scruggs, Pritchard? Didja enjoy the show?" His voice dripped with sarcasm.

"Yes, it was good."

"So damn good you couldn't be bothered to make your own show, is that right?"

Lula Mae and Hank just sat there, flashing me sympathetic looks.

"I'm sorry about that, Doc," I said. "I'm really sorry."

"Yeah, well, I'm sorry, too. Sorry my so-called performers are so busy watching other peoples' shows they can't find the time to be there when the curtain goes up. Maybe I should just hire Flatt and Scruggs. Would you show up then?"

I didn't say anything at all.

87

He leaned forward a little. "Tell you a little secret, Webb. You're in luck. Yep, today's your lucky day, you might say."

Now I looked at him.

"You see, I don't have anybody at all to go on tonight. Do you want to know why? I fired 'em, that's why. I fired 'em all!"

He was shouting now, swinging around so everybody in the coffee shop could hear him. Half the people having breakfast were hungover cast members.

"They're all fired because they're all a bunch of no-good drunks!"

Now he swung back around. "But you, Pritchard, you're no drunk. I'll say that for you. I'm gonna give you a second chance. The only one you're ever gonna get from me. Ask around, I don't give no second chances. A man's fired off the Hayride, he's fired. So you're gonna be walkin' on eggshells, my friend. Thin little eggshells. Don't fuck it up."

Now he seemed to notice Lula Mae for the first time. "Sorry, ma'am," he said, dipping his hat. Smothering a laugh, Lula Mae tried to look offended.

He jabbed a finger at me. "So where'll you be tonight, about seventhirty? You gonna be over at Flatt and Scruggs?"

"Nossir," I replied. "I'll be at the Cow Palace, Doc."

"Good. That's what I like to hear. Man who values his job. Not like the rest of 'em."

He turned to go, then seemed to have a thought. He came back.

"By the way, how were Lester and Earl, anyway?"

"Sit down and I'll tell you all about it," I said, making room for him in the booth.

"Don't mind if I do."

That night, everybody showed up and everybody went on. Doc and the cast of the Hayride were in the same precarious, hilarious position: he couldn't fire us because then he wouldn't have a Hayride, and none of us could quit because we had nowhere to go.

Except maybe Hank. He still had Opry aspirations.

"We're doin' that song you and me wrote, "Carry Me Back," tonight," he told me about ten minutes before the show.

"I didn't help write that song."

"The hell you didn't! You gave me a better title, and out of that idea, I wrote a better song. That song's gonna get Ole Hank back on the Opry, son."

"How's that?"

"It's the best thing I've done in a long time. I'm gonna polish it out here on the road, then you and me are goin' to Nashville and record it."

He looked quite pleased with himself.

"That's great, Hank," I said. "But first, it would help me—it would help us, that is, in the band—if you'd clue us in on how it goes."

He huddled us together and ran through it a few times. It was a great song, I'll admit. Even if it sounded a little rough the first few times out, it was going to be a winner.

"I'm savin' it for the encore," he told us.

The Cow Palace was nearly full. It wasn't a whole lot different from playing the Stock Show Arena in Denver. Same awful acoustics, same leftover cowshit smell. We did our first set, came off and rehearsed the new tune once again, in a sort of broom closet. It was already tightening up and sounding good.

Then it was my solo turn. I had almost overcome my stage fright, though not entirely. I always walked out there afraid I would forget everything and they'd start throwing tomatoes at me. This night I was extra careful not to play a single Scruggs lick, tune, or even think about such things. Not too hard, since I only got one song. I played "Cluck Old Hen." It wasn't like my first time out, when I played "Ground Speed," all dolled up with Bela Fleck licks. The applause was conservative.

I came off and there was Nancy, who planted a kiss on my cheek. "That was nice," she said.

"Not great, huh?"

"Well, you didn't set the stage on fire."

"I don't know if I can do that every night."

"You can with me. Later, Webb?" She smiled at me. My breath caught.

"You bet."

Muley Taggart walked up and grabbed Nancy by the arm. "We're on," he said roughly. He ignored me. Nancy shot me a helpless look as her father drew her away.

Hank was pumped. He paced around, back and forth, back and forth, waiting to go on again. He was sweating heavily. I wondered what pills he had taken.

Finally they announced us. "Let's go, boys!" Hank brayed as we rushed through the curtain. I hit my mark and stood ready. Hank counted off. We launched into "Carry Me Back," and it was magic. The audience came alive during the first few bars. Hank was in superb form, belting it out from his gut, his voice breaking in all the right places.

"Carry me back, all the way baaaack . . ."

But something was wrong. He had stopped singing. We kept playing, just keeping the time, going around a couple of times. A murmur swept the crowd. Hank swayed at the mike, gripping it with white knuckles. The sweat poured off him. His mouth opened but nothing came out. Somebody down front shouted, "Keep going!"

He crumpled and went down.

Jesus H. Christ. The bass player, Merle Daly, was the first to reach him. I was trying to get my guitar off, getting tangled in the strap, when that old feeling came over me. Oh, no, I thought. Not now. Not now, please . . . Everything kind of started humming, then the bright light, then the numbness. Whiteout.

I came to in my camper. I was back in the present.

10

I jerked upright on my bunk. The numbness hadn't left my arms. They still tingled. I could see it was high noon outside, but for the moment I was grateful for the spongy old curtains that kept the light nice and dim in here. The strange metallic taste filled my mouth again, coated my teeth, same as it had the last time I'd been yanked around the time warp. And my head hurt. Other than that, I felt all right. I guess.

Hank. Jesus, I'd left him lying in a heap on the stage. I knew he'd taken something; his eyes had that glittery look they got whenever he swallowed some funny pills, as he called them. God knows what combination of drugs he'd inflicted on his system this time. Hank had these close-set, beady little brown eyes. When he was high they somehow got even beadier. I knew the look. I should've seen it coming.

Had I disappeared right onstage? Were people in the audience wondering what sort of parlor trick Old Hank had introduced into his act? Hey, Hank, that was great, buddy. The way your guitar player just up and vaporized into thin air. Can you do that one for us again? Doc Mullican must've dropped his cigar.

Well, there was nothing I could do about it. That was the nature of this thing; I couldn't control it. No use worrying. Except I was sick with worry. I couldn't get the sight of Hank collapsing at the mike out of my mind. At least I knew he wasn't dead. That wasn't on the schedule yet. I couldn't change history. Or could I?

I swung my legs over the side of the bunk and sat there awhile, just thinking. Rubbing my bum knee, the way I do sometimes when I'm zoning out.

What day was it? I knew where I was, but not when. Had Marie given up on me? All I had were questions. A million of 'em. I stood up kind of slow. I'm too old for this shit, Hank. Why didn't ya pick on a younger guy? Somebody who could stand time travel better than me. This shit was wearing me out. I moved slowly over to the cabinet and took out a bottle of Advil. Shook two tabs into my palm and swallowed them quick, without any water. Then I set about making some coffee. That's my drug of choice most of the time.

I got out the jug of drinking water I had bought on the way down to Telluride. No mold in it. Nothing funny floating in it. I smelled it. It seemed OK. I turned on my little propane stove and started the water boiling. That should kill off any lurking bacteria, I hoped.

I sat back down on my bunk in the half light, waiting. When the water boiled, I let it go for a minute or two, then poured it through the filter of the little aluminum camp coffeepot that came with the camper. The smell of Maxwell House filled my little home. I put two globfuls of honey in my mug, poured the coffee, swirled it many many times with the spoon, brought it up to my lips and inhaled deeply. Aaaahhh. Then I took a sip. Ambrosia. Then another. Then a big swallow. The hot, sweet liquid shot down to my gut and ricocheted around my whole body till it came back up and zinged into my brain. Good morning, Webb. This is your caffeine speaking. I was human again.

My banjo case caught my eye. Over there in the corner. I dragged it over to the bunk, undid the latches and popped the lid. There she was. Lil Darlin'. None the worse for wear.

My fingers traced over her fine fretwork, touching her strings. My hand slid up and down her neck. I kissed her. Her smooth wood felt so familiar, like the body of a woman you've lived with a long time. Only hers never changed.

"Thank you, Hank," I whispered, laying the banjo back down into the case, easy as a sleeping baby.

I needed a shower. I needed a lot of things, but that would be a good start. I had asked Marie if I could use her bathroom, but I didn't think she'd be home. I was right. She wasn't. So I grabbed up a towel, a washcloth, some soap and a change of clothes and headed down the hill on foot, toward the campground. They had showers there.

The bluegrass festival was gone. Just a big bare spot with a few spare pieces of trash blowing around was all that was left of the four-day hoopla. So I'd been away at least a couple of days. Still, the camp showers remained, so I cleaned up in a hurry, as the hot water ran out rather quickly. Ever tried to take a shower under mountain water? It's so cold your head kind of freezes up and starts throbbing. First it's just cold, then it's really painful. It's like teeny ice crystals raining down on your body. I was covered in goosebumps and shivering as I dressed. I went out and sat in the high-altitude sun for a few minutes to get warm.

After that, I wandered over to the local bakery and got myself a big ham sandwich with Swiss cheese and a carton of milk, which I consumed as I walked up and down the main street. I noticed a clock: it was two in the afternoon. It was time to go find Marie.

Her store, she had told me, was called Crazy Quilts. It didn't take long to find it. A lady I asked pointed it out. Like many of the mom 'n' pop businesses in Telluride, it was located in a renovated Victorian house. All gingerbread and crystals hanging in the windows. Very cute. Cute town. Opening the wrought-iron front gate, I wondered exactly when Telluride had ceased to be a real place and become a concept instead. There's an old song, "All the Good Times Are Past and Gone." I was thinking, All the Good Places Are Past and Gone. They'd taken a perfectly dandy little mining town and turned it into a California wet dream. A place where a lift ticket and a couple of foreign beers would set you back sixty bucks. Hank would be shaking his head.

I opened the door and stepped into Crazy Quilts. It smelled like those little containers full of dried flowers, that and fabric. Quilts and knickknacks everywhere. All packed into a space so tiny you could hardly turn around. A woman's kind of store. This must be the living room, I guessed. Girlish voices floated out from somewhere in the back of the house. I headed that way.

Down a long, narrow hallway, then through the fine old high-ceilinged kitchen, I followed the sounds. I came out into a large, airy room full of women working around a huge quilt. Like my grandmother's quilting bees, I suppose, only these women didn't look much like my grandmother or her friends. No hairnets here. They all fell silent, looking up at me with raised eyebrows and inquisitive stares.

They didn't recognize anybody's husband or boyfriend. I felt like a party crasher.

"Webb!" Marie rose from her chair. She looked surprised. "Webb!"

The other women clucked approvingly and went back to their task. I had been properly disposed of.

Marie came over and grabbed my arm, pulling me into the kitchen. "I thought we'd lost you," she said, squeezing tight. Her touch felt good. Then her nails dug in. Ouch.

"I don't like being stood up for dinner," she whispered. "Carla didn't like it, either."

"You didn't think I'd desert you, did you?"

"Well, didn't you? Where've you been?"

"Wait'll I tell you. You won't believe it. I don't even know what day it is."

She looked back at her quilters. "I can't leave here now. This is a class. We're done at four. Meet me at the house." She reached in her skirt pocket and handed me a key. I took it and slipped it into my own pocket. It was warm from her.

I leaned down to kiss her, but she pulled away.

"See you at the house," I said. She was gone.

You know, it was good to be back in the nineties. A world I understood. A world with automatic teller machines, VCRs and microwave popcorn. Not that I had an ATM card, a VCR or a microwave oven, mind you, but if I wanted to get them, they were available. And that was nice.

None of this postwar rah-rah shit, either, an America On The Move. No billboards extolling the virtues of home, hearth, God and the U.S. of A. Nah, it was back to the age of good ol' cynicism and shallow values, and I was right in the heart of it, a place that worshipped spandex and cappuccino.

I was tired of Telluride.

It was beautiful, all right. A little too beautiful. And the people were all beautiful. A little too beautiful. What, was there a city ordinance against being ugly?

I hadn't seen a single overweight person the entire time I'd been in Telluride. Or anybody with zits or warts. Or hardly anybody wearing normal clothes like people buy at Target. Nobody even looked like they worked for a living, for Chrissakes. I needed a real place, like Tulsa, or Montrose, and real people, like my sister, Dot. The Oklahoma was coming out in me, and it wasn't pretty.

I charged into the Sluicebox Saloon, the place Hank had taken me forty-four years earlier, just last week, plopped down at the bar and did something incredibly daring. Dangerous, even.

"Budweiser," I said to the bartender, looking him straight in the eye. "I'll have a Bud."

His eyebrow shot skyward. His perfectly tanned face registered mild surprise.

"Sir," he said condescendingly, "We have Asahi from Japan, Boulder Beer from Boulder, Malanakani from Maui, six kinds of microbrew—"

"Bud."

No ifs, ands or buts. I stared him down, with an Oklahoma stare that said I meant business, pal.

It was a longneck. I smiled and took a long draught.

You know what? I don't even like Budweiser. I'm really a Miller man at heart.

When Marie showed up, at thirteen minutes past four, I was propped up on the porch railing with Lil Darlin' in my arms, picking lightly away at some old, long-forgotten tunes. It was all a pose, of course. I had been there, propped just so, trying to be Mr. Casual, oh, hello, I'm just picking some tunes here, since three forty-five.

She pulled up in her white Toyota, parking behind my RV, with Carla in the passenger seat. The child bounded out before the car fully stopped.

"Mr. Pritchard! Mr. Pritchard!" The blond hair was flying. "Where did you go?"

This was going to be interesting.

"Call me Webb, child. I was on the road, playing music."

She looked puzzled. "But your truck stayed here. Did somebody give you a ride?"

"Yes. Somebody gave me a ride."

"Is that why you didn't take us to dinner?"

"Yes. I'm sorry. We'll do it another time."

Marie came up the walk behind her. I could tell she was pissed.

95

She wouldn't look at me. But she said, "I bet Webb would like a beer after all his travels."

"That I would."

"I have some Miller. That be OK?"

"That would be mighty fine, ma'am," I said, trailing them into the house.

We settled out on the back porch, a place I hadn't yet seen. It didn't wrap around the house like the front, all grand and Victorian. It was a ramshackle affair, plain white painted wood, sagging a bit, and it overlooked a tattered back yard full of Carla's toys and playthings. The centerpiece of the yard was a huge truck tire filled with sand. I liked this view.

I sat on a plastic deck chair and Marie brought me a Miller. Another longneck. She had one herself. Carla bounded out into the cool yard and climbed on a swing set and began swinging. It was a fine afternoon.

"So what's the deal?" Marie said. "You're here, you're not here. You run off for three days without a word to anybody. The sheriff's been around, asking about your RV. I didn't know what to tell him. He's probably getting ready to tow it to Naturita."

She looked so fine. She was wearing a dark blue tank top, a print skirt and sandals. Her hair was pulled back in one of those cloth things women use to pull back their hair. I just drank her in.

I took another swallow of beer. I was already a little bit stoked from the Buds down at the Sluicebox.

"I went back in time again," I said quietly, so Carla wouldn't hear. "I went down to the woods to jam and it happened again, like before. Hank took me to Denver. We were in an outfit called Doc Mullican's Traveling Hayride and Medicine Show. I played in front of forty-four hundred people at the Stock Show Arena in Denver. It was fantastic."

"What year is this all happening?"

"1951."

She didn't believe a word I was saying.

"We went to Omaha, in Hank's Cadillac," I continued. "He's wasted about half the time. All the stories I always heard about him seem to be true. He drinks too much and he pops a lot of pills. But he's incredible. I've never met anybody before who has so much talent. He's just pissing it away. You know he died in 1953? Passed out in his car on the way to a gig and never woke up. He was only twenty-nine. Sad."

Marie set her bottle of Miller on the railing. "So, is he a ghost, or what?"

"I don't know. It sure as hell seems real when I'm there. I mean, everything in the real world is there in real time, like, I still have to shave and go to the bathroom and all. I eat and sleep. Hank's the only one who knows what's going on. The others, well, it's like it's their real lives happening. It's creepy. Hey, I met Earl Scruggs."

"Who?"

I looked pained. "Earl Scruggs. The banjo legend. The reason me and a million other people play the banjo. He was in Bill Monroe's band in the late forties, then left him to go with Lester Flatt. Flatt and Scruggs."

She looked blank.

" 'Beverly Hillbillies.' 'Foggy Mountain Breakdown.' 'Bonnie and Clyde.' "

Now she registered. "Oh! That Earl Scruggs."

I sighed. No matter how great his contribution to music, poor Earl was still remembered for the theme he played for a half-assed sitcom.

"Anyway," I said, "I met him. He was a young dude. Nice guy. Real nice guy, in fact. I had to watch what I played around him, because half the stuff I do is based on stuff he hadn't written in 1951."

"Mmm-hmm." Her face was stony.

"Yeah," I said bravely, pressing ahead. "It was tricky there a couple of times. But it was quite an honor to meet him and hear him play as a young man. Nobody else my age has done that."

"Is he still alive?"

I nodded. "Very much. He's mostly retired, but he's still around. I oughta write him a letter and say, hey, Earl, met you the other day. You and Lester were playing Omaha. Remember?"

"Take me back."

"What?"

"Take me back with you, Webb," she said sarcastically. "I want to see what it's like."

"You think I'm making all this up. I don't blame you."

"I just don't know why you'd jerk me around this way."

97

"All I can tell you is, it's true. Based on my reality, it really happened. And I couldn't take you back even if I wanted. Only Hank can do it. Besides, he finally told me what's going on. I mean, the reason he sends me back."

"And what is that?"

"He told me he wanted me to soak up the old music, the old vibes, so to speak, and bring 'em to people in the present. He says that old-time feeling's been lost."

"And so it has. You saw the festival here."

"I'm a man on a mission. A Mission from Hank."

She shook her head. "So how do you plan to carry out this mission, Mr. Pritchard?"

"Well, I've thought about that. I think Hank means for me to go ahead with what I had planned to do all along when I got out of prison, which is to go on the road and play the old stuff. Only now I guess I'll have the guts of the music in my head, and play with more feeling."

Marie was staring at me now. "Prison?"

Oh, shit. Dammit to hell.

"Ah, yes. I, uh, I'm out now."

Her face turned to pure flint. "I see that. I hope it wasn't an escape."

"No."

"Not jail. Prison. That's serious. What did you do, Webb?" Her voice had gone flat.

No use lying. I took a breath. "Oh, I shot this jerk who came to steal my tools. I hit him in the kneecap, I didn't kill him. I wasn't aiming to kill him. I just wanted to stop him from burglarizing my home."

"So why'd they lock you up? Why not him?"

"That's not how it works in the real world. I shot him, he was unarmed, so they nailed me for attempted murder. He was a little doper with a long criminal record. A real winner. He's in prison now, for trying to rob a 7-Eleven. He's a dirtbag."

She toyed with her beer bottle. "How long were you in for?"

"Four years. At the state penitentiary in McAlester, Oklahoma."

"When did you get out?"

That was the one I really didn't want to answer.

"Nine days ago. I think. What day is it?"

She stood up. "Carla!" Her daughter looked up from the sandbox. "Come in, now. We're going to make supper."

She turned to me and said, "I think you should go."

"I'm not a bad guy, Marie. Give me a chance."

"You've got to admit, that's some heavy baggage."

"I admit it. You're right. My life hasn't been perfect."

"You shot somebody! With a gun! I can't believe it."

I didn't say anything.

"You're a convict! What other secrets are you hiding?"

Instantly, I thought of Nancy.

"None. At least, that's the worst one. I never served time before, till that happened. I've never hit a woman, never hurt a child. Never stole anything. I've always worked. I'm not a deadbeat. I'm twice divorced, but I already told you that. And those didn't end because of any violence. The first time, we were too young and just drifted apart. The second time, the woman was cheating on me. I've been in my share of bar fights, but nothing serious. I have a gentle nature, Marie. Honest. I'm forty years old and I'm starting over. If you want a character reference, ask my sister Dot in Montrose. She's known me all my life. And she won't gloss over the rough spots."

It was about the longest speech I'd ever made. Marie picked up the beer bottles and prepared to go into the house.

"Carla! Now!"

She turned to me and said, "I need to think."

I did, too. I got up and headed back to my RV, still parked out front. I needed to hold Lil Darlin' awhile. Was it time to get out of Dodge?

11

I decided to move the RV. Get the whale out of Marie's sight for a few days. Now that the festival was gone, a spot shouldn't be too hard to find. Or so I thought.

The first place I tried, the town campground, was full. It looked half empty, but the guy running the place told me all the spots were reserved. Drat.

"And if you try to park that thing anywhere around town for longer'n four or five hours, the sheriff'll have you towed to Naturita," he said. Great. I was beginning to think Naturita had something on Telluride.

I was running out of money. I checked my wallet: $112. Desperation time. By now, nine or ten days out of prison, I had hoped to be hooked up on the bluegrass festival circuit and at least making enough bread to eat. Instead, I was stuck in one of the most expensive places in America, with a hundred lousy bucks and no place to go. Dot, maybe you were right, I thought. This crazy idea might have been just that. Crazy.

I rolled the RV slowly through town, pondering my options. I couldn't go back to Marie's. I could keep on driving and go home to Dot's in Montrose, eighty miles away, and regroup. Nah. That was stupid. She'd just feed me and say I told you so. I didn't need that.

What I needed was a parking spot.

Telluride consists basically of one long main street and tributary streets running off from that. It dead-ends in a box canyon and there's really only one way out of town unless you're in a jeep or on a mountain bike. So you can scope out the place pretty quick. Which I did. Guess what? There was no place to hide an RV.

I swung the whale—I now decided to name her Orca—around a corner and headed down one of the side streets. There was an alley on my left. I eased her in. She barely fit. I had no idea what I was doing. Just hoping the gods would smile on me.

And there it was. A big fat parking spot behind an old red brick building. Nothing out back but a dumpster and a screen door. If I parked there, I wouldn't be blocking anybody in and I wouldn't be blocking the alley. It was nice and private. There were no signs saying I couldn't park there. That's what I'd tell the sheriff, if he came around. But Officer, nobody told me this was off limits.

Cutting the wheel and backing up a few times, I was able to get Orca lined up perfectly. I was home free, at least for a while. I had bought some time.

"Hey! You! You can't park there!"

A guy in kitchen whites was leaning out the screen door. He had wild red hair and a huge bushy beard. He held an onion in his hand.

"I can't?"

"No. This is private property, buddy. We need this space for deliveries. You'll have to move."

"Who owns it?"

"The Sluicebox Saloon."

"This is the back of the Sluicebox?"

"That's right. Sorry. Try the campground."

"I already did." Suddenly I had an idea. "May I talk to you a minute?" I stepped out of the cab.

"Now, look," the red-haired cook said, brandishing the onion. "I'm trying to be nice. You just can't park here."

"I understand that," I said. "I'm not a tourist. I'm looking for a job. I'm a musician. I play the banjo. Sing, too."

"We don't have live entertainment."

"You don't now. But you could. Where's your boss?"

"I'm the boss."

"You own the Sluicebox?"

"My wife and I do."

"You don't look like the boss," I said, instantly regretting it. But he burst out laughing.

"Well, I am," he said. "I look like the head cook and bottle washer, don't I? I'm Red Sweeney. And you are?"

"Webb Pritchard."

He switched hands with the onion and we shook. His fingers were like callused vise grips. His blue eyes were kind.

"How long you been in town? Did you wash in with the bluegrass festival?"

"Yeah. Met a friend here and she let me park at her house for a while. But I wore out my welcome. I'm not ready to leave yet, but the campground's full. I meant no harm pulling in here. It just looked like a good spot."

"It's been tried before."

"Well, would you be open to a little audition?"

"No," he said. "But I always kinda liked banjo music. Come on in and meet my wife." He held open the screen door. I might get a paying gig out of this yet.

"Have you been in the Sluicebox?"

"Yes, I have. Today, in fact. Nice place."

We stepped into the kitchen. A boy about twelve was peeling potatoes over a sink while a woman stirred soup or something at a big industrial stove. They both looked up.

"Mattie, this is Webb Pritchard," Sweeney said to the woman. She wiped her hands on her white muslin apron and reached out to shake mine. "Mr. Pritchard, my wife, Mattie." She was plump and pretty, with laughing eyes. Her dark hair struggled to stay tied up in a bun. Gravity was winning.

"He was trying to park out back."

Mattie shook her finger at me. "We throw people in jail for that. Several people are already serving life terms."

Sweeney turned to the boy. "Our son, Mark." The boy didn't smile, but nodded slowly at me. I nodded back.

"Pritchard here's a musician. He wants a job playing in the restaurant."

"May I audition, Mrs. Sweeney?"

Mattie stifled a laugh. "But we don't have live entertainment," she said.

"So your husband said. But if you heard me you might change your mind."

The Sweeneys looked at each other with the kind of deep understanding married couples often share. Their faces betrayed some kind of secret glee. They were definitely up to something.

"You don't have any other gigs right now, do you?" Red asked me.

"No. Nothing on the agenda."

"Go get your banjo."

My hopes rising, I fetched Lil Darlin' and tuned her up. The Sweeneys were busy preparing for the dinner crowd, so my audition didn't take much time. In fact, I stood in the alley and played while they all kind of leaned out the screen door and watched. I played "Ground Speed" and then launched into "Ragged but Right," an old vaudeville number that dates from early in the century. It somehow seemed appropriate.

> "I come here to tell you people I'm ragged but right.
> I'm a thief and a gambler, I get drunk every night.
> Get a porterhouse steak three times a day for my board,
> That's more than any loafer in this town can afford.
> Big electric fan keeps me cool while I sleep.
> Little baby girl to play around at my feet.
> I'm a rambling gambler, I get drunk every night,
> I tell you, boys, I'm ragged but right.
> I go everywhere, I don't pay no fare.
> I could ride a freight train just anywhere.
> If I win or lose, I don't get no blues,
> Just a gambling life for me."

I finished with a big flourish, and bowed deeply. The Sweeneys clapped. Red motioned me over. He looked like he'd already made up his mind.

"Webb, may I call you Webb? That was great. You certainly can play that banjo. Here's the deal: you can play a fifteen-minute set at eight-thirty and another one at ten-thirty. Six nights a week. You can have Monday off. I'll pay you $125 a week. But there's a catch."

"What?"

"I don't need a banjo picker. I do need a dishwasher. You'll work from six to eleven. The music comes on your breaks."

My jaw dropped.

"That's about four dollars an hour. You get dinner, too. And a beer at the end of your shift. Take it or leave it."

Wash dishes? At my age? With my potential? Was I crazy?

"Can I park here?"

Red looked at Mattie. She shrugged.

"OK, we'll see how that works out. But you gotta move it when deliveries come, and that could be a problem. I can't promise anything. For now, I guess you can. I'll square it with the sheriff."

"When do I start?"

"How about right now?"

They handed me an apron and within five minutes I was up to my elbows in greasy suds.

Ragged but right, indeed.

My fingers were all wrinkled for my first set. By now I was sweaty and grimy from standing over the big stainless steel Hobart for two and a half hours. My face was all red. I had grease spatters all over me and I smelled sour. I took off my apron and put on Lil Darlin'. I warmed up for about twenty seconds in the alley. I didn't want the sound of the banjo to hit them till I was ready for it to hit them.

The Sluice had no stage, so I stood at the back of the room in a little cleared space about six feet by eight. No amplification. No mikes. No sound system. No Hank. Just me. Truly acoustic, the way bluegrass music used to be played. Of course, I wasn't really playing bluegrass; that's an ensemble music. I was playing Webb music, just me and my banjo. Somehow acoustic seemed to be just right.

I was nervous. This was my debut. All the stuff in the past, well, I knew it was real, but this was realer. That was then. This was now.

There were maybe about a dozen people in the restaurant and bar, all told. Hardly the Stock Show Arena in Denver. "Good evening, ladies and gentlemen," I said, as loudly as I could without seeming to shout. The bartender cranked up the blender for a couple of margaritas. I talked louder.

"My name's Webb Pritchard. Thank you for being here."

I wanted to say, "I play with Hank Williams most nights," but instead I said, "Here's a Hank Williams tune I hope you enjoy."

Hank's songs aren't really banjo numbers, but hell, you can work 'em out. They're good songs. I played "Jambalaya," and found to my delight my fingers had loosened up considerably during my ten days or so on the road with the Hayride. Man, I was cooking. After that, I did "Ground Speed," and followed with "Theme Time," two instrumentals. Then I did "Soldier's Joy," a perennial favorite with the traditional music crowd. I had no clue what these people thought. He's good but he's no Kenny G, probably.

I finished with "Ragged but Right," my singing maybe not so hot. But the folks seemed to enjoy it. When they applauded, it was much more rewarding than when I played with Hank. It was all for me. This is what I had hoped for when I got out of McAlester.

My fifteen minutes of fame were up. Red was beckoning me from the door to the kitchen. I took a bow and returned to the Hobart and its hot, sudsy rhythms. Top of the world, Ma! I wanted to jump on the dishwasher and shout. Scrape 'em off, stack 'em up, run 'em through, do it again. The dirty dishes kept coming back in a never-ending stream. Cripes, how much could these people eat? They're all so thin. After eleven million dishes, it was ten o'clock and time for my second set. My fingers were even more wrinkled. I repeated my first set because I was too tired to come up with anything new. They liked it. At least nobody threw tomatoes. I took my bow and rushed back to the kitchen. The dirty dishes had piled up in my absence.

My steamy kitchen world was ninety-eight percent of my existence; banjo picking was two percent. I stood on a black rubber mat under buzzing fluorescent lights and looked at a lime-green-colored wall. A radio was permanently tuned to Rush Limbaugh. I couldn't believe Red and Mattie liked that shit but I think they didn't really hear it. It was background noise. The boy, Mark, sullen and silent, moved about the kitchen like a ghost. Once every few minutes I caught a glimpse of the warm, homey atmosphere out front. That's where I wanted to be.

At eleven, Red came over and said I was done. Saying no thanks to my shift beer, I tore off my apron and walked like a zombie out the screen door to Orca the RV. I collapsed onto my bunk. I had started my day with Hank in the coffee shop at the Plainsman Inn in Omaha, 850 miles and forty-three years ago. I fell asleep so fast I didn't know what hit me. It was dark, dreamless sleep.

* * *

At least my days were free. Red had somebody else who washed dishes during lunch, thank God. I would've had to draw the line.

But without any money, free days hang heavy on a man. That's when a lot of people, not me of course, would fall back onto booze or drugs. I quickly realized I'd have to find something to do, or leave Telluride. I couldn't allow myself to become the town crazy.

"Lookit that man there, Pa. He just wanders the streets all day."

"Yes, isn't it sad."

I washed dishes and picked the banjo at the Sluice for two whole days before I screwed up my courage and went back to see Marie. I walked over to the quilt store. Her white Toyota was parked in back. I went in the front door.

She was alone this time, reading a book behind the cash register.

"Hello," I said.

She looked up. She neither smiled nor frowned. I couldn't read her face.

"Hello, Webb."

"What's new?"

"Well, I hear the Sluicebox has a new dishwasher."

"Didn't you hear the rest? They have live entertainment, too."

Now she smiled. "I heard."

"Course, it's the washing dishes part I'm really up for. A man could go far."

"Indeed. Y'know, you don't have to do this."

"Do what?"

"That. Wash dishes so you can stay in town. I know you want to go on the road, and you should. You're a wonderful musician and you should follow your heart."

"My heart leads me to you."

Tears welled up in her eyes.

"Aw, come on," I said.

She looked at me like she would a child. "Now, how long do you really think you can stand living in an alleyway and washing dishes for minimum wage?"

"Well, I can't live forever parked out front of your house, running in and out to use the bathroom."

"Where are you showering?"

"The campground. It's fine. A bit cold at the end."

"Carla's been asking about you. This time I told her the truth."

"About my time-travel fantasy?"

Marie shook her head. "She knows Mark, their son. He told her about you."

"He's a strange one."

"Yes. They've had problems with him. . . ."

We were silent for a moment. I fingered some blue and white quilt material lying in a basket.

"You thinking of getting into quilting?" she asked.

"Yes, in fact that's exactly why I came in. I'll be needing some quilting supplies. Fix me up with everything."

She came out from behind the register and came into my arms. I held her tight and kissed her passionately. The kiss lasted a long time. I got lost in it. At last we broke apart.

"I'm still mad at you," she said. "You stood us up. If you don't want to tell me where you really went, OK. I can deal with it. But the prison thing . . ."

"How can I redeem myself?"

"Quit disappearing into thin air. And dinner would be nice."

"Deal. But I'm working nights now. I've got to wait for a day off."

"How long are you going to stay there?"

"For now. For a while. I won't impose on you anymore." She started to say something but I cut her off. "Look, it's fine. Red and Mattie are nice, fair people. And besides the music, the job came with one giant perk."

"What's that?"

"A parking place."

Now we both laughed. It was great to see her finally smile at me. "My big plan now is to find a day gig," I said.

"Doing what?"

"I don't know. Something not too taxing. Washing dishes wears me out."

"I may have an idea."

"Now you're talking."

"Webb, this is Daniel. Daniel, meet Webb. Betty, this is Webb. Webb, meet Betty. And this is Horace, and this is Andrew, and Bernard, and Angie."

"For crying out loud, don't people name their dogs Blackie and

Spot anymore? Or at least Muffy? Don't we have a Muffy here some-where?"

"No, we do not, Mr. Webb."

"It's Pritchard. But call me Webb."

"All right, Mr. Webb."

Mrs. Tarantella, Patsy Tarantella, was my new boss, my daytime boss. I walked rich peoples' dogs. This was Marie's idea. She knew Patsy, she knew everybody in town, and this was the only paying gig available she knew of. Mrs. Tarantella ran a deluxe boarding kennel and pet grooming service. The previous dog-walker, some airhead babe from California, had met a fitness-video producer and run off with him to Santa Fe. I wished them all the best.

The dogs, an Airedale, two Labs, a golden, a collie and a plug-ugly mutt who looked suspiciously like a pit bull, swarmed around me, yap-ping on their leashes. I felt like Ward Bond on *Wagon Train*.

"So I'm supposed to just basically walk them?"

Mrs. Tarantella looked exasperated. "Yes, Mr. Webb, that's the idea. Take them out, and, *walk* them. It's not brain surgery. Now you'd better go."

"Where?"

"I'm sure you'll be creative. Go!"

I guided them all out the door, or rather they dragged me out, and off we went. Me and Daniel, Betty, Horace, Andrew, Bernard and Angie. I looked down at the pit bull. Horace.

"From now on," I said, "you're Muffy."

12

I was settling into Telluride, and I did not like it. Washing dishes and walking pit bulls named Muffy was not my idea of the bluegrass life. Somehow, I had got off track, and badly.

I blamed Hank. It was Hank who'd thrown me this giant curve that had got me stuck in the first place in this highfalutin ski town. Now I wanted to leave, but Marie's sweet smile was keeping me here. Women. Maybe it was her fault. Marie and Hank. Between the two of 'em, I was spinning my wheels.

It was a Wednesday afternoon, a glorious afternoon when everybody turned out in their best spandex or old hippie duds. The women in spandex had braided their long blond hair, and the women in old hippie duds had unbraided theirs and let it float down their backs. That kind of day.

Being ornery, I retreated into the darkness of Orca the RV. Drew the spongy old curtains and locked the door. I pulled out Lil Darlin' and set her on my lap. Stroked her fine old wood. I wanted answers. It was time to conjure Hank.

I sat there, holding my banjo love, trying my darnedest to be, I don't know, spiritual. I blanked out my mind. Concentrated on just being. Connecting to the inner light of nothingness.

Aw, shit.

It wasn't working.

Maybe I'll play an old tune, I thought, and that'll bring Hank around. So I noodled around for a few minutes until I hit on an old number that was perfect. And Hank wrote it. "I Saw the Light," in which he sings about a blind man wandering along in the dark.

That was me, a blind banjo picker looking for the light. I let the notes ring off into silence and shut my eyes real tight, waiting for the numbness to hit. Waiting. And waiting. And waiting.

Nothing.

I opened my eyes. It was still me, the Webb Pritchard of the nineties, hiding out in his dank old RV on a sunny afternoon. Nobody else was there. I felt like a fool. I put Lil Darlin' away, figuring that when Hank was good and ready, he'd make an appearance.

Or maybe he couldn't. I had considered that. He could be in a hospital in Omaha, or lying unconscious in our hotel room. God, maybe he was frozen in time, still slumped onstage at the Cow Palace. I hoped that wasn't the case. He couldn't be dead; it wasn't his time yet.

I left the RV and went walking through town. I was restless. My shift at the Sluice didn't start for a couple of hours. I'd already walked the damn dogs. Marie was working. I was taking things nice and slow with her. She didn't believe me, well, why should she, for crying out loud? But if Hank yanked me back again it was going to be damned hard to explain. I had to make her believe. But how?

I cared for this woman; not that I didn't care for Nancy, but every time Nancy and I made love I wondered if I were screwing a ghost. I half expected her to dissolve into fairy dust right in my arms. Maybe she would one day. Maybe I'd never see her again. But I hoped I would.

I thought about what Hank wanted me to do. Inspire people with the music. How was I going to pull that off? I'm a fair banjo picker, but inspiring, well, no. Bela Fleck's inspiring. Tony Furtado. Alison Brown. Not Webb Pritchard. I was like most players, I'd mastered the basic licks and rolls and could improvise a little. Do a little single-string work if called upon. Play up the neck. When I was warmed up, I could go pretty fast, pretty smooth, and dazzle people as long as they weren't banjo players, too. I could more than hold my own in a jam session. I felt comfortable onstage. I could even sing when I played, which a lot of banjo players can't manage. But inspiring? You gotta be kidding.

The folks who seemed to break all the rules and still stay true to the nature of the instrument were the ones who made names for themselves. They were writers as much as players. I had never written a song in my entire life.

Maybe that was the answer I was looking for. Did Hank want me to write songs? He hadn't said that. He only said he wanted me to bring the old feeling to the modern world. Infuse my music with authenticity. Well, like I said before, I couldn't go back and be a poor southern boy raised in Appalachia. I had to do it on my own terms. I just couldn't be anybody but Webb.

I thought of Lula Mae. I wished she were here with me now. The wise old hen from Brooklyn, New York, would know what to do. I had wanted to tell her the real deal, who I was and what was going on, but something held me back. It didn't feel right yet, if it ever would. Nobody knew but Hank and me. The people in the past, I didn't want to spoil things for them. Screw it up. Hank had never told me not to tell, but I knew I couldn't. The closest we had come was the speech Hank gave in front of Earl in the motel room. I was surprised he had done that. That was Hank: close to the edge.

I wanted to go back again. I was sick of washing dishes. At least Doc Mullican never made us do that. I'd been at the Sluice now for a week. Living in the alley, cold showers at the campground. I couldn't quit; I didn't have enough money to go anywhere or do anything. I couldn't even take Marie out, except for a beer. I had gone to the grocery and stocked up on fruit, cheese, bread and peanut butter and jelly. That and coffee generally held me until dinner, when I got a free meal at the Sluice. Mattie never hesitated when I asked for seconds. She knew.

I headed up the main drag, passing throngs of tourists, walking against the flow. I was angry at myself for becoming a fuckup again right out of prison. It wasn't supposed to be this way, dammit.

"Look out!"

I was lying flat on my back on the sidewalk. It happened that quick. My head hurt, I must've hit it on the curb. Something dark and furry filled my vision. A warm, wet tongue was all over my face. A dog's breath. Yuck.

"Horace! Horace! Let the poor man alone!"

Horace? Wasn't that Muffy the pit bull? I wasn't about to let a vicious killer dog make hamburger of my face. I rolled over onto my stomach. Oh, man. Pain shot through the back of my head. Shit. It hurt.

"Sir, are you all right? Let me help you up." A hand gripped my shoulder. Mustering every bit of strength I had, I somehow got into a crouch and from that I slowly stood up. My bad knee cried out.

"What happened?" I asked. For some reason, I kept my eyes shut. Maybe I didn't want to see the blood and brains splashed all over the sidewalk.

"You took a nasty spill, sir. Nasty." A man's voice. British or something.

"And how did that happen?" Eyes still shut. Maybe I was afraid I'd be blind.

"Ah, well, my dog tripped you up, I believe. He tangled you up in the lead, somehow. Terribly sorry. Clumsy of us. I say, are you all right?"

Now I opened my eyes. It was Muffy, all right.

"You little shit."

"I beg your pardon?"

"I meant the dog. Muffy. I mean Horace. I know your dog. I walk him every morning."

"Oh! No wonder he's so friendly! He usually doesn't take to strangers."

I raised my eyes now and looked at Muffy's owner. He was a portly fellow of about fifty, balding, gray beard, gold earring in his left earlobe. He wore a too-loud sportshirt, and his spindly white legs came out of walking shorts and ended in Birkenstocks. My savior.

"Reginald Sandhurst," he said, offering his free hand. "My friends call me Tex."

"Your friends call you Tex?"

"It's a long story. Really, we must get you to a doctor. I think you're injured."

"I don't have any insurance."

"Come with me."

He was very authoritative, and I was addled at the moment. He led me down the street and around the corner. The town clinic was there, in a renovated Victorian house. Of course. The doctor took a look at the back of my head and said I needed stitches.

"I don't have any insurance," I said feebly.

"He's under my care," said Sir Tex, or whatever his name was.

"I am not under anybody's care!" I spluttered, but they made me lie back down and be quiet. My head really did hurt like hell. The doc, a young guy wearing bicycle shorts and a ponytail, shined a little light into both my eyes, asked me a couple of questions, had me perform a few dexterity tests like the cops do when they pull you over, and sewed me up. He did it fast and neat. A real pro. He gave me some pills.

"These are for pain," he said. "Take—"

I had already opened the bottle and popped four into my mouth. I swallowed.

"You won't be having any pain problems," he sighed, and turned to the next patient, a tourist with a piece of glass stuck in her foot.

Sir Tex and I walked out the door. Horace was waiting patiently where he had left him, his leash tethered to a bike rack. People tend not to fuck with pit bulls.

"I must apologize for this terrible incident," he said. "Just terrible. Horace apologizes, too. You said you walk him every morning? So you live in town?"

I gingerly touched my stitches. Ow. The pills wouldn't kick in for another twenty minutes.

"Yes, for now," I said.

"Well, please accept my apology and an invitation to dinner. It's the least I can do. I never caught your name?"

"It's Webb. Webb Pritchard."

"How very western! Right out of Zane Grey. Your real name?"

Oh, boy. "Yes. But . . . Tex?"

He laughed heartily. "I know I don't look the part at all, but I'm a Nashville record producer. Country music. I started in London in the late sixties, all that British invasion stuff, but after I came to America I saw more opportunity in Nashville. Chet Atkins gave me the name. It's a bit of a joke."

"You live in Nashville?"

"And here."

"What have you produced?"

"Now don't tell me. You're a musician! Down on your luck, and all you need is somebody to listen to your demo."

"As a matter of fact . . ."

"Say no more, Mr. Webb Pritchard. We'll talk over dinner. Eight tonight? The Lotus?"

"Sorry. I work tonight."

"Too bad. Tomorrow, then?"

"Actually, I work every night. At the Sluice. If you come by at eight-thirty, that's when I go on."

"You really are a musician, then? Dear, dear."

"Afraid so. And looking for a break."

"Aren't they all. Well, we'll see. Perhaps. Eight-thirty?"

"Eight-thirty. And ten-thirty, too. I do two sets."

He turned to go. "Come, Horace. We've had enough excitement for one afternoon."

So had I.

The pills kicked in good. A little too good. I wandered back to the RV to rest my aching head, and fell asleep. I was awakened by pounding on the flimsy door.

"Hey! You in there?"

It was the boy, Mark. He had hardly spoken to me since I arrived. I got up and opened the door.

"What's the matter?"

He peered past me into the camper. "It's past six-thirty. My dad wondered where you were."

"Oh. Sorry. I'll be right there."

Christ, they probably thought I was drunk, sleeping in the middle of the day. I put on a shirt and shoes and got my ass into the kitchen. A mountain of dishes, and the mighty Hobart, awaited.

Red greeted me curtly. Mattie nodded. Everybody was in a real fine mood.

The small of my back began hurting about fifteen minutes into the shift. My head still felt OK, but I noticed Mark staring at my stitches.

"I fell in the street today," I said. "Tripped over a dog leash. Doc had to patch me up."

"Dumb-ass," he said to me. His parents had gone to the dining room.

"Hey, what's your problem?" I asked. "You got an attitude, son."

He gave me the finger.

What could I do? He was twelve. His dad was my boss. I turned back to the Hobart. I thought about Sir Tex. I knew what he wanted from me, all right, but if his story was true about being a Nashville record producer, he could be my ticket out of here. Not that I was willing to do anything but pick the banjo and sing for him. That would have to suffice. If it didn't, well, there was always another opportunity somewhere. I hoped.

Eight-thirty at last. I rushed out to the RV, wiping the steamy sweat off my brow, and grabbed Lil Darlin'. I felt energized. My head was hurting again. I took another pill.

I walked out front and did my introduction, searching the crowd for Tex. I didn't see him. It was a busy night for the Sluice, maybe fifty people were there. I had mixed feelings: more people, more applause. More people, more dishes.

I had honed my little act all week. I decided to do my dazzle-'em-with-bullshit set, the one that featured lots of hot picking and not so much singing. In case Tex was there, after all.

Like always, it was over too soon. I took my bow and trudged back to the confines of the kitchen. I had never spotted Tex. Maybe I'd been just another passing fancy.

I ate my dinner on the back steps, pinto beans and Mexican rice. I always had to eat in a hurry, because technically, my dinner break was during my set. But Red and Mattie never pushed me.

Mark was hanging out in the alley.

"Why are you here?" he said, doing a handstand in the gravel.

"I'm hungry," I said. "Man's gotta eat."

"I mean why are you here in this town?"

"Lotta reasons," I said. "I came when the bluegrass festival was here, and I stayed on awhile."

"Why don't you leave?"

"Do you want me to leave?"

He shrugged. "Your music's stupid."

"So some people say. I happen to like it."

"You suck!" he shouted at me, and ran off into the dark. It was time for me to go back and wash some more dishes.

Which I did, a hundred million of them until it was ten-thirty and time to be famous again. I always wondered how many regulars out there knew what I was doing. Probably all of them.

Maybe Tex would make it to this set. I yanked off my apron, went out to the RV and put the key in the lock. Somebody had been here. The door was unlatched.

I pushed it open slowly, and quickly saw no one was inside. I stepped in. Nothing looked disturbed. This was weird. Then I reached for Lil Darlin'. Her case was unlatched, too. Oh, no.

I flipped open the lid. She was there. All her strings were cut.

Shit. Why would that boy do this? I wondered as I took her out of the case and checked her over. She was all right. But a banjo has six strings. It would take me many minutes to restring all of them. Time I did not have.

I carried Lil Darlin' into the Sluice through the kitchen, and found Red up front, by the cash register. I showed him the damage. I didn't tell him who I thought did it.

"Can I have a little time to restring her, then do my set?" I asked.

He frowned. "How long will that take?"

"About ten minutes."

He looked around the restaurant. There were still a lot of people. I didn't see Tex.

"Lotta dishes, Webb. Don't know if I can spare you."

"I'll hurry. And I'll only do one or two songs. How about that?"

"All right."

I rushed back to the RV and set about restringing Lil Darlin'. Thank God I wasn't out of strings. It took awhile, my fingers working feverishly. I didn't want to think about the time. Or the dishes piling up. Or the boy.

A full set of strings really needs to set awhile to sound good, settle in, but that wasn't possible. I got her as tuned as she would go and ran like a deer with her to my spot at the back of the dining room. I was out of breath. It was ten forty-five.

"Good evening, ladies and gentlemen," I said, trying to look calm. "My name's Webb Pritchard and I'm going to play you a little banjo tonight."

No Tex yet. I launched into the same set I'd played earlier, the dazzle-'em set, and Lil Darlin' tried, bless her, but she really wasn't herself. It sounded, and felt, like I was playing baling wire. No finger grease on the strings yet. The tension was all out of whack. I probably needed to adjust the neck and the head. Damn that kid.

I was going into my second song when there was some kind of commotion at the front of the room. I kept playing. It was a bar fight. We didn't get too many of those, I gathered. In fact, this was my first at the Sluicebox. Two or three guys, I couldn't see, were bashing someone else. Red went rushing up. The whole room turned away from me and focused on the fight. People started standing up. Guys started heading that way. A woman squealed. This could get good.

I felt like the piano player on *Gunsmoke*. But I gave it up. Hell, I had to see, too. I shoved Lil Darlin' under the bar and worked my way up until I could see what was going on. Fists were flying. Two guys in flannel shirts and jeans had somebody down on the floor. They were pounding him good.

It was Sir Tex.

He had helped me out today. One good turn deserves another. I climbed up on the bar and leaped off in a flying swan dive, like on TV, and landed smack on the back of the guy on top of Sir Tex. He snarled like a bear when I hit him. I got off one good roundhouse punch.

"Oh heavens! Omigod!" Sir Tex was screaming, curled in a fetal position and kicking his legs. There was blood on his mouth. Red was trying to pull the other guy off him.

"I'm here, Tex!" I yelled. "It's me, Webb!"

That's the last thing I remember. Things kinda went black right after that.

13

Seems like I was always coming to. Coming to in the past, coming to in my RV. This time I came to in the clinic, with the ponytailed doc restitching my head.

"You have a way of putting yourself in the path of trauma, Mr. Pritchard," he said as he bent over me. Last time I saw him he had on bike shorts. This time he was wearing a tuxedo. Man led an interesting life.

"You mean I get popped a lot. I guess so. Ouch!"

"That's it. You'll be okay. Now please take it easy."

I sat up and swung my legs over the side of the examining table. A very large person in a khaki uniform instantly blocked my path. Had to be a cop. It was.

"Come with me," he said, and took my upper arm in a grip so firm I thought my blood vessels were being squeezed dry. I tried to yank away.

"What's going on?"

"You're under arrest. Assault and battery. Disorderly conduct."

"Gimme a break! Why don't you arrest the guys who started it? I tried to save my friend."

He didn't say a word, just "helped" me to the door. The young guy was so much bigger and stronger than I was, I let the reasonable, middle-aged, head-hurting Webb take over. I kept talking. He kept bringing me along.

"Look, Officer." I hadn't said those words in a long time. They felt nauseatingly familiar. "A fight started while I was entertaining the crowd at the Sluice. I'm a musician. A friend of mine was getting the shit beat out of him. I went to help. That's all I remember. Somebody punched my lights out."

The sheriff's deputy, for that's what he was, didn't even bother to handcuff me. He just led me out to his car, opened the door and indicated I was to get in. Being sane, I did. We drove exactly three blocks and got out in front of a low, tan building. The jail.

"What happened to my friend? He could be dead!"

I was photographed, fingerprinted, booked, and put in a cell. Nobody had told me a fucking thing.

"What time is it?" I yelled out. I couldn't see anybody, but I figured they could hear me.

"Twelve-fifteen."

So it was after midnight. I must've been out cold for a while. No wonder my head hurt. Where was Sir Tex? Who had hit me? Why was I in jail and the bad guys weren't?

"I want to make a phone call!"

I was ignored. After a while, I was so worn out I just lay down on the bunk and fell asleep. Hell, it was a softer bed than my bunk in the RV. I slept for what seemed like a long time. When I awoke it was still dark outside. Footsteps. Somebody was coming down to see me.

"Pritchard!" It was a barked command. It wasn't the deputy who arrested me. It was an older guy. Older than me.

"That's my name."

He stopped in front of my cell and stared at me. "Didn't know we had a hardened criminal on our hands."

"Do you?"

"You oughta know. Been out of prison less than two weeks. Don't you guys ever learn?"

"Hey, I already explained, I got jumped when I tried to help my friend, who was getting the shit beat out of him at the bar. There's a million witnesses."

"That isn't quite the way we heard it."

"Oh yeah, well, what is the way you heard it?"

"You assaulted one of the pillars of our little community, Mr. Pritchard. Andy Lanier is not a man you want to cross. He says it was the other way around, that you jumped him—literally. Says you landed on his back after taking a swan dive off the bar. He could have whiplash. Or worse."

"Come on! Him and his buddies were hammering my friend, he was down on the floor—"

"Your friend says he started it. He apologized to Mr. Lanier."

"Tex! Apologized? They were gonna kill him!"

"He apologized for the incident and Mr. Lanier will not press charges. Your friend went home, I believe."

"This is outrageous. He's badly hurt. I want to make a phone call."

The deputy unlocked the cell door and led me down the hall to a pay phone. He stood there while I fished for change. Of course, I didn't have any. My pockets were empty.

"I can't believe I'm the one who got arrested. You got any change?"

He handed me a quarter. "You owe me."

"Thanks." I slipped it into the phone.

Now, who should I call? Marie? Red? Dot? Tex? How about Hank?

I hung up and the quarter was returned. I didn't know anybody's number.

"Now what's the matter?"

"I forgot the number. Do you have a phone book?"

He sighed heavily. "Back to the cell. I'll go get you one."

He locked me in and went to get it. I looked up the number. He let me out and we walked back to the pay phone. I dialed the number. It rang several times. It must be three or four in the morning by now.

"Hello?"

"You sonofabitch, when I get out of here you'll wish you only had whiplash!"

I hung up and looked at the deputy. We both burst out laughing.

"You got some balls, Pritchard," he said. "Now get back in the cell."

Red came and got me out the next morning. He looked pretty sheepish. I thought he'd be pissed.

"Hell, no, it wasn't your fault," he said as he signed the papers. Because he was a local and my employer, they let me out on a PR bond—personal recognizance.

"Usually, we don't do this," said the deputy. "But in this case . . ."

"Thanks," Red said, and we walked out.

"How'd this happen?" I said as we headed for the Sluice, about six blocks away. "You were there. Those other guys started it, my friend Tex was down on the floor getting the shit kicked out of him, and I go to help and get thrown in the can? What's the fuckin' deal here, man? I can't believe this."

"Calm down. The deal is, Andy Lanier is an asshole but a very important asshole in this town. Your friend, as you call him, put the moves on him and he didn't exactly appreciate it. Andy told him to fuck off and he responded by dumping his beer on Andy's head. Wrong move."

"But they were pounding him!"

"Yeah. But when you jumped on Andy's back, that was too much for his bodyguard. That's when he started using your head for a basketball."

"His bodyguard? This guy has a bodyguard?"

"You have a lot to learn, Webb."

"Who is Lanier?"

"He's a porn king who also happens to own half the town. The Downhill Lodge? That's his. So are those condos next to the lodge. The Eatery, that's his. The Fourth Quarter bar. Oh, yeah, and he's a partner in the bank."

"Gee. That all?"

"No, he also owns a ton of real estate around here that hasn't been developed. Yet. Flies in and out all the time on his private jet. Spends half the year in L.A."

"Where he makes dirty movies."

"Right. He owns Bridger Entertainment, maybe the biggest X-rated video company in the country. He's probably worth close to a billion. Who knows?"

"And I jumped on this guy's back. I hope I hurt him. I hope I crushed his vertebrae."

"I hope he doesn't sue the bar."

"Thanks for getting me out."

"I need a dishwasher."

"I need to showcase my talent."

"Right."

I retrieved Lil Darlin' from beneath the bar where I had stowed her just before the fight got nasty. She was all right, thank God. I carried her out to the RV, made myself some coffee and ruminated on last night's events. I felt I should call Tex. This whole thing was partly my fault; I invited the man to the bar, after all. And I had my interests at stake here. I wanted him to hear me play. If he wasn't bullshitting, he might be able to help my career. Though I doubted it. Beat-up forty-year-old ex-con banjo pickers aren't exactly the hottest ticket in Nashville.

But what the hell. I went back into the Sluice and looked him up in the phone book. Right before I made the call, I changed my mind. I decided to go see him instead.

Tex lived up on a hillside just outside of town, in a house with a lot of glass all around. It wasn't a fancy house by Telluride standards. Probably only worth half a mil. I swung the Orca up his steep driveway and parked her next to a shiny new black Porsche. Whatever he did for a living, he wasn't doing too bad at it. I got out and heard barking. Muffy the pit bull.

I rang the bell. After what seemed like too long a time, the door opened.

"My God," I muttered. Tex was a mess. His right eye was blacked, all puffy and swollen many colors. His left cheek was bruised yellow-purple. There was a hell of a scrape across his forehead and his lip was cut. They'd done a number on him.

"I thought you might be dropping by," he said through the lumps and bumps. "Come on in."

"I heard you apologized. What kinda bullshit is that?"

"Want a drink?"

"No thanks."

He led me into a living room that overlooked the valley. Big fireplace, big sofas, big windows. Big pieces of art hung on the walls. I felt uncomfortable in such a house. Tex fixed himself a big Bloody Mary and eased himself onto one of the sofas. I stood over by the fireplace, rocking on my boot heels.

"How was our town jail? They treated you well, I trust?"

"How could you apologize to that asshole?"

"It seemed the prudent thing to do."

"They coulda killed you."

"And nearly did. Thank you for coming to my rescue."

"Well, I'm not apologizing. Except maybe to you, for bringing you into that situation."

"It was entirely of my own making, I assure you. How's your head?"

"More stitches. I'll live."

"As will I. I propose we put this nasty incident behind us and move on."

"Hope Lanier can do the same."

"Yes, well, that remains to be seen. He's not one to mess with, from what I know."

"What do you know?"

He shrugged. "You must've heard by now. He's very rich and very corrupt. Runs a pornographic film business."

"Why'd you proposition him, anyway?"

"I was drunk, dear boy. What can I say? A lapse in judgment."

"I'll say."

"I didn't get to hear you play last night, at least, nothing I can remember. Did you bring that banjo?"

"Yeah, it's out in the RV. But I really just came over to see if you were OK. I felt partly responsible."

"Well, go get it. I'd like to hear you. Really."

"I'd rather you hear me perform in front of a crowd, but . . ."

"Go!"

I fetched Lil Darlin', and tuned her up out on the driveway, where I spent a few minutes warming up my fingers. In the back of my mind, I still wondered if this guy was bogus. He said he was a Nashville record producer, but I didn't know that to be a fact. He did have a nice house in Telluride and a fancy car, but so what? He could be another porno king like Andy Lanier, for all I knew. Or maybe he was a dope dealer. He sure as hell didn't look like no Nashville dude to me.

I walked back into the house and he was sitting on the sofa with a fresh drink. I stood in front of the fireplace and took a bow.

"Ladies and gentlemen, or rather just gentlemen, or rather sir, my name is Webb Pritchard and I hail from the Great State of Oklahoma. Without further ado, I'd like to pick you a little banjo music."

And I lit into "Ground Speed," my standby whenever I was nervous. When that was over I laid a little Bela Fleck on him with "Whitewater," a nice jumpy little number I'd been dying to try out on the Hayride and couldn't. I finished up with "Doug's Tune," a slower piece but very nice. My chops were up from playing every day. I knew I sounded like a pro.

"Bravo, my man, bravo," Sir Tex said, standing up and waving his drink in the air. Did this guy always wear loud Hawaiian shirts and baggy shorts? "Simply superb. Where did you learn to pick like that?"

"Here and there. I've been in some bands."

"You sing, too, I'm to understand?"

"Some. I enjoy singing, but to be honest it's not my strong suit. I do mostly instrumentals."

He circled the room, looking out the windows at the spectacular view. The ice clinked in his glass and he drained it.

"We need a gimmick here," he finally said.

"Beg your pardon?" Jesus, this sounded like Hank and the comedy routine. No way, Jose.

"I must be honest with you, Webb. You're a fine fellow and a helluva banjo player, but that's not enough. You're too old to be the next Garth Brooks, if you don't mind my saying so. And you're not much of a vocalist, as you freely admit. Pickers aren't the stars in Nashville. They're the sidemen. Especially banjo players. Banjos haven't been at the forefront of country music in more than forty years. You realize that."

"Of course. My sister keeps reminding me. My heart really lies with bluegrass, but for now I'm solo. Guess I just don't fit in anywhere, do I?"

"You tried the festival circuit?"

I laughed. "That's what I was planning to do when I got here two weeks ago. Hook up with somebody at the bluegrass festival. But I got sidetracked." If he only knew.

Sir Tex plopped back down on the couch. "I'd like to help you. I really would."

"Why?"

"I like you."

"I hope not too much."

He roared with laughter. "Nothing like that. You're not my type, Webb. No offense."

"Hey, none taken. You aren't exactly my type, either. So why help me out?"

"As I said, I like you. Do I need another reason? You seem like a decent man who needs a break. And I feel badly, too, about what's happened. First you're nearly killed by my dog's appalling lack of sidewalk manners and then you're nearly killed again on account of my drunken escapades. It's the least I can do. I can't promise anything.

But my advice is expert, free and given from the heart." He laid a hand theatrically over his breast pocket.

"You really are a Nashville record producer?"

"Ever heard of TipTop?"

"That's you?"

"That's me."

TipTop wasn't a big label, but its pedigree was beyond reproach. They produced a handful of stars who routinely shot into the Top Ten on the country music charts. A small indie, but quality all the way.

"I've heard of you."

"Now. Let me think on this a bit. Do you write?"

"What?"

"Write songs. Do you write songs?"

I thought about Hank. "Haven't really tried, but maybe I could. Why?"

"Well, if you did it would be a helluva lot easier to get you started. You must do original material, my boy. That's a given."

"I'd have to work something up."

"And from what I can see, you don't really have an act. That's what I mean about a gimmick. You need . . . something. You can't just get up and pick a banjo and say thank you and leave. Nobody wants to see that."

"So my sister says."

"She speaks the truth! Ever watch the Nashville Network?"

"No."

"Take a look sometime. They don't play a lot of videos of middle-aged men doing old Earl Scruggs numbers."

I sighed. "I know. But I'm not a rocker like Garth and I don't have big hair like Reba."

"So what do we do? How do we make Webb Pritchard a star?"

"I'm not sure I want to be a star. That wasn't exactly what I was aiming for."

"A musician who doesn't want to be a star. Never heard of such a thing. Then what do you want?"

I paused. "I want to play the music I love and bring it to as many people as possible. And have them feel it like I feel it. Get away from the plastic side of country music. What it's become. Computerized shit. Get back to what it was. Close to the bone."

He stared at me.

"My, my. Didn't know we had tapped such a deep well."

"Fuck you."

"Sorry."

"I mean what I say. You ever listen to Hank Williams?"

"Senior or Junior?"

"Senior."

"Not lately. But sure. Why?"

"Can you feel what he's feeling when you hear him?"

"He was the best, wasn't he?"

"Damn right," I said. "He knew what it was all about. He couldn't help himself. He was what he was, and he was the real thing. And the people loved him for it. No gimmicks."

"Forgive me, but you're no Hank Williams."

"No, but I know what he felt. I want to bring that to audiences."

He sucked on an ice cube. "Times have changed. Half the people who ever heard Hank Williams are dead. The other half are on Social Security. You've got to hit the MTV audience. Their attention span is about a nanosecond.

"I'm in the recording business. That's my end of it. I think you need some more road experience before we bring you into the studio. You need to work up a real act, not the slam bam thank you ma'am you're doing now over at the Sluice. We need a gimmick here."

"Stop saying that!"

"I don't mean we should set fire to your banjo. I simply mean you need to show me something nobody else has, nobody else is doing."

"Nobody else is playing old Earl Scruggs numbers. You gotta admit."

He shot me a look and went on. "Something fresh. You need to write some songs. In short, Webb, you need to get to work. Then maybe I can introduce you to a few people around Nashville. Where are you staying?"

"In my RV. It's parked out in your driveway."

He smiled. "A travelin' man. Travelin' light. I like that. Maybe we could use that to our advantage. Part of your image. I'm goin' to Alabama with a banjo on my knee. I don't know that we can market you to a younger audience. They'd never understand where you're coming from. But there're plenty of women over thirty-five who would go for your type. They buy a lot of country music. Maybe we can turn you into a Tommy Lee Jones type. Here's a man with a past. Older, rugged, lonely. Yes, I can see it."

"Well, I sure as hell can't. Sounds like a buncha bullshit. I'm no Hollywood actor. The music's the thing with me. That's what I'm about."

"I think you're wrong, Webb. If you want to bring your music to the people, as you said, you can't hide away down here in a box canyon at the Sluicebox Saloon. Playing to fifty people a night. Being true to yourself. You've got to hit the road. Write some songs. Develop an image, an act. We'll talk again."

He stood up abruptly, a bit unsteady on his feet. It was my cue to leave.

Sir Tex headed for the kitchen, I assumed to make another drink. I let myself out. I cranked up old Orca and we cruised back down into town, nice and easy. I had a lot on my mind.

Marie. Did she know about last night? I figured she did. Damn small towns. Now she'd really think I was a thug. Maybe I was. Yes, I have this dark and violent side, Marie, but let me just pick you this little ol' tune here before I slip off your panties . . .

Shit. Everything had turned to shit. I washed dishes for a living and my fingerprints were on file at the local cop shop. I had pissed off Mr. Big. I was broke. Now some faggot alcoholic record producer was trying to turn me into Garth-Reba. We need a gimmick here!

But Tex was right about one thing. I needed to write some songs, a song, any song. I wasn't going to get anywhere just doing others' material. That's a given, dear boy, he'd said. He was also right that I needed to "work up an act." I had no idea where to start. When I was with the Hayride, everything was so simple, all laid out. You'll do one song, Doc Mullican said, and I got up there and the audiences had never seen a video or a laser light show and it was enough that I got up there and picked my banjo.

I missed Nancy and her beautiful clodhopper shoes and sweet smells.

Marie Nancy Marie Nancy Marie Nancy Marie . . . Nancy.

In sudden haste, I drove Orca over to the local market and picked up what I needed. Sometimes only a homemade enchilada dinner will make things right.

Melt the shortening in the pan. Heat up the Hatch chile sauce. Chop the onions real fine, grate the cheese. Lay the tortilla in the oil just long enough so the edges snap. Flip it over. Take it out with the tongs and sink it into the Hatch sauce. Let some of the grease roll off. Let it get soft. Pick it up and lay it flat on the plate, throw some onion and cheese on it, start another tortilla. Make four. Layer 'em like pancakes. Now pour what's left of the Hatch sauce on top, sprinkle with last of the cheese. Put an egg on top.

My RV stunk to high heaven. Grease spatters on the paneling. On the ceiling. I didn't give a shit. I ate with solid gusto, thanking God I was alive. I thought things over as I ate, and I came to some decisions.

Orca was pulled over on a side street, exactly where I hadn't been able to park when I first came to town. Now I started her up and took her over to the Sluice, trailing a pungent grease smell through the town as we went. She smelled like a roach coach. I parked out front, not in the alley. I went in and found Red doing some paperwork in his office.

"I've done some thinking, Red."

He looked at me.

"I can't wash dishes anymore. I just can't. It's not for me. Sorry. But I'm beefing up my act and I'd like the chance to do a real set, say forty-five minutes. Six nights a week. Two sets a night. Pay me what you can. If it works out, you can pay me more. I need a couple of days to fine-tune this thing."

"I have to let you go, Webb."

"That's OK. I won't wash dishes anymore."

"No. All of it. The music, everything."

"Why?"

He looked embarrassed. "One of Andy's boys came around."

"You're kidding."

"No, I'm not. He said if you ever showed up here again Andy'd see to it my liquor license got yanked."

"He can't do that!"

"The hell he can't. His brother sits on the damn board. And everybody in town owes him."

"We'll fight him! We'll—"

"Sorry, Webb."

I looked at the floor. Ah, well. The enchiladas had suddenly turned to lead in my gut.

"You're a square guy, Red. I like you and your family. Thanks for what you did for me."

He fumbled in his pockets and peeled off two twenties. "Here's what I owe you."

I turned and left without another word. I drove over to the quilt store.

"What's past is past, huh?" Marie said. "Doesn't look like it to me."

"I went to help a friend. They started it. They jumped me!"

"I heard you jumped on his back."

"Well, yes, but—"

"That's enough, Webb. I think you'd better go."

I walked out to Orca and got in my captain's chair and looked out the big, wide windshield. Box canyon to the left. A dead end. Highway to the right. The only way out. The town suddenly looked tiny, Lilliputian. A toy town full of toy people.

"Head 'em up, move 'em out," I muttered.

Rollin', rollin', rollin'.

14

When you try to cut ties to people, they often stretch out and snap you back like a rubber band.

I was fifteen miles gone from Telluride when I realized I'd have to go back. Not right now, mind you. My jaw was set and my foot was mashed to the pedal, and I was a Man on a Mission. A Mission from Hank. To hell with your town, I thought. To hell with all of ya. But I knew I'd be back. I had unfinished business there. A lot of it.

I was trying to make it to a cheaper gas station before the tank ran dry. Gasoline in Telluride was about four dollars a gallon, and Orca was a thirsty bitch. I needed a town where everybody wasn't a millionaire in a Land Rover.

Fortunately, Naturita had a Conoco that wasn't too steep. Real people lived here, I guessed, when they weren't busy towing cars from Telluride. I filled 'er up, used the restroom, bought a pop and climbed back into the cab. I figured I could get a hundred miles or more before I stopped for the night.

I slid a Hot Rize tape into the deck and had gone about thirty miles into the countryside, when I heard a noise. A definite noise. A scraping and moving about. What the . . . ?

That's when the boy popped out of the storage cabinet.

Mark. Red and Mattie's kid. The one who hated me.

"Holy Christ! Where'd you come from?" I cut the wheel and jerked Orca over to the side of the highway. The kid climbed out of the cabinet and stood there, wiping his nose. Looking at me.

"Mark?"

He didn't say anything.

"Want to tell me what's going on?"

Visions of state troopers with shotguns swarming over the RV swam into my head. Kidnapping. Probably sexual assault on a minor. Why else would a man take a boy these days? Now I was a pervert on top of everything else. Child molester. I had to rectify this situation, and fast.

"Let's step outside, shall we?"

I got out of the cab and motioned him to follow. He started crying. Aw, shit. He was afraid I was gonna leave him.

"I'm not gonna ditch you, OK? Now come on out. We gotta talk, kid."

He finally got out and stood there in the afternoon chill, a thin twelve-year-old in a T-shirt and jeans.

"Don't you have a jacket?"

He shook his head no.

"What's the story? Wanna tell me?"

"I want to go with you."

"Why?"

He shrugged. "I don't want to be there anymore."

"Where?"

"Back there."

"The Sluicebox? With your folks?"

He nodded.

"Why?

He shrugged again. "Don't want to."

I looked at him. "I kinda thought you and me weren't exactly buddies."

He didn't say anything.

"Well, you can't come with me, kid. You don't belong to me. Your folks'll come after you. The law'll come after me. I could get in as much trouble as you. You understand?"

Mark looked down at the asphalt. A big tear rolled down his cheek.

"Aw, come on. What's the matter? Your parents are real nice people, Mark. What is it that's got you upset? Listen, I'm gonna have to call 'em. You know that, right? I'm gonna have to call 'em."

We were out in the middle of nowhere. Hardly any traffic went by. Nothing around but miles of wire fences and high Colorado pasture. I knew if he bolted, he couldn't get anywhere. But the problem was, if he did, my old bones couldn't catch him. I prayed he wouldn't run.

"Tell you what, kid. We'll head on to the next place. We'll get us Cokes and cheeseburgers. We'll call your folks. That's my best offer. Come on."

He hesitated, but when I moved to climb in the cab he went around and got in on the passenger side. The little shit even buckled his seat belt.

I could've turned around and headed back to Naturita, toward Telluride, but we were so far out I thought maybe the next stop could be just up ahead. A closer phone, a closer cheeseburger. So we rolled on, and watched the stars come out as the evening began to creep over the mountains.

I didn't need this complication. Red and Mattie wouldn't think I'd swiped the boy. They knew their son was messed up. He'd probably run away before. Hell and damnation, why did this shit always have to happen to me?

I turned on the headlights. The dashboard glowed green. "You know, I didn't exactly appreciate you cutting those banjo strings. Why'd you do that?"

He stared straight ahead.

"I don't have any kids of my own, so I don't always understand the things they do. But that hurt me. You found my one soft spot. Did you know my banjo has a name? I call her Lil Darlin'. She's my sweetheart. It's true. She's really all I've got. And she's not so young anymore. She's kinda fragile. So when somebody damages her, it's like they're damaging my best friend. My true love. A man doesn't like that."

"I . . . don't hate you."

"Well, there's some progress. I could've sworn you did."

I looked over at him. He was trying hard not to smile.

"Now what on earth possessed you to hitch a ride with me? Did you sneak in when I was talking to your dad?"

"Yeah. You never saw me."

"I sure as hell didn't. You're a slick little devil. Wasn't it kinda cramped in that storage locker?"

132

"Yeah. I stayed real quiet. I was hiding."

"I know. You're a good hider."

"I think I need to go to the bathroom."

"Should be someplace right up ahead. Can you hold on that long?"

"I think so."

"If not, holler and I'll pull over."

I put a little more speed on and turned the Hot Rize tape back up. The bluegrass music filled the cab. I hoped we wouldn't be heading away from Telluride much longer. This situation could turn on me at any time. I kept checking the rearview mirror for state troopers.

About ten miles later, lights flickered up ahead. Good. It was a gas station and a little roadside restaurant called Angie's. It didn't look too busy. I pulled in and parked.

"Think Angie knows how to make a cheeseburger?" I asked Mark. He scrunched up his thin shoulders and raised his hands, palms up.

"Shall we find out?"

He nodded violently.

"All right then."

The lady put us in a booth. We ordered double cheeseburgers and double fries; I got a Coke and he got a chocolate milkshake. There was a phone by the door.

"You're in charge of the food," I said to the boy, and walked over, fishing for quarters. I dialed the number. As it rang, I had this imaginary conversation in my head:

"Sluicebox Saloon."

"I have the boy."

"Omigod! Is he all right?"

"He's fine. But only as long as you do exactly as I say."

"What do you want?"

"The job. No dishes. Just banjo. That gig we talked about. Six nights a week, two forty-five minute sets. If you don't cooperate—"

"Sluicebox." Man's voice.

"Uh, Red?"

"I'll get him."

I turned around. Mark was fiddling with the silverware. All was well.

"Red Sweeney."

"Red, it's Webb. Mark's with me. Seems he decided to hitch a ride without telling anybody. He's fine. We're in, I don't know, a cafe about forty miles out of Naturita."

Big sigh on the other end. "That damn kid. We were worried sick. I told the sheriff he was missing, but we hadn't started a search yet. Figured he'd turn up at dinnertime. He's all right?"

"He's all right. We're having burgers right now."

I heard Mattie coming up on his end, chattering excitedly. She got on the line.

"Webb! Mark's with you?"

"Yes, ma'am, and he's fine. He hid in my truck and popped up in the middle of nowhere."

"Thank God. Put him on the line, please?"

"Sure. Hold on."

But the kid refused. When I told him his mom wanted to talk to him, he looked away and wouldn't look back. I returned to the phone.

"Mattie, um, he won't come. He's sitting right here in a booth here, looking stubborn as hell. I can't make him come to the phone."

"Well." I could hear the little catch in her throat. "Well, then. He's all right?"

"He's fine. A little hungry, I think. He's inhaling a double cheese-burger and a shake."

"Want us to come get him?"

"No. We'll eat and I'll bring him back. Should be there in about two hours or so. That all right?"

I could hear her talking to Red. She came back on.

"That's fine, Webb. Thank you. I'm so sorry you had to put up with this."

"No problem. If you don't mind my asking, he's done this sort of thing before, hasn't he?"

"Yes. Many times. But he never got this far."

"Uh-huh. Well, we'll see you in a bit. And don't worry. He's fine, really. See you soon. Good-bye."

The food had arrived. Mark's face was buried in his cheeseburger. After he took a bite, he'd stuff several fries in on top of it and slurp down some milkshake. Whatever was eating at this boy, it sure hadn't hurt his appetite.

"Hungry?" I carefully poured a dab of ketchup on the side near my pile of fries.

He looked up at me over the burger mashed between his hands, eyes popped open wide.

"Mmmmpphh."

"Well, enjoy." I was thinking, I hope your folks bawl the tar out of you when you get home. If he was my kid that's what I'd do. Yank his ear so hard he'd remember next time. Remember not to fuck up. This kid was screwing up my plans.

I decided to mess with his head a little.

"Bet you didn't know I was a time traveler."

He surfaced long enough to get a breath.

"Huh?"

"Time traveler. I travel in time. Why, just the other day I was in Omaha and it was 1951."

"Right."

" 'S true. I played the Cow Palace. Big crowd. Ever hear of Hank Williams?"

"Nope."

"He was famous. Real famous. Way before your time. Played country music in the forties and fifties. He died in '53."

"How?"

"Well, he was man who took a lot of drugs and drank a lot of whiskey, sometimes both together. That's basically what did it."

"Just say no."

"What?"

"That's what they tell us in school. Just say no."

"Somehow I don't think that woulda worked with Hank."

"It doesn't work with Bobby Lanier. He does drugs."

"He does?"

"Yeah. I've seen him smoking joints after school. Everybody knows it."

"Uh-huh. Well, it'll catch up to him one day."

"Do you do drugs?"

"Me? No. I mean, have I ever? I'd be lyin' if I said no. But I don't recommend it."

"What'd you do?"

"I've smoked joints. Popped a few pills. But I found that reality was much more interesting than anything on drugs. Drugs just slow you down. Garble you up. Make you stupid. Know what I mean?"

"Are they fun?"

Smartass kid.

"Well, now that's a question that uh, that uh, it uh, they can be, but no, I said I wouldn't recommend it." Dumb-ass grown-up answer. How do people who went through the sixties and seventies tell their kids, Hell, yeah, we had a fucking blast, but you can't do it?

"My dad says drugs are a dead end."

"He's right. Listen to your dad."

"But they're fun, right?"

I swirled a fry in the ketchup. "Look. I can't say I never had fun when I was high. But it wasn't really worth it, is what I'm trying to tell you. The world of drugs is a false world. It's not real, son. Plus you can get your ass thrown in jail. And you can become dead real easy. Is that worth it? I would say no." Christ, I sounded like some kind of school counselor. "You can have fun other ways."

"Bobby Lanier gave me a joint."

I should let Red handle this.

"Well, like I said, I wouldn't smoke it."

"Let's smoke it now!"

"Shut up and eat your hamburger."

Great. Now we were carrying drugs. What else did this kid have on him?

"Your friend. His name's Lanier, you said?"

"Yeah. Bobby. He's not really my friend."

"His dad wouldn't be Andy Lanier, would he?"

"Yeah. Why?"

I sat back in the booth and pondered the possibilities. Life had just taken a turn for the better.

"Mr. Pritchard?"

"Yeah?"

"Why'd you leave?"

I ate my last fry. It was cold. "Oh, lots of reasons. I was tired of washing dishes, for one. I didn't see much happening for me in Telluride. It was just time to move on."

"Are we going back now?"

"Yep. I gotta take you home."

"Where are you going?"

"Wherever the road will take me."

"What are you going to do?"

"Pick the banjo, son. Let's get out of here."

I got up and left the tip. We got back in the RV. The night air was chilly in the San Juans, even in late June. I gave the kid my jacket. He put it on and buckled himself in. Good little soldier. I'd still yank his ear if he were mine. We got out on the highway and headed back toward Telluride.

"Mr. Pritchard?"

"Yeah?"

"Tell me about that guy."

"What guy?"

"The dead guy. Hank Williams."

It took us more than two hours to get back. I kept getting stuck behind hay trucks and old pickups doing about twenty. It was close to eleven when we pulled up in front of the Sluice. Mattie ran out to greet us.

"Mark!"

The kid slid out of the camper and into his mother's arms. He squirmed away from her and ran inside.

"Oh, Webb. We owe you for this. I'm so sorry," she said, looking embarrassed.

"Don't worry. I'm just glad everything turned out all right. He's a good kid. Just a little mixed up."

"Come on in."

"I—"

She took my elbow and led me into the saloon.

Mark was nowhere to be seen. Red came up. He clapped a beefy hand on my shoulder.

"Thanks. What can I say?"

"You don't have to say anything. No sweat. But I might ask you for a beer."

"You got it."

"And maybe one other thing."

"Sure. What?"

"It's a bit late to be heading out again. Mind if I park out back just for tonight?"

Red laughed. "Hell, no. Least we can do. Be our guest."

I drained two Killians in fifteen minutes and called it a night. I was asleep before my head hit the pillow.

The next morning, I got up early and drove over to the little market to get bagels and coffee. After I ate and the caffeine kicked in, I did some checking around. Andy Lanier kept an office in the bank building. That's where I went.

Telluride's a pretty casual place. Nobody wears ties, nobody seems to have receptionists. Lanier was the exception. I rode the elevator to the third floor and found his office guarded by a goon in a black suit. I'm not kidding. A black suit.

"I'm here to see Lanier."

"Who the fuck are you?"

"Is that the standard greeting around here?"

"Beat it."

"My name is Webb Pritchard. Are you the one who kicked me?"

Now his eyes glittered. He smiled.

"What do you want, asshole?"

"Telluride's such a friendly little town, isn't it? I'm here to see Lanier. On business."

"He's got no business with you."

"Maybe he does. I want to star in a porno film."

"Fuck off."

"Go ahead. Hit me."

He looked like he wanted to. We were standing there eyeballing each other when the door to the inner office opened and Lanier stepped out.

"What's going on, Ned?"

Ned?

Before his goon could respond, I turned toward him and said, "I'm Webb Pritchard. Remember me? We need to talk."

"I have nothing to say to you, Mr. Pritchard. Except good day." He turned away.

"It's about Bobby."

Now he stopped. He turned and looked at me. He didn't say a word.

"Your son. Isn't his name Bobby?"

His face was expressionless. He jerked his head toward his office. "Two minutes."

I brushed past Ned and strolled into the inner sanctum. Lanier's office was a spacious, wood-filled cocoon. Beamed ceiling, polished floors. Indian rugs. Brown leather sofa, brown leather easy chairs gathered around a carved wooden coffee table. A place where deals were made. I was about to cut my own.

He didn't say, "Have a seat."

"Well?"

Lanier was close to my age. He had that corrupt look that comes from too much easy living at other people's expense. It wasn't in his body, which was hard and lean, no doubt from many sessions with his personal trainer in his personal gym. No, it was in his face, a cruel, slack face that betrayed no trace of compassion for other human beings. His hair was California coifed. I hated this guy.

"I knew you were a sick fucker, Lanier, but I thought your specialty was dirty movies. Didn't know you were in drugs, too."

"You have about ten seconds."

"Your boy. Bobby. He's selling drugs at school. Didn't you know that? Are you his supplier?"

"What do you want, Pritchard? Money? Get lost."

"I have proof your kid's a dope dealer. Isn't that nice? How old is he? Fourteen? Fifteen? A real chip off the old block."

Lanier's eyes flickered for just an instant. A cord in his neck raised up.

"How would that play in this town, Andy Lanier's kid the local dope pusher at the school? Mr. Pillar of the Community? Of course, you're already a porno pusher, so I guess it'd be pretty hard to damage your reputation. Might not matter."

"You're fulla shit, Pritchard. Beat it."

"It's not just weed, either. It's pills, and hash, and guess what? The little shit's been showing other kids how to shoot up. Needles, pal. Now we're not talking juvenile probation. Now we're talking jail time. State reformatory for your little darling. Couple of kids I know'll be happy to testify."

"What do you want?"

"My job back."

He laughed wickedly. "Washing dishes? You're dumber than I thought."

"Not that. The music. I want to pick up where I was so rudely interrupted the other night."

"Your faggot friend got in my face. He deserved to get pounded."

"Maybe queers are drawn to you. I could see that."

"You can't get to me that easy, you fuck."

"How about it? I get to keep my job at the Sluicebox and your kid gets to keep his job as a schoolyard dope pusher. And I want the charges against me dropped."

Lanier sat down in one of the easy chairs. He took a lemon drop from a dish and popped it in his mouth.

"You're nothing to me. I could have you killed and your body dumped where they'd never find it."

"How many people have you offed, Lanier? Or maybe a better question would be how many lives have you ruined?"

"Lately, just yours, I guess. Tell you what. Go back to the Sluicebox. See if Red'll have you back. It's up to him."

"Right."

"Get out."

"Charming boy, that Ned."

I slammed the door on the way out.

15

Well, I got my banjo gig back, but the dishes came with it. It was a package deal, Red said. Take it or leave it. Seeing as how my previous escape from Telluride had barely got me past Naturita, I was coming to believe this town held some kind of fate for me. I was stuck in a time warp at both ends.

I parked old Orca out behind the Sluicebox again, and plunged straight back into kitchen duty. What fun. You ever wash dishes? Or do any kind of really monotonous work? I guess washing dishes is better than some gigs. I knew a guy once, older than me, who decided when he was seventeen that he didn't need to go to college or anything like that. He was too smart. Had it all figured out. So his dad said, OK, son, here's a job for you, and put him to work in a slaughterhouse for the summer.

"My job was to stand there at the bottom of a chute, and cattle heads would come thumping down that chute and I had to put 'em in a kind of vise and then slice their face in half," he told me. "Guy who showed me how to work the machine had a hook for a hand. I looked around and saw all these old guys in their fifties, standing in the slop and the blood, and I decided it was time to go to college."

So washing dishes had its appeal. I could've been cleaning up dog shit at a kennel, or mopping up vomit at a nursing home. Or stepping through cow guts in a slaughterhouse all day. Or stuck in prison.

Instead, at the age of forty, I had landed in the Switzerland of

America, where some people lived fantasy lives but where I, at the very bottom of the food chain, scraped bits of hamburger and chili sauce off of plates and stuck 'em in a Hobart and picked a little banjo on the side. The dog-walking gig? I had kind of let that slip for the past few days, since my little run-in with the law. I thought about it and decided to let it slip altogether.

I had needed to fill my time before, but now I didn't have enough time. I had to kick-start my career. I had to start writing songs.

Hank made it look so easy. Get naked, put on a hat, go for it. Somehow I knew that approach wouldn't work for me. I'd sat on my bunk in the RV with Lil Darlin' on my lap, trying and trying to come up with a tune. Everything I played sounded like something I'd already heard before. Probably because I had.

So I stood there at the mighty Hobart, staring at the dull green walls and trying to think up a song. This might be the problem, I thought. Hank didn't have to stand with his elbows in greasy dishwater and stare at a blank green wall while he was trying to write songs. He just lived. That was the secret. He just zoomed through life like a car out of control and when he slowed down to take a breath, he took off his clothes, put on his hat and let it flow. He didn't have to wash any damn dishes.

I wished my life were different.

"Break this plate, oh my Lord, and set me free," I sang to the tune of "Take These Chains from My Heart," one of the last songs Hank ever recorded.

> "Break this plate, oh my Lord, and set me free,
> This dishwater's grown cold, it no longer cares for me . . ."

"Whatcha doin'?"

"Huh?" I blinked out of my reverie. Mark stood there.

"I said, whatcha doin'?"

"What's it look like I'm doin'? I'm up to my ass in dirty dishes, is what I'm doin'."

"Was that a Hank song?"

I kept stacking. "Kind of. I mean, it was a Hank tune, he sang it, but not with those words."

"Did he write it?"

"Nope."

"I thought he wrote a million songs. You told me he did."

"Yeah, but he didn't happen to write that one. He just sang it."

"What's it called?"

"Break This Plate."

"Beat it," I said.

The kid was hanging all over the Hobart, crowding me.

"Do a Hank song. A real one. One that he wrote."

"Nooo . . ."

"Yesssss!"

"After I'm done here. I gotta lotta dishes, kid. Work to do. Later."

The boy scampered off. He wasn't a bad kid. We'd had a long talk on the ride back to Telluride. His problems had become clearer.

"I'm adopted," he had told me.

"I didn't know that," I'd said.

"Red and Mattie aren't my real parents."

"They are, in a sense."

"They don't love me."

"That's bullshit. Of course they do."

"No they don't."

"Why do you say that?"

"Because they never told me. That I'm adopted. They were lying."

"Whoa. Now hold on. What are you talking about?"

"Somebody at school told me. Then I asked 'em."

"And?"

"My mom, I mean Mattie, said it was true. But they didn't want me to know."

"You don't call your mom 'Mom' anymore? Now she's Mattie?"

"She isn't my real mom. My real mom is . . . I don't know. Dead. She's dead."

I shifted in the captain's chair and glanced at the gas gauge. We had plenty. We started the long descent into Telluride.

"So you just found out you're adopted. Is that what's been bugging you?"

He didn't say anything.

"Look," I said. "You're lucky as hell. Two people who really wanted you took you in and gave you a home and everything. Who your real parents are, that doesn't really matter at this point. Whatever happened back then is history, kid. You hear me? Your parents are Red and Mattie. Me, personally, I think they're pretty great people."

He still didn't say anything.

"Why didn't they tell you before this?" I asked him.

He shrugged. "They lied."

"I wouldn't be so hard on them. They must've had their reasons. What'd your mom say?"

"She just said my real mother had made a hard choice to give me up. And they didn't want to tell me because they just thought it was better I didn't know, I guess. It'd be easier. But it's not."

At that point, the boy had begun to cry.

Aw, shit. I handed him a Kleenex from the little box I kept on the dash and kept driving. He simmered down and we made it back to town and you know the rest.

Anyway, it didn't seem to me to be quite as bad as it could've been. Hell, they might've been beating him with rubber hoses back in the storage room or something. Or even worse. So my faith in Red and Mattie was restored, not that it ever really went away, and the kid, well, he'd have to work this one out on his own. I even felt a little sorry for the little bastard.

"So you never told me exactly why you took it upon yourself to cut my banjo strings," I said to him later. We were sitting out on a packing crate in the alley. I had Lil Darlin' out and was polishing her wood. I like to do that sometimes, even when she doesn't really need it.

"I don't hate you."

"I know. You already told me that."

"You wouldn't understand."

"You're damn right I wouldn't understand. Helluva thing to do to a man. But I want to know why you did it."

He jerked his head toward the bar. "For them."

"For them? What do you mean?"

"I thought if you couldn't play, the bar wouldn't do as well and they'd have to close it."

"Are you kidding me? You think I keep this joint afloat?" I started laughing.

"I thought it would hurt them."

"Well, that's what I call convoluted thinking, kid. You ended up hurting me and Lil Darlin' here and nobody else. Thanks a whole heap. Next time you want to do a number on your folks, leave me out of it."

"Do a Hank song. You promised."

"All right. Lemme think."

I noodled around a bit, and tried "Jambalaya." He liked that.

"Did Hank write that one?"

"He sure did. One of his best, in my humble opinion. But I need to be writing my own songs. Met a guy who told me that. Said I'd never get anywhere unless I became a songwriter and jazzed up my act. What do you think?"

Mark reached out and touched Lil Darlin'. He ran his fingers over her strings.

"I think he's right, Webb."

"You do?"

"Yeah. That stuff you play here?"

"Yeah?"

"It's stupid."

"Hey, I appreciate the thought. Thanks."

"No, it is. It's like, I don't know, like everything else you hear. It's not, it's not, you."

"You mean it's not uniquely, fabulously Webb Pritchard?"

"Yeah. It sounds like what everybody else plays."

"You may be right, kid. I need to do my own stuff. I need to listen to my heart."

I thought about "Carry Me Back." Wondered if I could remember it.

"Here, lemme try this one. It's brand new. In a way."

I'd only done this tune a couple of times. My fingers fumbled for a few seconds, and then the melody came flooding back. That night at the Cow Palace . . .

"Carry me back . . . all the way back . . ."

Mark's eyes lit up. "Yeah!" he said. I kept singing.

"Carry me back . . . all the way back . . ."

Lil Darlin' began to shake and shimmy in my hands, and the alley behind the Sluicebox Saloon began to fade away. The bright light washed over me as the music took over, and the song seemed to be playing itself. The banjo felt absolutely weightless. I knew where I was, but I didn't.

"Jesus wept, boy, I thought we'd lost you."

I opened my eyes and looked down at Hank, sprawled in a hospital bed, white and drawn as a ghost. He clutched his cowboy hat on top of the covers. The door opened and a trim little nurse came in. She moved soundlessly about the bed on her white rubber soles, fussing with the sheets.

Hank let out a horse laugh and slapped me with his hat.

"Welcome back to the real world, Webb. You ready to roll?"

Hank insisted on leaving the hospital, but they wouldn't check him out. So he snuck out, with my help. He sent me to fetch the car and then I half carried him down a back stairwell. We made a clean getaway.

"We still in Omaha?" I asked him when we'd pulled out of sight of the hospital. Looked like a cow town to me, but hell, most places the Hayride played did.

"Yeah. But we're leaving tonight. That's why I had to get out of there."

"What happened?"

"When?" Hank sank back into the Caddy's upholstery. He looked weary.

"When you collapsed onstage. And when I disappeared."

"Nothing. I started singing that new song, and then I don't exactly remember much. Is that when you took a powder?"

I nodded. I looked at him. He looked gray. "You all right?"

"No, goddammit. Pull over."

So I did. Hank got out and hurled right there, at the curb. People saw him and turned away. I sat there and let him finish. He climbed back in. He smelled like puke.

"You should be in the hospital."

"No I shouldn't. They made me sicker in there. Goddamn doctors."

"Why'd you collapse? What's wrong with you?" Like I didn't know.

"I don't know. I never know why I do, I just do sometimes, that's all. It's in my nature."

"What'd Doc say?"

"Said I was fired. But then I acted like I was dyin' on him, you know, breathin' real hard and goin' stiff in the bed, so he hired me right back. Said it woulda looked bad for the Hayride, havin' Hank Williams die on it. Right after he got his skinny ass fired."

"You're a fucking mess."

He closed his eyes and pretended to sleep all the way back to the Plainsman Inn.

"You coming?"

Lula Mae was at the door.

"Where?" I was sitting on the narrow bed, waiting for Hank to finish up in the bathroom. Sometimes he took forever.

"Where, he says. You're so green. Where do you think?"

"I swear I don't have a clue, Lula Mae."

"Totsy's!"

"What's Totsy's?"

She looked like a kid with candy to spare.

"A place. A honky-tonk, kid. Best party in town. We always hit it on our way out of Omaha. Can't miss Totsy's."

"Where we headed after that?"

"Don't you know?"

"If I knew I wouldn't ask."

"Nashville."

"Nashville! That far? Don't we stop somewhere along the way?"

"Not this trip. Doc says we gotta get back."

And she was gone.

It took us about another hour to get out of the tiny room where I felt I'd been living the last twenty years. It even smelled like us now. God, Hank was slow. He took a shit and read *War and Peace*. All of it. He took a bubble bath. He shaved. He spent fifteen minutes combing his hair. He changed his shirt three times. Then he just admired himself in the mirror for a while. Finally I couldn't stand it any longer.

"For crying out loud, will you move your ass! They're gonna be in Nashville before we even get to Totsy's!"

"Gotta look sharp."

"You get any sharper you're gonna cut yourself. Come on!"

At long last, we loaded up the Caddy. Hank got behind the wheel and rolled her out of the parking lot. I'd had my fill of the Great State of Nebraska. I wasn't in much mood to party, I was itching to get going away from this place, but we had to make a courtesy call, at least.

"Where is Totsy's?"

"Out a ways."

"How far is a ways?"

"A ways."

Well, it was damn near fifty miles. Out in the middle of absolutely nowhere, and Nebraska has a lot of nowhere. We're barreling along a two-lane blacktop, natch, and it's pitch dark out there where the cows must be, and then there's lights up ahead and about a million cars. All clustered around a low white clapboard building with nothing but a little old beer sign over the door. Your classic roadhouse.

I could hear the music before we got out of the car. Sounded like Kit and the Kaboodles. As we walked up to the door, it flew open and this sweet little thing huffed out, pissed off as hell. Right behind her was some cowboy, moony-faced.

"Don't talk to me!" she hissed.

"But honey, I—"

"Don't talk to me!"

Ass twitching, she arm-pumped her way on her high heels over toward the dark end of the parking lot. Her boyfriend loped along behind.

Hank grinned. "Looks like a fine evening, yessir!"

We hit the door and it *was* a party. Packed to the rafters, smoky and hot and loud. Not that big a room, but there musta been two hundred people, easy, squeezed into the joint. Kit and his boys were cooking like gumbo. When they weren't playing the Hayride, he liked to do dirty songs, and he was doing one now. About a dozen people were trying to dance in a postage-stamp-size square up front. Everybody from the Hayride was there.

Me and Hank eased over to the bar and got us a couple of brews. He was going to start off slow, it looked like. Sometimes he jumped right in with a bottle of scotch.

He lit a cigarette, turned around and faced the room, and checked out the scene. Pretty women everywhere. Dim lights, thick smoke, and loud, loud music, as the country song would say years later. Red neon through the haze, beckoning us to crash on the rocks.

Back in those days, people knew how to have fun, I thought as I eyeballed the room. Nowadays, I mean in my own time, everybody was so cool they couldn't loosen up. Watch out, don't say anything not cool. Don't wear anything not cool. Don't be anything not cool.

Don't touch when you dance. Eyes just laser slits. Order the right beer. Drive the right car.

These people didn't give a fuck. They were just having a good time. Drinking, smoking, touching, belching, farting, laughing, being human. Where'd that go in the nineties? I was born too late.

I felt a tickle at my elbow and turned around. My heart skipped a beat.

"Hello there, stranger!"

"Nancy!" I bent forward and scooped her up, giving her a huge hug. Ah, this was nice. Oh, yeah. I didn't want to let go.

"I can't breathe!"

"I don't care!"

I set her down and we just stood there, looking at each other. I could smell her even over the beer and cigarettes and everything else. Hell, everything else just faded out.

"God, I missed you," I said.

"What?"

I realized that all the time I was gone was probably half a day to her. Only Hank knew how long it'd been.

"I mean, I just miss you when I don't see you, sweetheart. Minutes seem like days."

"Oh, bullshit."

We both laughed.

She had on a pretty yellow dress. "Let's dance," she said, pulling me along. I followed willingly.

Now, I'm not much of a dancer. But like I said, in those days you didn't worry about being cool, so I just whirled her around and tried to keep time. It was easy. She was light as a feather. She made me look good.

"Where's your dad?"

"What? I can't hear you!" She cupped her ear.

"Muley!"

She pointed. I saw him across the room over in a booth, deep in conversation with Doc Mullican. They didn't see us.

"Will he come over and kill me?"

"I hope not!"

Kit launched into some other raunchy tune and the music got faster. Our feet were a blur. There wasn't any room, really, so we jarred and bumped the others and they crashed into us. A fifties mosh pit. I started laughing and I couldn't stop.

Finally, it ended, and we fell onto chairs at a nearby table. It was a miracle we found one. Lula Mae joined us.

"Now what do you think of Totsy's?" she asked me.

"It's a hummer."

"We always have a good time here."

Now Kit left the stage and Hank and Daniel Eberhardt got up and did a drunken duet. It was a hoot. The crowd was egging them on. Nancy took my hand.

"Let's do one of our songs, Webb," she said, starting to get up. "Come on."

I gently pulled her back down. "No, not now." I didn't want to. I wanted to sit here and drink and soak it all up. The music, everything. Nancy settled back in her seat.

Lula Mae gave me a funny look over the top of her beer bottle. A look I'd never seen before. She'd had a little bit to drink.

"I've got your number, Webb," she told me.

"You do?"

"I do, indeed." She winked and took a swallow.

"What number would that be?"

"1994."

16

The bottom dropped right out of my stomach.

"What's 1994?" I asked innocently, reaching under the table to take Nancy's hand. Mine had suddenly turned all sweaty.

Lula Mae tilted up the bottle and drained her beer.

"Oh, I think you know," she said.

"Well," I said, "I don't. Honest."

"You've come a long way, Webb. Longer than I ever thought possible."

"What are you two yakking about?" Nancy said irritably. "Is this a private conversation?"

"No," I said, and stood up. "Let's dance."

As we moved away from the table, I glanced back at Lula Mae. She was looking at me and shaking her head.

I was freaking out. I'd sort of wanted to tell Lula Mae about myself, what was really going on, but had decided not to. It just wasn't right. I didn't want to mess up these people's lives. No reason to. Now things were getting weird.

Nancy and I danced two more dances, and then I couldn't keep her out there any longer. We had to go back to the table. Lula Mae was still sitting there. Nancy excused herself to go to the ladies' room. Lula Mae and I were alone.

I didn't say anything. If anybody was gonna bring it up, it had to be her.

"So," she said after a few moments, when the band was quiet. "Hank told me."

Shit.

"Hank told you what?"

"When he was in the hospital. I went up to see him and he told me about you."

"What are you talking about? What did he tell you, Lula Mae?" I was shitting bricks.

She leaned over and put her hand on my arm. "I didn't believe him at first. Who would? But . . . maybe it adds up."

"What adds up?"

"C'mon, Webb." Now she was whispering. "You show up out of nowhere. You're forty years old with a background in music but nobody's ever heard of you. Sometimes I can see you're a fish out of water. Trying to pretend you understand what's going on." She leaned in closer. "He said you were from the future. That you're really living in 1994, and you've traveled back in time to be with us."

I was so cool on the outside, I could've won an Academy Award. Deliberately, I rolled my eyes. "What? Are you kidding? Do you know what kind of drugs that man is on half the time?"

"Sure do," she said. "Done some of 'em myself. But I believe him."

"Well, he's crazy. You're all crazy. I can't believe you'd buy into that notion. Do I look like somebody out of *The Twilight Zone?*"

Oops.

"What's the Twilight Zone?"

Jesus. "You know, outer space or something. I'm real, Lula Mae. I'm here. People don't just drop in from the future." I laughed, and hoped it sounded real.

"What year were you born?"

Oh God.

"Uh—"

"Aha! You don't know. Who doesn't know what year they were born? I bet you're not even born yet!"

"What the hell year were you born?"

"None of your business."

"See? You're a space alien!"

I looked at her square in the eyes. "Lula Mae, this is ridiculous. You read too much science fiction. 1911. I was born in 1911." Man, I was treading on dangerous ground here. I wanted this conversation to end.

"I've read a lot of stuff about this, Webb," she continued. "Past lives. Reincarnation. Flying saucers. I know most people think it's bunk, but I think one day we're all gonna find out. And what we find out isn't gonna be what most people expect. But it will be the truth."

"I'll get us another beer." I stood up real fast and went over to the bar. Hank was there, schmoozing with a blonde. I took his elbow and turned him away for a sec.

"What the fuck, oh hey, Webb! Wantcha to meet my new friend. What's yer name, honey?"

"Not now, Hank," I said rudely, ignoring the girl. "Listen. Did you talk to Lula Mae? In the hospital?"

"Huh?"

"Did you have a conversation with Lula Mae, while you were sick in the hospital? She come to see you?"

"She come to see me."

"What'd you tell her?"

"About what?"

"Me, goddammit. She thinks I just dropped in from the future. Now where in hell did she get that nutty idea?"

"She thinks what?"

It was like talking to an idiot.

I stood on tiptoe to get closer to his big jug ears, and spoke slowly and clearly.

"Lula Mae is saying you told her all about me. Who I really am. Where I really come from. Did you?" I knew he must have. How else would she know?

His brown eyes got scared and childlike. "I don't remember doing that, Webb. I did that?"

"Shit, Hank, it looks like you did. We've got to stop her. She can't go blabbing that shit all over the Hayride."

I was wondering who the hell else he had talked to. Hi folks, I'm Webb Pritchard, banjo picker and resident alien. I'm not a man with a future, I'm a man from the future. Christ. They'd probably lynch me.

"Come on. We're gonna go talk to her."

"Wait for me, honey," he called to the blonde, but I was yanking him along.

I brought Lula Mae a fresh beer. Maybe alcohol would erase her memory. Nancy was over in a booth talking to her father. A lucky break. Hank and I sat down.

"Now, Lula Mae, Webb here's mighty upset," Hank said. "Says you're talkin' like a lunatic. Says you think I told you he's from the future. A space creature or somethin'. Well, I want you to know right now, it's all true."

I looked at him like he was out of his mind.

Hank reached over and took her hand. "Yep. I had a, what you might call, a visitation from the beyond."

Lula Mae's eyes grew wide. My eyeballs hazed over.

"Yes, ma'am," he continued. "I was sittin' in my hotel room in Lubbock one night, naked as a jaybird, just my hat on—you understand." He stopped here and searched her face for affirmation. Lula Mae was spellbound.

"I was sitting there, trying to write a song, looking for the Great Speckled Bird to hit me, drop guano on me, so to speak, when this vapor came into the room"—Lula Mae's jaw went slack—"and I dropped to my knees, thinkin' it was the Lord come to make me atone for my sins—when out of the mist comes ol' Webb here," he said, and clapped me on the back. "Isn't that right?"

I was speechless.

"He had this banjo on, see, and he walks out of the mist, it was bluish, over to me, sittin' on the bed there," Hank went on. "Naked as a jaybird, just wearin' my hat.

"And he says to me. And he says to me—'Hank. Show me the way.' O'course, I have no idea what he's talkin' about. Show you the way? I thought you was the Lord, gonna show *me* the way, but no, he says, I want to know the way of truth. In country music.

"So I'm showin' him the way. I got a mandate from the Great Beyond. The Great Speckled Bird laid this egg on my doorstep and I'm gonna see it through." He looked off into space for a second. "Till it hatches. I don't know where he's from, or who he is, but it's okay with me as long as he shows up on time and is sober. And so far, he is."

Lula Mae stood up, scooped up her beer bottle and put one hand on her hip. She looked down at Hank with total female scorn. I know this look.

"Hank Williams, you are the bullshittingest bullshitter that ever bullshitted a bullshitter. In the hospital, I believed you. Drugs and all. There was something about the way that you said it, I believed you. Maybe I wanted to believe it," she said, looking at me. "He's—something's not right about this one. I don't know what. But don't take me for a fool," she said, and toddled off toward the bar.

"Now there's a woman knows too much," Hank said, tossing back his scotch. "Dangerous. We gotta keep an eye on her. Hey, where's that little blonde?"

"Great Speckled Bird, my ass," I said, and knocked his hat across the room.

The Hayride was headed for Nashville. Doc Mullican had to see a man there about making a recording of the Hayride cast. I was told we didn't even have a gig lined up there yet. We were all on Doc's own wild-goose chase.

Everybody was real familiar with the place except me, of course. I'd never set foot in Nashville, Tennessee. (Another sinister clue for Lula Mae to pounce on.) I had planned to make a pilgrimage there at some point, like all country music fans hope to do, but somehow I'd never made it. You know how it is.

Now I'd get a chance to see the real, genuine article. Before the Grand Ole Opry moved out of the Ryman Auditorium downtown and into a glitzy theme park in the 'burbs. Back when the Opry wasn't a collection of star-spangled has-beens, but the Holy Grail of country music. Folks'd pile into the family Ford and drive 250 miles on county roads to get to the Saturday night show, when all the big stars were there, live and in person. The people would pack into the Ryman's church pews and fan themselves in the stifling heat and just about pass out from the excitement.

Who could blame them? These were *shows*, in the best vaudeville tradition, long after Hollywood had killed off real vaudeville. Guitar pickers hotter'n Tabasco sauce, country fiddlers, singers belting out heavenly three-part harmonies as they stomped their shoes on the beaten wooden stage. Comedians in blackface cracking up the crowd. One act after another, each one different. All of them performing right there in the flesh, riding the music's unpredictable heart, unencumbered by Dolby sound systems, laser light shows and overdubbing.

The thing of it is, human beings just aren't digital. We're much messier than that.

There are still some real pickers and singers around, the ones who can really nail it to the wall without any help, but probably the only ones who ever get to hear them like that are their close friends and families, and their bandmates on the bus. Otherwise, onstage and in the studio, even the best are filtered and digitalized and compressed all down into tiny computer bytes. The fans are so far removed from the real thing they wouldn't know it if they heard it.

I wished they could hear it.

I wished everybody could be as lucky as me.

It's all become far too clean for my taste. Sometimes I just have to put a scratchy old George Jones record on the turntable, pour a glass of Jack Daniel's and listen to George wrench through the heartache. No CD can give me George the way George really sounds.

The closest kind of music to the way it used to be is bluegrass, which is still played on acoustic instruments but is virtually always performed through a sound setup.

I said virtually. Once in a Blue Moon of Kentucky . . .

One of my fondest memories is of Bean Blossom in '87. That's Bill Monroe's own festival down at Bean Blossom, Indiana. He invites all his friends. The best pickers and singers alive. The stage is set up among the trees on some of Bill's property, and the seats are just rough planks. The year I went it rained. It was day one. Warm enough, but wet. Anyway, the sound system wasn't working. Maybe they hadn't turned it on because of the weather, or maybe they just hadn't got it ready yet.

So we're all sitting out there in a June shower, under umbrellas and ponchos and what have you. Huddling under trees. Patient. Lord, bluegrass fans are patient. Nothing's happening. We don't care. The music will come.

Then Bill walks out onstage, clutching his ancient mandolin, his long flowing white sideburns sweeping down from his white cowboy hat, elegant as hell, and addresses the gathered flock.

Only we can't hear him. He's leaning into the main mike and we can see his lips moving. He's nearing eighty, and it takes him a second or two to realize the sound's not getting through. So he steps away from the mike, totally unperturbed, and hollers out, Welcome, friends, how about we play something for you till the sound people get this fixed? Would that be all right?

Hell, yes, Bill, that would be all right.

So his Blue Grass Boys come on out and commence to playing. Sans microphones. No sound system. No amplification. Just Bill Monroe and his band, playing in the rain to several hundred spellbound listeners edged up close around the stage.

It was the best concert I ever went to. I was sorry when they finally got the electricity up and going.

Half drunk, half asleep and half assed, the Hayride finally stumbled out of Totsy's and into the harsh morning light of the Great Plains. We had a long way to go. There were no interstates. Imagine driving nine hundred miles on back roads. Doc insisted we all go in a convoy. He didn't want anybody straying from the flock.

This had happened before. Once, on a trip from San Antonio to Mobile, Kit and the Kaboodles just up and disappeared. Somewhere after Lake Charles, Louisiana, they weren't in anybody's rearview mirror anymore. There were rumors of a wild party out in the bayou, with alligators and underage girls, and when Kit finally turned up three days later, Doc fired him and told him it better not happen again. You know how that goes.

So Doc would lead us to the Promised Land, nearly fifteen cars in all, with Muley Taggart and the Taggart Family bringing up the rear in their broken-down bus. Me 'n' Hank were kind of in the middle, which Doc insisted on, because Hank was so unpredictable. But of course Hank wanted none of that.

"I can't be in the middle of this here caravan, Doc," he told him in the parking lot at Totsy's. "I've gotta be at the back."

"Gee, now why would that be, Hank?" Doc asked him.

"I get claustrophobica."

"What in the hell is that?"

"You know, claustrophobica. If I'm cooped up, I go nuts. I can't be responsible for what might happen."

"You're not responsible now. Get in the car, Hank."

So we were wedged in behind Daniel Eberhardt's flawless Buick, the one he polished every ten minutes, and Lula Mae's ancient old Dodge.

"Daniel, keep an eye on 'em," Doc said. "Lula Mae, don't let 'em out of your sight."

One by one, the cars rolled out of Totsy's, headed straight into the sun. Top speed: thirty-five miles an hour. The Hayride was on the move.

We breezed along in the big Caddy, just letting the prairie air flow through the car. We weren't fifteen miles out when Hank turned to me and said, "We're cuttin' out."

"What?"

"I said, we're cuttin' out. I can't stand this no more. Feel like a bird in a cage."

"Christ, we've only been gone half an hour."

"Oh, we're not gonna do it right now. We're gonna bide our time. Watch for an opening." He hunched over the wheel, staring out at Daniel Eberhardt's rear bumper like it was some gorgeous piece of ass.

"Once we cut out," I said, "then what're we gonna do? Got any big ideas?"

"No," Hank said. "We'll go where the road takes us."

"I thought you wanted to get back on the Opry. We're all supposed to be making this recording in Nashville. How will this help? You're gonna screw it all up again."

"Boy, you think too much. You just stick with Ole Hank."

Great. We'd probably get our asses arrested in the middle of Iowa, and then Doc would fire us for real. The future looked bright.

"Hank. I want to go to Nashville. I've never seen it."

"We'll go to Nashville, boy! We just may not get there with the rest of the crowd. Hell, we may beat 'em."

For the next two and a half hours, we stayed right on Daniel's tail, rolling past cornfields and grain silos and Burma Shave signs. Small boys with cane fishing poles stopped to stare as the convoy swept past. Kit had his band's name painted on his car in bright yellow, and Doc had the Hayride logo painted on his. Half the cars had big bass fiddles strapped to their tops. We must've looked like some kind of wacked-out funeral procession going by, as Doc was setting a snail's pace.

Hank honked the horn.

Then he leaned on it. Daniel stuck his hand out the window and gave him the finger.

"Move your ass!" Hank cried. "By the time we get to Nashville it'll be Christmas, goddammit."

He fumbled in his pocket and brought out a small bottle of pills. He steered with his knees while he unscrewed the cap and shook two capsules into his palm.

"Webb. Hand me that bottle back there, please."

I reached back and took hold of an elixir.

"This shit?"

"That very shit. Thanks."

Still steering with his knees, he opened the bottle of vile brown liquid and poured some down his throat. I could see his Adam's apple bobbing up and down, up and down as he swallowed.

"Jesus. How do you stand that stuff?"

He corked the bottle and drew his sleeve across his mouth. Hank was sharp-looking onstage and when he chose to be, but sometimes in private he was the biggest slob I ever met.

"Ambrosia, son, pure ambrosia."

"Gag me with a spoon."

"That one of those modern phrases?"

"You got it."

"Gag me with a spoon?"

"Gag me with a spoon."

Hank leaned on the horn again, just for fun. Now Lula Mae got into the spirit, honking at us. Daniel was shooting us the bird and we were shooting the bird at Lula Mae. Then Hank decided he'd give Daniel a scare. He pulled up so close on his bumper we practically touched it. We were mere inches off that hunk of chrome. Daniel saw us in his rearview mirror and looked terrified. He was really proud of that car. I wanted to say something but I was laughing too hard.

"Watch this," Hank said.

He swung the Caddy out into the oncoming lane and acted like he was going to try to pass Daniel. But of course we were in this long convoy. We got up alongside him and I looked over. Daniel was furious.

"What the hell are you trying to do?" he yelled at me. I just kept laughing.

"Hey Daniel! Gag me with a spoon!" Hank hollered.

Daniel just frowned and speeded up. Hank speeded up right with him.

Lula Mae decided girls could play as rough as boys and she closed the gap. Now she was right behind Daniel and we had no place to go.

That's when I happened to look up and see the tractor. Dead ahead.

"Hank! Look out!"

He swung the wheel hard right and smashed into Daniel's left side. The perfectly polished Buick made a terrible scraping noise as it bounced off the Caddy and went sailing into a ditch, with us right behind. We bounced ten feet into the air before landing hard on the edge of a cornfield. The car settled on its springs and seemed to sigh as one of the tires sprang a leak. Ssssssssssss.

"Well, damnation," said Hank. "It's a hell of a thing when a man's friends cut him off in traffic."

17

After Muley pulled the cars out of the ditch with the help of a farmer, after Daniel held Hank's face under the mud so long we all thought he'd killed him, after Doc fired Hank, me, Daniel, and Lula Mae for good measure, and after the Iowa Highway Patrol came and threatened to throw us all in jail if we didn't get the hell out of their state, the Happy Little Hayride continued on its way toward Nashville.

This time, me 'n' Hank had to drive right behind Doc. Second from the front. Daniel, poor Daniel in his now bashed-in Buick, they put way at the back, as far from Hank as possible. I'm not sure where exactly Lula Mae was. Somewhere in the middle, I suppose.

"It's all that damn tractor's fault," Hank said to me after we'd been back on the road awhile. "Damn farm vehicle on a major highway. Somebody could get killed."

We crept out of Iowa and meandered down the back roads of upper Missouri the rest of the afternoon. There were about a dozen or more vehicles in our caravan. If somebody had to stop to pee, we all stopped to pee. If somebody stopped for gas, we all stopped for gas. Doc finally decided to call it a day down near Kirksville. Driving his big yellow Ford, the one that said *Dr. Mullican's Traveling Hayride & Medicine Show* on the side, he led the caravan into the potholed parking lot of the Chief Hosa Trailer Court Motel. It didn't look very hospitable. There wasn't a soul around. Looking down a sad, long row of rooms overhung with a sagging porch, I was reminded of the Bates Motel in *Psycho*. Was that a sinister shadow at the window of the big house up on the hill? Was Norman lurking somewhere with a carving knife, waiting for me to step into the shower?

"What kind of shithole has he brought us to now?" Hank muttered as he got out to stretch his praying mantis legs.

I got out, too, and immediately sank into mud three inches deep. It sucked at my boots and swallowed the tops. Dammit. Major cleaning job. We stood around waiting for Doc. Eventually he emerged from the tattered little office. All of us gathered around to hear what he had to say. I kind of hoped the place was full. I knew it wasn't.

"Well, folks, we camp here tonight," Doc said. "Hot baths, soft beds, and they told me there's a pretty fair little diner not a quarter mile down the road."

His face twisted into a dark scowl.

"Now hear this. There will be no shenanigans tonight. I want you all to go eat and get to bed. There ain't no Totsy's around here. Don't go lookin' for one. Manager said he don't allow alcohol in the rooms, either. No noise after ten o'clock. Get the picture?"

He looked at Daniel first, and then Hank. "And you two. Whatever's boilin' up between you I want it on the back burner tonight. Got it? Forget today. It's past. We're up early tomorrow."

Doc handed out room keys and the little crowd dispersed. It didn't surprise me that the Chief Hosa Trailer Court Motel had no guests but us. It had to be the sorriest-ass place in Missouri. Looked like it was built in the twenties and never been fixed up since. Peeling paint, bad smells. Water ran brown out the tap. My bed had a damp, unpleasant odor.

"Hey, Hank, wanta switch beds? This one's too soft for me."

"OK. Whatever."

He plopped down on it and started to stretch out.

"Jesus, what died?" He was up and out of there in a flash.

"I ain't sleepin' there," he said. "Gimme my bed back."

"What's wrong?"

"What's wrong, my asshole. Somebody died in that bed."

"Get outta here."

"I ain't lyin', Webb. I've smelled it before. I know what a dead man smells like."

"Well then, why should I have to sleep there?"

"So between us two, you think it's gonna be me?"

"I'm older. I'm forty."

"Shit, if I were alive, I'd be seventy!"

"You are alive."

"I'm a bigger star, then. And you know what else?"

"No. What?"

"I'm better lookin' than you."

"Yeah, then how come I'm popping Nancy and you're not?"

That shut him up. For a second.

"Aw, I guess I could. But I know her daddy too well to do that. Muley's a close friend."

"Yeah, hell of a guy. Has a way with a tire iron."

Hank laughed. "You better watch it, boy."

"So where am I gonna sleep? I can't sleep in that bed. It fucking stinks."

"I'm telling you, man died in that bed. Died violent, too. Stabbed, most likely."

"Thanks, Hank. Thanks a lot."

"Pretty recent, I'd say. Maybe even last night. It was 'bout midnight. He was sleepin' so sound . . . then . . . BOO!"

I jumped; there was no stopping it.

"Hey, Hank."

"Yeah." He lit a cigarette.

"When we get to Nashville, you gonna go try and get back on the Opry?"

He stretched out on his bed and I sat in a chair. I wasn't going near my Bed of Death.

"My contract with Doc isn't up for six more months. I signed through this year."

"That's not what I asked you."

He kind of half smiled. "Well, it wouldn't surprise me if I turned up one night at the Ryman. But they don't want me back. Not now, anyways."

"What would it take?"

"They need me, you know. I bring 'em in like nobody brings 'em in, son. Ole Hank packs the house. Oh, it would take me having another big hit, I guess. They couldn't refuse to put me on. Not then. The people wouldn't allow it."

"So that's all you gotta do. Get another hit record."

"Like fallin' off a log, son."

"Well, you've got the song. "Carry Me Back." Wish I had a song like that."

"You can have it."

"Nooo . . ."

"I don't want it. It's all yours, son."

"Bullshit. It's a great song. It's the one that'll put you back on top."

He sat up and blew smoke rings. "Aren't you still washing dishes or something back in that chickenshit town?"

"Well, yeah," I said defensively. "But I'm working on things."

Hank snorted. "You ain't never gonna get out of there if you don't put a better act together. Why don't you take 'Carry Me Back'? Get you started. I ain't gonna give you another one."

I stared at him. "You're serious."

"As a heart attack."

"You'd give away that song? It's fucking great, Hank. I can't do that. Not when you're, when you're . . . like . . . this."

"You mean down and out? You mean, stayin' in a shithole motel in Outback, Missouri, where men die in their beds and the water runs brown? You mean, I need it worse than you?"

I just nodded.

Hank moved so fast I never saw him. I was just all of a sudden on the floor with him on top of me, his hands around my throat. Squeezing. He bent his sharp face down until his burning cigarette was almost touching me. I couldn't breathe.

"Look, you little shit," he hissed. His ashes flicked down on me. "Let's get one thing straight. I am Hank Fucking Williams. Hank Williams!" He banged my head on the floor. His cigarette dropped on the carpet beside my head.

"You know how many great fucking songs I've written? How many more I'll write before it's over? I can write songs in my sleep. I can write songs when I'm screwing. When I'm taking a dump. When I'm drunk. When I'm half dead in a hospital and they've all given up on me."

I tried to say something. I couldn't. My windpipe was shut.

"Listen to me!" he screamed. "You need it worse than I do, my little friend, make no mistake. Because if you don't take it you're gonna be washin' goddamn dishes the rest of your sorry life. You can take that to the bank."

I was starting to black out. He let go. I sucked in the foulness of the dank little motel room like it was a fresh mountain breeze. Hank rocked back on his boot heels.

"I didn't appear in your goddamn life so you could stick your ass in a kitchen somewhere, Webb. You've got a mission. Don't let me down."

I rolled over onto my side, coughing. The carpet was foul.

"Take the song," he said. "It's all yours. Now let's go get some eats. I'm starving."

He bought my dinner. Steak and eggs. And he was right, we were both starving. We'd been on the road more than thirteen hours that day, if you counted the wreck with Daniel, and everybody on the Hayride was basically a basket case. People sitting around in the Big Top Diner on Route 6 with glazed eyes. I was so road-wasted I barely noticed Nancy, sitting over in a big corner booth with her family. I was keeping my distance with Muley around. She caught my eye and waved once, with a dazzling smile, but I'm afraid all I managed was a weak finger-lift with a half-assed wink. Not too swift. Ah, well. When a man's past forty . . .

Two things happened at the diner. One was, Lula Mae stopped by and told Hank he was a stupid idiot and almost got everybody killed out on the highway. She said her piece, patted me on the shoulder, and left. I wasn't quite sure what the pat was all about. I think she thought I was in dangerous hands. Which was probably right.

The other thing was, Daniel came over. It was inevitable. I mean, he was there. We were there. The thing couldn't be avoided.

"Hank, don't say anything," was the first thing he said as he slid into our booth. Daniel Eberhardt was real young, about twenty, with smooth brown hair carefully greased up into a modest pompadour at the front. White, even teeth, nicely tailored clothes, kind of anal-retentive if you asked me. Very meticulous about his person, about how he looked, same as he felt about his Buick. The now-wrecked Buick. Hank's problem, not mine. I sat back to watch.

"Webb, first of all, I blame this whole thing on you," Daniel said to me, fiddling with a heavy glass sugar pourer.

"What?" I was incredulous. "On me?"

He set the sugar pourer down and folded his hands. I noticed his cuffs were immaculate. He must've showered and changed already. Now us, we were road-ragged.

"I know Mr. Williams here"—he indicated Hank with a wave of his hand—"is often not responsible for his actions. We all know that. That's precisely why"—I mean, how many people on the Hayride would have used the word *precisely*, for crying out loud—"I hold *you* responsible. Doc put you with Hank to be under his wing, I understand that, but I also understand he put you two together so you would keep Hank out of trouble. You failed."

I looked at this kid and sighed.

"Daniel," I said, "look. I am not Hank Williams' baby-sitter. He was driving. I am sorry about your car"—I very nearly said "your fucking car" and thought better of it—"but there was nothing I could do. It was an accident, OK? We were having a little fun, you know, Hank pulled out to pass you, or pretend to pass you, and this tractor—"

"How are you going to pay to fix my car?"

"Excuse me?"

"How are you going to pay to fix my car?"

"Excuse me, but I am not going to pay to fix your car. Daniel, I didn't run your Buick into the ditch!"

"You were supposed to keep an eye on him."

Jesus, I thought he was going to cry.

"I am not supposed to 'keep an eye' on him! Christ, he's a grown man! It happened, OK? It was an accident, OK? Nobody got hurt. Don't you have insurance?"

Daniel looked bewildered.

"Insurance. Car insurance?"

Hank leaned over and whispered in my ear.

I looked at this earnest, pissed-off kid and sighed. He would be a big rock 'n' roll star in ten years. Then he'd flame out fast. In the nineties, I'd see his Greatest Hits collections collecting dust in the cut-out bin at Kmart.

"Daniel, you're a decent enough guy," I said. "Hank's awful sorry about what happened." I kicked Hank under the table. "Aren't you, Hank?"

"Who's going to pay for my car?" Daniel asked.

"Well now, that could be a problem," I said. "I don't have the money to fix your car, and I don't know that Hank does, either. But I'm sure there's a way to work this out."

I had no clue how to get out of this.

Suddenly Hank came to life.

"Your car? What about my car? What about my nice Cadillac? Who's gonna pay for that? Hell, it's as dinged up as yours."

Oh, boy.

"Now look," I said, "let's not get angry here. What happened happened. How much damage you think you got, Daniel?"

"At least five hundred dollars."

"Five hundred my ass!" Hank exploded. "Then my car's got a thousand. At least."

"I think you're both wrong," I said quietly. "It's not gonna be nearly that much. But I have an idea. . . ." I thought real fast and sketched it out for both of them. It would have to wait till Nashville.

I didn't go near the Bates Motel Death Bed that night. I slept on the floor wrapped in two blankets and a bedspread. Sometime during the night I woke and thought I heard something outside the room, but it was only the wind. I think.

Doc came around banging on everybody's door about six. We all stopped for coffee and doughnuts and were back on the road by a little after seven. Hank let me drive. When Doc wasn't looking, we managed to slip into the very rear spot in the caravan, hanging back until we were trailing the Taggart Family bus. Muley shot me a look as I walked past him to the Caddy, but he didn't say anything.

Hank fell asleep almost as soon as we hit the highway. He slouched down on the cream-colored upholstery, let his hat fall over his eyes and began snoring.

It was a hot summer day. The Hayride caravan rolled through Missouri and southern Illinois at a lazy pace. Sometimes Nancy would appear at the back of the Taggart Family bus and wink at me and stuff like that, but mostly I had no distractions. So I decided to use the time to write myself a song.

I always had these good intentions about writing songs, but couldn't seem to get around to doing it. Something always got in the way. I'd be standing at the dishwasher at the Sluice, trying to conjure one up, and then Mark or Red or Mattie would come around. I'd sit in my RV and noodle around on the banjo and nothing would come. My stomach would rumble and I'd start thinking about pot roast or something. Sometimes I decided that Dot was right, that going on the road as a musician was completely half-assed. Maybe I should get some tools together and go work construction again. That's when I'd get depressed. I wanted it so bad, the freedom of the road, the music. But I kept dragging myself down. Dammit. What was wrong with me?

I looked over at Hank. His jaw hung slack. A fleck of drool hung on his lower lip. Guy's IQ was probably at least thirty points below mine, and here he was, the big star, making it all look so easy. Not only was he low IQ, he was lazy and he possessed not one shred of common sense. If you opened up his brain there'd just be pictures of women and shots of Johnnie Walker. And yet, his instincts took him right to the top, while mine led me to the back of a kitchen. Some people win in spite of it all. I didn't want to lose because I tried too damn hard.

That's what I was doing and it was killing my career. C'mon, Webb, I told myself, just flow that song right out. It's in there. Just . . . flow it out. Be the song.

That made me laugh out loud. Hank woke up.

"Go back to sleep," I said. "I'm trying to be the song."

He barely roused, and settled back down. Good. I didn't need his genius screwing me up right now.

OK. Here we go. Right brain. Be the song. *It's a long way to Tipperary . . . I wanna hold your hand . . . Jumpin' Jack Flash is a gas gas gas . . .*

Did anything rhyme with "future"?

I've come a long way, longer than you know,
And my path was filled with pain.
I was lost in the dark until I found you
And then it began to rain.

Boy, that was a real right-brainer.

How'd these dumb-ass hillbillies come out of the woods and write these great songs? Well, they felt them. They didn't put too much on them, they just put their feelings down and it was true. Like Bill Monroe, who's written about a million great songs, wrote one called "True Life Blues." Now what's simpler than that?

Write what you know. Should I write about washing dishes? Walking dogs? Being in prison? Nah, already too many prison songs. Living in a little RV? Time traveling? Shit.

We kept rolling and Hank kept dozing. My left forearm began to sunburn from hanging out the window. I started thinking about Marie. About how she probably deserved better than me. I wanted her, but I didn't want to ruin her life, know what I mean? I wasn't meant for Telluride, and I was pretty sure she wasn't meant for my kind of life. How to reconcile all these things? I didn't know. I didn't know shit.

And then, out of the blue Illinois sky, the song came to me. Just like that.

18

We got into Nashville after dark, so it didn't look like much to me. Doc had arranged for us to stay at a downtown hotel, the St. Regis, which sounded pretty uptown until we all saw it. A real Depression flophouse, it was a four-story crumbling orange brick building down on Sixth, and the lobby smelled of urine and stale cigars. The elevator didn't work. The manager, Mr. Detweiler, didn't think too highly of show people but I think outfits like ours kept him afloat. We weren't too far from the music clubs and I could hear somebody upstairs practicing a guitar riff.

"So you're the Hayride, are you?" he asked gruffly when we all crowded into the lobby. "Hmmph."

"We are indeed, and it's purely a pleasure to be back in Nashville," Doc replied, and signed us in. Detweiler was chewing on a dead cigar, which he kept moving around as if he couldn't quite find the right spot for it. It looked to me like he was eating it.

There were thirty-one of us, all told, and we took thirteen rooms, on the third and fourth floors. Place was a real firetrap. Ratty carpet curling at the corners, and some of the drapes were in shreds. Early Cigarette Burn decor. My room with Hank was about what I'd expected. No one had died in my bed here, but when you lay down in it the middle swallowed you up in a hole. I began to wish for my little RV. At least she had a tape deck. And air-conditioning.

"So this is the big town," I said, looking out the window at the street below.

"Yep," said Hank, "this is where dreams come true." He started laughing. "Shit, if I'd known I'd be staying in places like this after I became a big star I'da stayed a nobody."

"How far's the Opry from here?"

"Couple blocks."

"I'm going down for a look."

"I'll go with you."

So Hank and I left the St. Regis to check out the home of the Grand Ole Opry, where he had been kicked out the year before. It was a Tuesday night and we didn't think anybody'd be around.

The Ryman Auditorium, where the Opry had its home from 1943 to 1974, was originally built as a gospel tabernacle in the late 1800s. A hulking red brick edifice down on Fifth between Broadway and Commerce, it had stained glass windows that reflected down on rows of oak pews where the faithful gathered on Saturday nights to see and hear the Opry. The show was broadcast over the whole eastern United States on powerful WSM. I had read up on the old Ryman, and I knew it had been restored and still hosted occasional musical events. The Opry itself had moved out to a suburban theme park, Opryland, after the powers that be decided they could make more money by glitzing things up and moving into the modern era. Now I'd never been to Opryland, as I'd never been to Nashville until now, but the whole idea of a country music theme park with shiny hotels and gift shops selling whoopee cushions made me wistful for an era long past. Hell, I like air-conditioning and comfortable seats as much as the next guy, but the Ryman held the magic.

They cut a piece of the stage out of the Ryman and transplanted it to the stage of Opryland but I don't think it worked. Once the Ryman was closed, the ghosts and echoes of what had transpired here stuck around, never to leave, sunk into the pews and the red brick like indelible ink.

Me and Hank walked over to the place and I sort of got the tingles when we came around a corner and looked down the hill. There she was. Big and ungainly, even kind of ugly. Like a blind date set up by your sister.

"Well, ladies and gents, I'm here in Nashville with two icons of country music," I said out loud. "I give you Hank Williams and the Ryman Auditorium."

"To hell with you, I ain't no eye-con," Hank said, and walked up the broad steps to the front doors. They were locked. We'd expected this. "C'mon," he said, and went back down the steps and around the side of the building.

We went down the alley and came to an arched doorway set into the brick and stone. It looked medieval. Curving steps led up into darkness. Hank led the way. We stepped through a plain door and I was suddenly on hallowed ground. The hair on my arms stood up. The Opry had hold of me.

The light was fairly dim, but enough to see a little, and I followed Hank down a hallway past an office. The door was open and the light was on, but nobody was there. We went around a turn and up a few steps and suddenly we were onstage.

It was dark. I could just make out the curved rows of pews before me, and the balcony, too, and imagined the audience stomping their feet and hollering for more. God, I had to play this place. I had to. No way I couldn't.

Hank walked slowly to the center of the Ryman's broad stage and looked out past the darkened footlights. He sighed.

"Hell of a thing," he said softly.

Then he began to sing, very low, almost so I couldn't hear him and I was standing not ten feet away.

"*Amazing grace, how sweet the sound,*
That saved a wretch like me.
I once was lost, but now am found
Was blind but now I see."

"Who's there?" a voice called from the darkness. Hank and I both started.

"Who is that?" the voice called.

"It's nobody," Hank replied. "Nobody a'tall."

"Look here, mister, you cain't be walkin' in here, we're closed," the voice said, getting closer, and suddenly a young man holding a broom emerged from the shadows at stage right.

"Good God Almighty! That you, Hank?"

"Dinger?"

"I'da reckonized that voice anywheres!"

"No you didn't! You was gonna throw me out, you little fart!"

They slapped each other on the back and shadowboxed around the stage.

"Webb, this here's Dinger Purdy. Been with the Opry since he was knee-high to a gopher. Place'd fall apart without him. Dinger, this is my buddy Webb, Webb Pritchard. Plays banjo. He's all right."

"Pleased to meetcha, Mr. Pritchard."

"Same here, Mr. Purdy."

"Call me Dinger. Everybody else does. What the hell you doin' here, Hank? They hire you back on?"

"No, Dinger. I'm still fired. I'm back in town with Doc Mullican's Hayride. Just thought I'd swing by and check out the old home place."

"Well, we're still here. Hangin' on. More trouble'n ever. Wait'll you hear. C'mon back. I may have a snort somewheres." Dinger disappeared into the darkness.

We sat around the tiny little office, sharing a bottle of moonshine while Dinger regaled us with tales of the Opry, how Sam Preston had got drunk and punched out Bill Whittier just before showtime last week and how Peggy Smith was pregnant and everybody knew it wasn't her husband, and Old Uncle Fred the fiddle player's arthritis was so bad they were gonna have to tell him he couldn't be on any more and that would most likely kill him. And oh yeah, they had a new sponsor, Aunt Handy's Candies, and Will Taylor's wife just had a baby and it was ugly as sin, too, but of course you didn't say anything, and the Carolina Brambles were breaking up 'cause the lead singer's momma was in an iron lung and he had to go take care of her just about full time.

"Nothing's changed," Hank said.

"We miss you, Hank," Dinger said. "You gotta come back."

"I'm too big a risk right now. That's how they see it."

"I'll talk to Jim. Tell him I seen you and you're bright-eyed and bushy-tailed."

"No. I'll get in touch when I can. Don't say anything. You ain't seen me."

Dinger looked disappointed. "Awright, Hank. But you know you got a friend here if you ever need one."

We said our good-byes and wandered back to the St. Regis. I swore to myself I'd play the Ryman, with or without Hank.

And that meant one thing: I'd get on the Opry.

The importance of the Grand Ole Opry in country music back then is hard to translate to the modern era. So many things have changed. The Opry no longer makes or breaks stars. But in 1951 it was Ground Zero. The Saturday night live show featured the biggest stars and hottest acts and drew fans from all over the country even as it was broadcast over the radio to millions. If you could manage to wangle your way onto the Opry, you had made the bigtime. A lucky few were asked to join the cast, that is, be a permanent part of the proceedings, welcome anytime. Bill Monroe, the Father of Bluegrass, joined the Opry in 1939 and was still on the roster in 1994.

"If you ever leave the Opry, it'll be because you've fired yourself," Monroe says they told him after his first appearance.

Doc Mullican's Hayride, a pitifully puny outfit compared to the Opry, sure as hell wasn't gonna be playing no Ryman. So I had to make my own arrangements.

We were only staying in Nashville a week or so before we headed for dates in Alabama, so I had to move fast. This was already Wednesday, and the big show was Saturday night.

I had my song, the one I wrote in the car while Hank slept. But beyond that I'd need some help. I went to Lula Mae.

"You're gonna what!"

"Play the Opry. And you're gonna help me do it."

"You'll never get on and if you did Doc'd fire you faster'n a minute."

"So what? Then I'd be on the Opry."

"Not necessarily. You could have one shot and blow it, kiddo. You wouldn't be the first."

"I won't blow it."

We were hanging out in her stuffy little room at the St. Regis, having Cokes. The heat of the afternoon wafted in the window.

"We'd all like to be on the Opry, Webb," she said, easing herself back on a bunch of pillows scattered over her bed. Her hair was up in curlers and she was wearing a beat-up pair of slacks and an old shirt. She picked up a well-thumbed Hollywood movie magazine and began fanning herself. "I used to be on it, remember? I know the Opry inside out. But then they said I wasn't good enough anymore. Not funny. They had to make room for somebody new. And the Hayride saved me."

Thank god for *Hee Haw*, I thought, which would someday save her again.

"The Hayride's fine," I said, "but if you were me, wouldn't you try to get on?"

"Yep."

"There you go."

"Y'know, I'm still curious about those things Hank said in the hospital," Lula Mae said, out of the blue. I hated when women did that. They were good at throwing you a damn curve. "I wasn't kidding when I said I believed him, even if he did make fun of me at Totsy's."

I spread my hands apart, palms up. "What do you want me to say? We already had this conversation. I am not a space alien."

"I'm not saying you are. I'm just saying some things don't add up."

"You gonna help me or not?"

She sighed. "Yeah. Of course I am. Does Hank know about this?"

"Nope."

"Good. He'd just fuck it up."

My jaw dropped at Lula Mae's foul mouth and we both started giggling like kids at a slumber party.

"Now the first thing you'll need is some clothes," she said, getting up from the bed and almost spilling her bottle of Coke. "You look like a Hayride reject. We gotta get you looking like an Opry star."

"I want me a suit of mirrors. I see myself as a cross between Liberace and Elvis." Now I did that on purpose, just to mess with her head.

Lula Mae looked at me.

"One day, Webb Pritchard. One day. Now shoo. Let me get dressed. Meet you downstairs in five minutes."

We headed out into the midday heat of Nashville's un-air-conditioned summer. The sidewalks rippled in white waves, and the people had all opened their collars and rolled up their sleeves. Musta been ninety-plus. Mr. Take Me Back to the Past was wishing mightily for a cool mall. Instead, we wandered over to Second Avenue, where all the shops were. Lula Mae knew just where we were going.

First we went into Bert's, a men's clothing store, but nothing they had suited her.

"I knew we weren't going to find anything here, but I thought maybe . . . I used to shop for Bob here all the time," she said, mentioning her late husband. She fingered a stack of checked shirts. "No no no, this is all wrong. We're going to have to go over to Brannum's."

"Brannum's?"

"Brannum's," she said firmly, and steered me out the door.

The place was much larger than Bert's, and the clothes were much nicer and much more expensive. Relatively speaking. A summer suit here was $12.99. My modern-day Levi's, the stonewashed ones I liked, cost forty-two bucks, for crying out loud. And that was at Target.

"What are we looking for, Lula Mae?"

"I'll know it when I see it."

"I was joking about the suit of mirrors."

I must've tried on sixteen outfits. A brown suit. Plug-ugly. A bright yellow cowboy shirt. Made me look like a fairy. Blue satin. Ugh. Plain white. Too plain.

"Here it is!" she cried. The salesman rolled his eyes. She'd said this fifty times.

I walked over and decided she might be right. Lula Mae held up a dark blue cotton shirt with white piping. Very country, but very, well, subdued. Classy.

"With a black neckerchief, and black trousers," she said bossily, addressing the salesman. "And nice black boots." I had nixed the cowboy hat idea early on.

Well, it took another forty-five minutes to pull all that together to her satisfaction, and when the guy rang it up the total came to $43.49. Practically a fortune. The boots were what jacked it up so high.

"Now I'll have to get on the Opry or I'll be broke," I said after I paid in cash. My money was running awful short.

Next, she took me over to the barbershop, where the guy cleaned me up a little. Trimmed up my thinning hair, splashed on the lilac water and even buffed my fingernails. I was getting into Hank territory, I told her.

"Now comes the hard part," she said. "Getting somebody to put you on the Opry."

"So we spent all my money and I may not get my foot in the damn door?"

"That's right. But you'll look so nice now on the Hayride."

"Thanks a bunch. 'Preciate it."

We were having ice cream at a little sidewalk stand.

"You gotta know somebody," she said.

"Who do I know?"

"Nobody. But I do."

"They fired you."

"Thanks for reminding me. I mean, I know somebody who knows somebody."

"Ah."

"You got some nickels on you?"

"Yeah."

"Wait here."

She went into a drugstore across the street. She was gone a good twenty minutes, at least. I stood around under an awning getting heatstroke. I had another vanilla cone. Finally Lula Mae came back out, and she was grinning. A good sign.

"What happened? I'm the opening act?"

"It's a good thing I kept some friends in this town. I called around and finally got hold of Hub Jenkins."

"Hub Jenkins!" He was an Opry regular. He hosted one of the segments.

"We go back a long ways. Told him what the deal was. Bullshitted him into believing you're an up-and-comer he ought to see. You're to go to the Ryman tomorrow afternoon at three-thirty."

"Jesus, Lula Mae! It was that easy?"

"No. I had to tell Hub you were a big hit out on the California circuit or he wouldn't have bought it. So you're gonna have to skate around a little."

I leaned down and kissed her a big one, right on the mouth. She backed away, laughing.

"Stop that, Webb. Now you just do well. Don't shame me. That's all I ask. What song you gonna do?"

"I finally wrote one."

"What's it called?"

" 'True Gold.' "

I took her arm and we headed back over to Broadway, our heads full of dreams.

I hid my new duds back in the hotel room. No need to get Hank all suspicious. I sat there on the bed, practicing my song over and over, nailing down the licks, getting it perfect. If Jenkins wanted to hear some more, I had a couple of good ones in mind, old tunes that I felt would go over well on the tradition-minded Opry. I laughed to myself, wondering what would happen if I laid some Bela Fleck on him. He'd probably swallow his tobacco juice.

In a way, I knew this was crazy. What if the unthinkable happened and I passed the audition? Would I leave Hank and the Hayride and strike out on my own here in Nashville as an Opry star? But this was the past, not the present. Maybe Hank was essential to the plan. Maybe I wasn't supposed to be doing this. Maybe I was screwing things up.

There was nobody I could talk to except Hank, and I couldn't talk to him about this. He'd kill me if he knew I was plotting to get on the Opry while he was stuck on the Hayride.

A knock on the door.

"Come on in."

The door opened and Nancy came flying into my arms. We tumbled back on the bed and she was all over me, kissing my neck and lips and everywhere.

"Whoa, girl!"

"Webb! Whatcha doin'?"

"Kissing you, it looks like."

"Workin' on a song?"

"Yep. Wanna hear it? I need an audience. A sympathetic one."

She rolled off me and off my banjo and sat up, smoothing her skirt.

"What's it called?"

" 'True Gold.' "

"Oooh, I like it already. Is it a love song?"

"Sort of. Now don't tell anybody. This is a work in progress. I'm keeping it to myself for now."

"OK."

I played and sang, kind of soft, and when I got around to the chorus for the second time she joined in on high harmony. It sounded great.

"Webb! That's wonderful! Hold on." And she was gone, leaving the door open.

She was back in a minute with her fiddle. She tuned it and sat up straight and brought the instrument up under her pretty chin.

"Do it again."

So I did, and she swirled a lovely line underneath the banjo, always staying real close to the melody but going off in her own direction. Whatever she did, she sure made my song sound better.

The last line faded away, and she held the note. The little room fell silent.

"Wow," I said.

"You should record that," Nancy said. "It's real good. You'll knock 'em dead on the Hayride with that one. We should do it as a duet."

"First song I ever wrote."

I had a thought.

"Nancy," I said, "can you keep a secret?" What a dumb question. Has anyone ever said no? I was bursting to tell somebody.

"Yes, of course."

"C'mere." I patted the bed beside me. She put down her fiddle and sat close. The bed creaked.

"Now nobody can know this. OK? This has to stay between us."

"Cross my heart and hope to die."

"I'm gonna try out for the Opry."

Her eyes flew open wide. "What?"

"You heard me. Tomorrow at three-thirty. Down at the Ryman."

Tears bubbled up in her eyes and she began to cry.

"Aw, what's the matter?"

"You're leaving the Hayride."

"No, I'm not," I lied. "I just want to see if I'm good enough. They won't take me, believe me."

She dabbed her eyes. "You're leaving me."

I held her tight. Didn't say anything.

She pulled away and suddenly looked different. The tears were drying up.

"I'll go with you!"

"No, I—"

"Didn't we sound great just now? I'll go to the audition and back you up. We'll go as a team. It's my big chance, too!"

Oh, man. The water was getting deeper and hotter.

"I've been waiting to get away from Daddy for a long time," she said, standing up. "He still thinks I'm a baby. The stupid Taggart Family. This is it. The chance I've been waiting for. The Opry." She twirled around with her arms outstretched. "Freedom!"

Well, the song did sound better with her in it. No denying that.

But the Opry wasn't expecting two people. They might throw us out before we hit the first note. I tried to tell her this. She wouldn't listen.

"What'll we call ourselves?"

"Nancy—"

"I know! Webb 'n' Nancy."

"Hey, that's a good one. How about Dead Meat, after Doc and your dad find out what we've done?"

She looked at me with shining eyes. "I've gotta go pick out an outfit. I can't wear that hillbilly stuff I wear with the family. I've got a lot to do."

"No. C'mere." I wanted to pull her clothes off. But she ran out the door, and I was left to sit there and wonder why my life always seemed to be operating in a Cuisinart set on high. I wasn't there very long before Hank came in.

"Well, the recording session's all set," he said, unsnapping his sweaty shirt. "We'll do a run-through and then the real thing. Doc couldn't get the studio for longer'n that. So we gotta do it right the first time, I guess." He threw his shirt over the chair.

"When's that?"

"Tomorrow. Three-thirty."

19

T hree-thirty!"

"Yeah, over at Castle Recording Studios." Hank pulled off his boots and sank back on his bed. His feet stunk up the room.

"I don't have to be there, right? I mean, they're not recording the whole damn cast, are they?"

"Way I understand it, we all have to be there, 'cause Doc hasn't quite decided who's gonna be doin' what, exactly. Man hasn't thought this through, if you ask me."

"Well, I can't make it."

"Whaddaya mean, you can't make it. You gotta make it. This is a big chance for you. Besides, if you're not there, he'll fire you."

"I can't make it, is all."

Hank sat up and stared at me. "Well now, the boy's got somethin' cooking here, don't he. Somethin' mighty damn important. Would he want to share it with ol' Hank?"

"No."

He sank back down. "All right. You go your own ways. Don't mind me. I ain't got no interest." He closed his eyes and pretended to doze. But I could see his eyelids flickering.

I went out and walked the streets of Nashville, not thinking, not wanting to think. There were so many things going on in my head I couldn't run them all down, so I didn't even try. I had reached a crossroads, that was for sure. I could just feel myself on the cusp of something big. You ever get that feeling? I do. Every time I've felt it, sure enough, something big did happen. Once, when that feeling turned up, I got married. Another time I damn near killed a man. I could feel it coming up again, and it was rare, and I knew it, and I decided after I had walked the evening away to just let things happen.

And that's how it went down.

I woke up the next morning real early. Way too early for the line of work we were in. Nobody at all was stirring at the St. Regis Hotel. Hank was so far gone I don't think a freight train would've woke him up. I pulled on a pair of pants and a shirt and slipped out, taking the stairs because the elevator didn't work.

I went over to the Ryman. There she was, just squatting there in the dawn, my future. Sometimes when you try to conjure up a special feeling about a place, or a time, it just won't go for you. You try and you try, and the forcing of it doesn't work. You can be looking at old family snapshots, and there isn't anything there, though you want it to be. Was that me back then, you think, was that Ma and Pa? There we all are, gathered at the river. And nothing's happening inside, and that makes you wonder what kind of person you are. Then other times, anything'll set you off. It might be a smell, or something somebody said. And there it was all the time, all bottled up inside somewhere secret and now it's finally letting go. Tears flowing. For no reason.

I was standing there on Fifth Avenue, trying to force the feeling, and nothing was coming. The Ryman. Big deal. A pile of bricks.

Whatever magic the Ryman held had got hold of me the other night, when Hank and I were there. Now, though, I just couldn't bring it back standing out here on the street, no matter how hard I tried. I sat down on the curb and drifted off in my head for a while. I came right back to earth when I heard a ping! and looked down and saw someone had tossed me a nickel. Time to leave.

The day dragged. I ate breakfast at a greasy spoon. Eight o'clock. Read the papers. Nine. Walked down to the Cumberland River and watched a barge work her way through the docks. Ten-thirty. Eleven. What was taking this day so long?

At noon, I wasn't hungry, so I went to a diner and nursed a cup of coffee until the waitress shot me a look that said, Beat it, buster, I'm trying to make a living here.

I finally went back to the hotel. For all the time I'd wasted, I hadn't figured out a way to sneak out for my audition. The part of my brain that was logical and figured things out for me left that little problem to the part of my brain that worked on the fly, and often fucked up.

I sat on my bed, tense. My palms rested on my knees. My back was straight. I stared at the wall. My breathing was shallow. Mr. Natural, that's me.

The door flew open. Hank strolled in with a little brunette on his arm. He looked like the cat that ate the canary.

"Hello, friend. May I introduce you to the prettiest girl in Nashville, Miss Linda Lou!"

I stood and nodded bashfully. The girl regarded me through long, dark lashes. She couldn't have been more than seventeen.

"She's comin' to our recording session. She sings. Right, Linda Lou? I may be able to get her a spot on the Hayride," Hank said, reaching for a bottle of scotch and two glasses he kept on the table. "Scotch be all right, Miss Linda Lou?"

"That will be just fine," she said. I'm certain she'd never tasted any. She'd probably been out of high school all of two weeks.

"One for you, Webb?"

"It's a bit early for me, thanks. Hadn't we better be getting ready for the recording session?"

"Huh? Yeah, later. We got time. Hey, Webb, think you might want to give us a little breathin' space here, for a little bit?"

He was asking me to leave.

"Uh, sure, okay, Hank. Gimme a sec."

Now I couldn't pull out my new clothes without raising all kinds of suspicion. I didn't know what to do. So I just gathered up Lil Darlin' and headed out.

I couldn't go to Nancy's room, either, or her pa might see me. I went to Lula Mae and told her what the deal was.

"Shit! We gotta get those clothes!"

"We can't. He's in there with a girl."

"To heck with that! This is your big chance, Webb. This is it."

"You go in there. Not me."

"I can't go in there!"

"Well, I'm sure the hell not. I'll just go to the Opry in my old clothes."

"You'll do no such thing. You've got to go back in there."

"How?"

"Just walk in. Get 'em and leave."

"I can't do that."

"You come with me, Webb Pritchard."

Lula Mae grabbed my hand tight and led me out into the hallway like a schoolmarm taking a kid to the principal's office. We snuck up to the fifth floor, where my room was, and we crept down the hall. Jesus, we could hear 'em halfway down. Moanin' and groanin'. Hank was having himself a fine old time.

Me and Lula Mae pressed up against the crumbling plaster, laughing so hard we almost lost it. I dropped to my knees and crawled along the Oriental carpet, inches at a time, until I reached the door. I raised up and slowly, slowly turned the doorknob. I knew it wasn't locked.

I turned that knob so slow it must've taken half an hour to get it around. Every tiny noise it made I cringed. But their caterwauling drowned it out. I finally got the latch to free and I pushed the door open about ten inches. Lula Mae was slumped on the hallway floor, shaking with silent laughter.

Staying low, I crept my way back into my room. Inch by inch. Fortunately, I had hidden my new Opry duds under my bed. If they'd been up high there would've been no way. Moving about two feet every five minutes, I slithered on my belly toward the target.

"Oh, Hank! Oh, Hank, baby, you're the best!"

"Yeah, darlin', come on, give it to me!"

I covered my mouth and nose with my hand. This was the hardest thing I'd ever done. Two more feet. One more. If they finished I was a goner.

"Ooooooh, baby!!!"

I snaked my hand under my bed and took hold of the box that held my clothes. Got a grip. Yanked it hard and dragged it out. It made a big noise. Aw, to hell with it. I stood up, leaned over and calmly picked it up.

Miss Teenage Nashville let out a scream, and it wasn't her orgasm.

"Excuse me, ma'am," I said, "I've come to collect my things."

Hank raised up long enough to catch a glimpse. But I was already out the door.

"Didja get 'em?" Lula Mae was breathless out in the hall.

"I got 'em all right," I said. "Got 'em in the act."

*   *   *

I sent Lula Mae to tell Nancy I'd meet her at the Ryman. I changed clothes at a gas station, slicking my hair with tap water and running a toothpick around my mouth. Lula Mae didn't think much of Nancy being in on the whole thing, but she knew it was a done deal and so she let it go, bless her heart.

This time, I went in the front door of the Ryman. It was three-fifteen. I knew Doc would be wondering where the hell I was, but tough shit. You only go around twice in life, I had found.

The Ryman was empty. I didn't see anybody as I came down a side aisle to the stage. Just as well. I was nervous and needed a minute. I set down my banjo case on one of the oak pews and breathed in the musty afternoon air.

So many greats had performed here over the years. Ernest Tubb. Patsy Cline. Roy Acuff and his Smoky Mountain Boys. Minnie Pearl. Little Jimmy Dickens. Johnny Cash. Jim Reeves. Hank Snow. Loretta Lynn. A thousand Saturday nights. "Keep it low to the ground, boys . . ."

I'd keep it low. Radar would never find me.

"Mr. Pritchard?"

I spun around.

"I'm Hub Jenkins."

The man who would decide my fate, Lula Mae's old friend, was a wizened old apple in a sweat-stained workshirt and a pair of dunga-rees. An Opry regular, though not a big star, he hosted one of the half-hour segments. I couldn't remember a single song he had ever done.

"Mr. Jenkins, a pleasure to meet you," I said, pumping his hand. "Thank you for giving me a chance."

He cocked his head back and looked at me. "I hear good things about you, son. You been tearin' up the West Coast."

"Well," I said, coughing slightly, "they do seem to like what I do out there." I had never been anywhere near the West Coast.

"And what is it you do, exactly? Lula Mae wasn't too strong on the details."

"I play banjo, sir, and sing."

"Banjer? Is this a solo act?"

I was about to reply when Nancy came flying down the aisle with her fiddle case. She rushed up to us, out of breath, and gave Hub Jen-

184

kins the most winning smile I have ever seen, in this life or that one.

"Mr. Jenkins hello my name is Nancy Taggart and I'm here to back up Webb," she said, curtsying slightly and extending her hand. He bowed low and kissed it, completely entranced.

"We'll be auditioning together," I said. "Webb 'n' Nancy."

"Fine," he said, never taking his eyes off her. "Take a few minutes and when you're ready, let me know."

Hub Jenkins turned and headed back into the dark depths of the Ryman.

"Looks like it'll be OK," I said, and unsnapped my banjo case.

"You're pretty sharp today," Nancy said, appraising my new outfit. "You oughta wear that on the Hayride."

"This is too good for the Hayride."

That hurt her feelings. Now I saw that she, too, was wearing something new, or at least something I'd never seen before, a pretty yellow dress. She looked like a sunbeam. And instead of her black clodhoppers she wore dainty little white shoes.

"You look great," I said. "They won't even notice me up there."

We tuned up and in a minute we were as ready as we were ever gonna be. We walked around back and up the steps to the stage. The canvas backdrops for the Opry were in place. My heart was hammering and my mouth was a little dry.

"Let's go get 'em," Nancy whispered.

We didn't rate a spotlight. The power didn't seem to be on anywhere. The stage was kinda dim, with only the daylight filtering down from the stained glass windows. We could see Hub Jenkins right there in the fifth row, sitting with two other men. They wore business suits.

"We're ready, sir," I said loudly. We had no mikes, either. My voice echoed out through the empty auditorium.

"Go ahead, son."

Nancy and I had decided to save "True Gold" for last. We started off with "Little Maggie," which sounded good with just banjo and fiddle. Trading licks and weaving our voices together, I was surprised at how good we sounded. The Ryman had great acoustics.

I was glad now that Nancy had joined me. A banjo alone sounds wonderful to my ear, but to a lot of people it's a little harsh—even country people used to the sound. Her fiddle smoothed it out perfectly. And my own singing voice, while adequate, was helped along considerably by her own sweet tones. We made a hell of a duet, to be honest.

But when we finished, they didn't clap. The men just sat there. I guess I should have expected it, but it was weird to play your heart out and not hear anything afterward. They whispered among themselves.

"Thank you, thank you," I said anyway. "That was 'Little Maggie,' an old favorite. Now here's another one you all know, 'John Hardy.' "

This one was real fast, the better to show off my banjo skills. I tore into it and Nancy stayed right with me, playing lickety-split. We only sang one verse and one chorus because I didn't want to bore these guys, who must've heard this song ten thousand times. But I felt they needed to see what I could do, and I showed 'em. If the Opry was looking for a new banjo picker, here I was. If there was anything running against me it would be my age. I just hoped my forty years didn't show up too sharp in this setting. I hoped Nancy made me look young.

I got off a nifty little tag lick I'd been working on and we got out of the song. Nancy did a little two-step there at the end. Clop-clop. I thought we were doing great.

"Thank you, ladies and gentlemen, thank you," I said to the three men sitting silently in the fifth row. "That was 'John Hardy.' And now here's one that I wrote—"

"Thanks, Mr. Pritchard, that'll be all," Hub Jenkins said, standing up. The two men with him stood, too.

I was freaked. "But Mr. Jenkins, I've written a song and I'd like you to hear it. It's brand-new."

"Mr. Jenkins, it's a terrific song," Nancy spoke up. "Just one more. Please."

"Well, I—" Jenkins started to say something but one of the men murmured in his ear.

"OK," he said, and sat back down. The men did the same.

Now I was rattled. I didn't know if they liked us or hated us. I looked at Nancy and she gave me a reassuring little wink. All right.

"Here's one I wrote. It's called 'True Gold,' " I said. Nancy started it by coming in with the fiddle line, and I joined in after four bars. We played the intro smoothly, and I began to sing.

"Memories are silver, tarnished or bright,
    The future, that story's untold.
    Yesterday's dreams are tomorrow's dreams, too,

But times spent with you
Are true gold."

We let the last line die away. I was proud of it. It was a good song. The men didn't do anything for what seemed like forever, then Hub Jenkins stood up and came down front. He looked up at us and said, "That was mighty fine, Mr. Pritchard. I like your sound. Come on down here and we'll talk."

Nancy and I looked at each other and hurried down to the front row. I was so excited I could barely contain myself. He liked us! Lula Mae would be pretty happy.

The two men in business suits came up and stood behind Hub Jenkins. He never said who they were.

"You're a pretty fair banjer picker there, Mr. Pritchard," he said. "Nice, clean sound. I do believe you've studied your Scruggs."

"Yessir," I said, smiling. "He's my biggest influence."

"And you, little lady," he said, looking at Nancy, "you have a way with that fiddle. You certainly do."

"Thank you, Mr. Jenkins," she said.

"But I've got a little problem," he said. "Right at the moment, I can't use a banjer picker. But I sure could use a fiddle. How would you like to join my band?" he said to Nancy.

This wasn't the way it was supposed to go down at all.

"But Mr. Jenkins," I said, "we're auditioning as an act, not to join somebody else's band. We're Webb 'n' Nancy."

His eyes went cold. "Sorry, Pritchard," he said. "It's the best I can do for you. Maybe somebody else can give you a better shot. So how about it, little lady?"

Nancy stood there looking lost. What could I tell her?

"I—" She faltered.

"I pay forty dollars a week. Plus room and board."

One of the men behind him was smirking. I wanted to punch his lights out.

"My father," she said. "He, I mean, I . . . Yes. All right. I will."

Hub Jenkins' face twisted into a dirty smile. "That's just great. It's Nancy, right? Nancy? Good. Good. Well, Nancy, we're gonna rehearse tomorrow night at my house. Be there at six-thirty. One of my boys'll give you the address."

I was crackling with anger. It surged through me like an electric current. I wasn't jealous of Nancy, I was just incredibly pissed that this guy had blown me off like that. I felt like breaking his head open with Lil Darlin'. A Ted Williams swing with a fifteen-pound bat. Right there in the Ryman. Brains and blood spattering over the pews.

As one of the men took Nancy aside, Hub Jenkins turned to me and said in a low voice, "She's over eighteen, ain't she?"

"Fuck you," I said. "You lay a hand on her and I'll kill you."

I stomped up the aisle and kicked open the door. The street outside was bright and hot. I looked at my watch. Just after four. Maybe not too late to get to Castle Recording Studios.

20

I had no idea where Castle Recording Studios were. It was hot, and my banjo was heavy, and I really didn't feel like schlepping it around all afternoon. I checked my wallet. Twenty bucks. I caught a cab.

"Castle Recording Studios," I said, wondering if the guy would have a clue. But he turned back around and gunned it, and we flew down the block. He made a right turn, then a left, and a right, and we were there. He'd taken me all of three blocks. The meter said I owed him seventy cents.

"I don't see it," I said, handing him a dollar bill. "Can you tell me where it is?"

"There," he said, pointing at the building across the street. "In the Tulane Hotel."

"Thanks."

After giving him a ten-cent tip, I hurried into the coolness of the hotel. I asked a bored-looking bellboy where Castle was.

"Seven." He pointed his finger up. Then he saw my banjo. "You're late, pal."

I rode up in the elevator and began to worry. Maybe this wasn't such a great idea. Doc was likely to fire me for real this time. But if I didn't show up at all it could be worse. Then again, if Muley Taggart saw me . . .

The elevator doors opened and I stepped out into a small reception area. I heard familiar voices in a nearby room. A tough-looking dame in a broad-shouldered suit looked up from some paperwork.

"May I help you, sir?" she said tartly, eyebrows raised in suspicion. Did I look like an ax murderer?

"Yes," I said pleasantly, "I'm an ax murderer and I've come to hack off your head."

No, actually I said, "I'm with the Hayride."

She tilted her chin up and looked down her nose at me. "Well, I'm afraid you're quite late. They've already started."

"Yes, ma'am, I'm aware of that," I said. "But I made it." Maybe I could become an ax murderer.

She shrugged, and pointed to a door.

I picked up Lil Darlin' and went in.

Everybody was there, and they must've been between takes because they were all hanging around, smoking and drinking cold pop. I slunk into the thick of things, trying to look invisible.

"Webb!" Lula Mae had spotted me. I held a finger to my lips, trying to shush her so Doc wouldn't hear my name. I steered her over into a corner.

"How'd it go?" She searched my face. "What happened? I can tell something happened."

I shook my head. "You won't believe it. We played three songs, including my new one, and then the sonofabitch asks Nancy to join his band and tells me to take a hike. He wants to get in her pants."

Lula Mae's face darkened. "Oh my."

"Yeah, he barely had time for me once he got a load of her. Asked me if she was underage. Asshole." I slumped against the wall. "I played my heart out, Lula Mae. I gave it my best shot. You shoulda heard us. We were great."

"So where's Nancy?"

I laughed bitterly. "She said yes. She's with Hub Jenkins now."

Lula Mae dropped her voice. "That's terrible. Muley's looking for her. He's madder'n a wet hen."

I just leaned against the wall, disgusted.

"What've you guys done so far? What've I missed?" I asked.

"Well, Doc's been breaking us up into groups and rehearsing a couple of songs. He says everybody in the cast'll have a chance to be on the record. I think he's gonna call it *Hayride Hoedown* or something."

"Well, he doesn't need me."

Lula Mae patted my arm. "Sure he does, honey. You wait."

"I'm gonna go take a leak."

I went back out through the reception area and into the hall. The men's room was by the stairs. I was just at the door when it opened and out stepped Muley Taggart.

He stopped short and drew a sharp breath.

"Where's my daughter, Pritchard?" His country-lined face was hard.

I weighed my answer for a split second. I couldn't buy any time.

"She's joined Hub Jenkins' band."

That truly startled him. "What?"

"You heard me. She auditioned for him over at the Ryman. Looks like your little girl's done gone over to the Opry, Muley."

I braced myself, half expecting him to pop me, but instead he slumped into himself. Suddenly he looked old and tired.

"Well, I'll be," he murmured, gazing at the floor. "I'll be."

He looked up at me. "You had something to do with it."

"Well, actually, I was the one trying out, and I just asked her to come over and help me out. It wound up being her they liked."

He smiled and rubbed his jaw.

"Your daughter's one hell of a fiddle player," I said gently. "She had a good teacher. She's gonna go far."

Muley Taggart sucked on his teeth for a moment, jerked his head in a nod and walked back into the studio without saying another word. I had stolen his daughter and sent her out into the world without his permission. None of it could be helped.

I took my time in the bathroom. My spiffy new Ryman duds now drooped. The armpits on my new blue shirt were stained with sweat. I looked at myself in the mirror and knew I could fool nobody. I was no Opry stud. I was almost as old as Muley, for crying out loud. You're just an old banjo picker from Oklahoma and you'll never be a star, I told the face staring back at me. Marie's gonna have to understand.

"You're fired, Pritchard," Doc Mullican said to me as soon as I got back into the studio. "Now come over here and help us out."

I went over to where he was standing with Daniel Eberhardt and a few others. Daniel nodded coldly.

"Now I ain't gonna ask where ya been," Doc said, " 'Cause there's a rumor goin' around you snuck over to the Opry. You're breakin' my heart, boy. Why would anybody want to be with that flea-bitten out-fit when he could be on Doc Mullican's Hayride? I ask you.

"But now that you've seen the error of your ways and rejoined the flock, here's the game plan. You're gonna back up Daniel here on 'Rocky Road to Heaven.' You boys work it out. We're gonna hit that button in fifteen minutes."

He walked away. Daniel looked at me and said, "How are you going to pay for the damage to my car?"

Jesus, this kid was Johnny One-Note. "Well, I—"

"You said we'd do it in Nashville. Well, we're in Nashville."

"OK, Daniel," I said, exasperated. "We'll do it tomorrow. How's that?"

He looked skeptical. "I'm coming to your room in the morning."

"Fine."

I had almost forgotten about the "plan" to get his Buick fixed. Some half-assed notion I'd had of going to a body shop and offering free tickets to the show in exchange for the work. The kind of work his car needed, we'd have to hand out five hundred freebies.

"Daniel," I said, "let's worry about your car later. Right now I think we'd better work on this tune."

So we did, picking a key and working it up with a few of the guys in his band. We didn't sound half bad. I was nervous, I guess, since I'd never recorded before. We were herded into the studio, a claustrophobic room with padded walls and a glass-walled booth off to the side, where the engineers and the producer sat in semidarkness. Was that Hank in there? He waved at me with a big, silly grin.

"Howdy, pard," he barked over the P.A. system. "Ready to make your big hit?"

I gave him a thumbs-up.

"I told 'em you're One-Take Charlie," Hank said, his voice crackling over a speaker near the ceiling. "Don't let me down."

"What's with him?" asked one of Daniel's band members.

"He's just trying to make me nervous is all," I said. "Don't pay any attention."

"Keep those fingers limber, boy," Hank said. "And above all, don't fuck up!"

Everybody looked at the booth, shocked. The producer pushed Hank away from the mike.

"Jesus, he's on a roll today," somebody muttered.

"All right, let's just do a run-through to get some levels," the producer said. "Anytime, guys."

We started, then stopped, then started and stopped again. It appeared to be Daniel who was nervous.

"Take your time," the producer said reassuringly, but we knew time was money here. He dimmed the lights way down until the studio was lit like a fancy restaurant. The only thing that stood out were the red glowing buttons on the recording equipment. Still, I could see Hank's ghostly face behind the glass. He was angry at me for some reason.

"I can't do this," said Daniel, stepping away from the mike.

"What's wrong?" the producer said.

"It's OK," I said. "He just needs a minute."

Finally we managed to do a take, but we all knew it wasn't any good. Daniel's vocal was off-key and really shaky. He sounded nothing like he did on the Hayride.

Suddenly Hank's voice came back on over the P.A.

"Show 'em how, Webb!" he hollered. "Do 'Carry Me Back'!"

I tried to ignore him.

"You know how it goes!"

"He's not helping," Daniel muttered. "Get him out of that booth."

I leaned into the main mike. "Could we have a little less of Hank, please? Thank you."

"Fuck you, boy!"

Doc banged open the door to the control booth and spoke to Hank. The producer was rubbing his forehead like he had a headache. Doc left the booth.

"All right, gentlemen," the producer said in soothing tones, "One more time, please."

Well, that time wasn't any good, either, but on the next one Daniel seemed to find his voice. We all began to loosen up.

"That was a good one, Daniel," I said to him. "Do it again."

And we nailed it. It was as good as it was ever gonna get, it seemed to me, but the producer demanded one more take, just for insurance. So we did another one, but it didn't sound quite as good, I thought. I hoped he used the other take.

When we were done, Doc came into the studio and came over to me.

"Would you do 'Carry Me Back'?" he asked.

"That's Hank's song," I said.

"I know," Doc replied, lowering his voice, "but he says he won't leave the booth until you do it. He's being damned ornery. Just run through it once and that's all we need. We don't even have to record it, Webb. Help me out, will ya?"

"OK. You want me to do this solo?"

"Hank insists."

Well, geez, we don't want to piss off Hank, now, do we, I thought.

"Gimme a sec," I said through the mike as I ran through the chords. I hoped I could remember all the words. Ah, well. It was for a good cause.

"I'm ready," I finally said.

The lights were still dimmed down. I liked it that way. My fingers were loose and I felt pretty good. I decided I'd give it a good ride. It was a great song, anyway.

"Anytime you're ready," the producer said. I could see Hank in the booth, grinning at me, the faint green and red lights of the control board coming up on his face, making it devilish.

I cleared my throat. Hit the opening lick. Opened my mouth. Began to sing.

"Carry me back, all the way baaaack . . ."

I was coming up on the second chorus when it happened. Right in the middle of the line, I could hear that damned P.A. system crackle to life above my head.

"I'm pullin' the plug on you, boy," Hank said.

My hands froze and my body began to tingle, and the familiar white light wrapped me in its unholy embrace. I fought it this time, something I'd never done before, but there was no staying. The light lifted me and took me away, and at the very end I swear I could hear Hank singing "I Saw the Light."

I knew right where I was. The hardness of the bunk and the closeness of the air told me I was back in the RV before I even opened my eyes. Home sweet home.

I sat up, swung my legs over the side and blew out a big breath. How long had I been gone this time? I'd soon find out.

I was no longer wearing my fancy Ryman duds. I had on my

stonewashed jeans from Target and a T-shirt. My feet were bare. My face had a three-day growth of beard. I didn't feel very clean. And I was hungry.

Peeking out the window, I saw I was still parked behind the Sluice. The story of my life. Was I destined to live in this stupid alley the rest of my born days? Would I become a huge star in the past, overtake Hank and headline the Opry, live in a big house in Nashville with a banjo-shaped swimming pool, only to be jerked into the present and be stuck behind a dishwasher scraping peas off a plate? Great.

Frankly, I was getting tired of this shit. Where am I, what year is it? Fuck. Prison was never this complicated.

I should do what Dot said, go back to Tulsa and work construction. Steady money. Play in a bar band on weekends. Find a nice girl. Smoke a little pot. Be normal.

I found my shoes and gathered up a towel and some other things, and headed over to the campground showers. Took a long, hot one, washing away the muggy heat of Nashville and the crazy events of the last twelve hours. Toward the end, the water turned icy, like it usually did, only this time I didn't even mind. I needed the jolt.

After that, I went over to this cafe I sometimes went to and ordered a hamburger and a bowl of soup. Then I hankered for pie, so the waitress brought me a slice of cherry. I ate it with my fingers. I picked the last bits of cherry skin off my teeth and sat back, deciding my next move. I felt human again.

I thought of going to see Marie, or going to see Sir Tex, or going to the Sluice, but Lil Darlin' won out over them all. I just wanted to be alone with her for a while.

I hoped nobody would see me around the RV, and nobody did. I fetched the banjo and walked back over to the campground, this time heading straight for the spot in the woods where I'd first met Hank. Hardly anybody was around; no festivals right now.

In the daytime the place in the woods didn't look nearly so mysterious. Just a little clearing around a fire ring. I sat down on a log and tuned her up. Ah, sweet lady. You're always so true. What did I do to deserve your love?

I played and played, thinking all the while. One thing about banjo picking, it lends itself to working out your problems. Your fingers fly and your mind roams all over the place, settling on things and turning them around and around.

I was mad at Hank, and I let that out, too, digging in with my fingerpicks and yanking out the music. Take that, you jerk. And that. And that!

After a while I eased off and just sat there, staring into space, cradling Lil Darlin' in my arms. Had I come to any hard conclusions? I wasn't exactly sure.

"Webb?"

I popped up out of my reverie. "Huh?"

The boy Mark pushed aside some leaves and stepped into the clearing.

"Mark!"

"Hi. I followed you."

"Have a seat, kid." He was the last person I'd seen just before I went back to the past. What did he know?

"What's cookin'?" I said.

He squatted at the fire ring and poked at the ashes with a stick.

"We were all worried about you," he said. "You got sick."

"I did?"

"Yeah. You were playing your banjo in the alley and you kind of stopped and fell over. My dad came out and put you in your camper. The doctor came and said you'd hit your head and that was probably it."

"What was the doctor wearing?"

"Huh?"

"The doctor. You remember what he had on?"

"Uh, I think it was mountain-climbing gear. Ropes and stuff. Yeah. Why?"

"Nothing. Then what happened?"

He shrugged. "You mostly slept."

"Well, I don't remember much," I said, lying through my teeth. "I think that bar fight must've caught up with me."

"What are you doing here?"

"Oh, just trying to find a way out."

"Out of what?

"Out of all the messes I've got myself into. My music's not happening, my love life's in a holding pattern. I wash dishes for a living. It all sucks."

He came over and sat on a rock near me.

"You know what?" he said.

"No. What?"

"You should just play your own songs, that's all."

"That's it? That's the answer?"

He nodded his head up and down, up and down, the way kids will do. "I told you before. Your music's stupid. What you play in the bar. You shouldn't play that, you should do your own thing. Do the right thing. Like Spike Lee. Like that song you were playing in the alley before you fell over."

"If I play that again I may fall over again."

Mark laughed. "You know what I mean. Try it. Be Spike Lee."

"I did write a song . . ."

"Do it!"

So I did, played "True Gold" for Mark there in the woods. Last time I played it I was at the Ryman with Nancy. The kid swayed back and forth while I sang. I finished and he clapped.

"Do another one."

"I'm afraid I don't have another one. You just heard my entire original-tune repertoire."

"So write another one."

"Don't know if I have another one in me."

"Yeah, you do. Write one about me."

"About you?"

"Yeah. I'm a pain in the ass."

"That you are. So it'll go, 'He's a pain in the ass, a snake in the grass . . .' "

" 'He drinks from a glass . . .' " Mark said.

" 'He passes gas . . .' " I finished. We were both laughing.

"Look out, Garth Brooks," I said. "Watch your back, buddy. Ol' Webb's gainin' on ya."

"It just seems like when you do your own stuff, it's better," Mark said. "You sound different. I like it."

"So all I gotta do is write tunes. Then my whole life will fall into place."

"Yeah."

"Somehow I think it's more complicated than that, kid. But it might be a start."

He stood up. "I'd better go. Mom doesn't know where I am."

So it was Mom now and not Mattie. A good sign.

"You run along. Tell everybody I'm back among the living. Sort of."

The kid scampered off into the woods, and it was all quiet again. If I was ever gonna get out of that stinking dishwashing job, it had to start with writing songs. If I failed at that, I'd say I gave it my best shot and go back to working construction. Maybe move to Montrose to be near Dot for a while. I could live there cheap. I could just park the Orca in a trailer park somewhere on the edge of town. Must be jobs around for a skilled laborer. I'd find myself a little bar band to play in on weekends. Wouldn't be a bad life. Montrose was a nice little place.

Fuck that.

I've backed up Hank Williams and tasted the Ryman. I've seen the light.

I dug in on Lil Darlin' and played that banjo till my fingerpicks wore my skin raw. I went up one key and down another, searching for the right notes, racking my brain for the right words. Sometimes they were there, sometimes not.

I thought about my life, and the women I'd loved, and my cell at McAlester, and how time dragged there. How I'd pissed away a lot of time, too much time.

I was out of time.

The shadows stretched longer and the late afternoon warmth gave way to the evening chill. On and on I played, never minding the cold, rocking the log along with the beat of the music. Lil Darlin' had hold of me, but it wasn't like the white light. It was tender and sweet. Rock me baby, all night long. Somehow I had found what I needed. I think it was there all along, really. I'd just been blind to it.

It was pitch dark when I quit. I laid Lil Darlin' in her case so gentle, and headed back through the woods to where I belonged.

I had written four songs, so now I had five. If you counted "Carry Me Back," I guess I had six. A good day's work. It was time to go conquer the world.

21

I didn't tell Sir Tex I'd just come off the road with Hank Williams. I didn't tell him about trying out for the Opry, or making a record with the Hayride, or any of that stuff. I just stood there in his living room and played my six songs—I had decided to include "Carry Me Back"— and let him be the judge.

He wandered around with a Bloody Mary in his hand, gazing out the big windows some of the time and watching me other times. I couldn't really read him; his face was a blank. I noticed he'd healed up quite a bit from getting kicked in the head. Tough old bastard.

I rolled right into the next song from the last, and when I was done I took a deep, silly bow and said, "And that, ladies and gentlemen, is the new Webb Pritchard."

Sir Tex stirred his drink with his finger. "A damn sight better than the old one, dear boy. A couple of those tunes have the spark of genius, I dare say. Sure you didn't steal them?"

"Hell, no. I wrote 'em all." Well, it was almost true.

"I like that last one. 'Carry Me Back'? And that other one. The one about true love?"

" 'True Gold.' "

"Yes. Very nice, indeed. A nice ballad there. You've come a long way in a very short time. And frankly, I'm surprised. I wasn't sure we'd be seeing each other again. Thought you might just hit the road in that caravan of yours."

"I stuck around. I wanted to see if I could do it. Write a song, I mean."

I'd kept my part of the bargain. Now I was curious to see if he'd keep his.

"What happens now?" I asked pointedly.

The older man plopped down on his marshmallow sofa and drained his drink.

"I'm thinking," he said. "You'd need to establish yourself as a live performer before we could record you in a valid setting. I'm a record producer, not a booking agent. But I have friends. Let me make a few phone calls."

Shades of Lula Mae.

"You mean you'd get me some gigs?"

He hesitated. "Well, all I can say is I could call a few people and see what they say. Get you an audition, perhaps. See what happens from there."

I began to wonder.

"This would be in Nashville?"

"I'd assume so, yes."

There was something wrong here. Maybe this guy was just an old fraud, after all. His voice had lost its bluster.

"Tex?"

"Yes, Webb?"

"You wouldn't bullshit me, would you?"

"What? Heavens no! What gives you that idea?"

"Just my bullshit detector going off. Wondering if you really can deliver. That's all."

He stood up. A bit unsteady on his feet. How many Bloody Marys had there been today?

"My credentials are impeccable, dear boy. You insult me."

He turned his back on me and marched into the kitchen to fix himself another drink. I sighed.

"Well, Tex, I'm afraid I've learned in life that money talks and bullshit walks," I called after him. "I want some kind of guarantee."

I could hear the refrigerator door opening, ice being plopped into a glass. The glug, glug of vodka being poured. Now the tomato juice. Sir Tex reappeared in the doorway.

"Oh, now he wants guarantees! Guar-an-tees! My boy, in show business, as in life, there are no guarantees."

I was more annoyed than pissed. "Look," I said, "I know you can't promise me stardom. I just want to know if you can really help me. Because if you can't, I'm outta here. I've already wasted too much time."

Sir Tex walked over to his biggest picture window and stood there, looking out at the valley. He looked ridiculous in his loud Hawaiian shirt, his old white legs sticking out of his shorts. A beached whale washed up on the snowy shores of Telluride.

"My mother died when I was ten," he said quietly. "We lived in Sheffield then. My father shipped me off to live with my aunt in London. I rarely saw him after that."

He turned and faced me. "Do you know what it's like to lose your mother when you're ten?"

"No."

"It makes you very weak, and then very strong." His voice rose. "Do you have any idea what it is to be homosexual at a school, a boys' school, back in the fifties? Where they torment you and the headmaster looks the other way? Where they whip you for being a pervert? Push you down on the football field and step on you in their cleats? Where the headmaster takes you into his rooms at night and—"

He was crying now. "No, you wouldn't." He crumpled to the floor, his Bloody Mary spilling across the new carpet.

I walked over and picked up the glass and set it on a table. Went into the kitchen for some paper towels. I blotted up the smeary mess as best I could. The carpet would have a stain.

"I'd better go," I said.

Sir Tex reached out and clutched my ankle. His fingers were cold. "No, no," he said. "I really can help you, Webb. Let me help you." He was still crying.

God, I hated shit like this. "You're in no shape to help me," I said, gently pulling my foot away. "You need help yourself."

"Hand me the phone."

I saw it on the coffee table. I picked it up and handed it to him. He punched in some numbers. I felt like bolting out the door.

"Jeremy?" His voice was strong, but his face was running tears. "It's Tex."

I decided to go out on the deck and leave him alone. Whoever Jeremy was, I doubted he could do anything for me. It looked like Sir Tex was a dead end. I would have to take my songs and break out somewhere else.

I waited a long time, probably half an hour. I began to think he'd passed out or something. Finally, Sir Tex came out on the deck. He didn't have a drink in his hand. No more tears. He looked pleased with himself.

"Well, my boy," he said, throwing an arm around my shoulders and squeezing in a manly way. "How'd you like to go to Nashville?"

I looked skeptical and didn't say anything.

"It's all set," he went on. "You're to see a man there named Art Peabody. He runs the Mockingbird Cafe. The biggest showcase for new talent in Nashville. Now that's all I can do," he said with fake modesty. "It's not much, but—"

"When?" I asked.

"He's expecting you tomorrow at four o'clock."

"Tomorrow! How do I get to Nashville by tomorrow?"

He laughed. "You hop a plane, dear boy. You go to our little airstrip in Telluride and you fly to Denver and then a great big airplane takes you all the way to Nashville."

"I have twenty bucks to my name."

He pouted. "Webb, you're so limited sometimes. Do I look like a pauper?"

"Come on," I said, "I don't mind you making a phone call, but I won't take your money."

"Of course you will," he said cheerfully, "You won't get out of here any other way. You can pay me back when you're rich and famous. Now go pack some things and get to the airstrip. I think the last plane out leaves in about an hour."

He practically pushed me out the door. I went back to the Sluice and told Red I had to leave town for a couple days. He wasn't happy about it. I asked him if I could leave the RV in the alley.

"Whatever," he said, rolling his eyes. "You're one strange dude, Webb."

"It's not me," I said, "It's all the shit that happens to me."

There was a taxi service to the airstrip for seven bucks. Now I was down to thirteen dollars. Not enough for a Nashville debut. But Sir Tex had pressed his platinum American Express card in my palm and wouldn't take it back, a huge temptation if ever there was one, so I guessed I'd be more than all right, money-wise.

I hate flying. The little Continental Express turboprop shook like an aspen leaf when the motors revved up. We taxied out and roared down the high-altitude runway, which looked way too short to me, and I pulled up hard on my armrests to help the plane get up as we shot into the evening sky. The mountains and valley dropped away below with sickening speed as the pilot banked over the San Juans, and we turned northeast toward Denver.

When Uncle Dave Macon, one of the early stars of the Grand Ole Opry, a man born in the 1870s who thought cars were the devil's invention, was once told he would take an airplane ride to his next gig, he balked a little. Naturally. But they got him on the plane (this was the 1940s), and as it zoomed over the Carolinas somebody asked the old man how it was.

"I b'lieve I'll lay with it," he said.

That's how I felt.

Back in Nashville, forty-three years after I'd just been there, I rented a Lincoln Town Car and drove straight to the Ryman. I wanted to see if it was the same.

It wasn't, of course. Oh, the building itself was preserved, but now it sat right across the street from one of those big ugly concrete-bunker convention centers. And next to it was a parking lot. I walked up the old front steps and remembered being here with Hank just the other day. Or was it yesterday? Standing here now, I wondered what had happened to Nancy. Was she still alive?

It was very late, way past midnight. The flight from Denver had been a long one. I wanted to go hear some music, wander the city, check it out, but my bones said no. There was a time when . . . but no. I found a Holiday Inn and fell asleep about thirty seconds after I walked into the room. I was hoping I'd dream of Patsy Cline, but I didn't dream of anything at all.

The next afternoon, after I'd bought some souvenirs at the Hank Williams Gift Shop and Museum—"Are you familiar with Hank's music?" the clerk asked me. "Not much," I replied. "I'm more of a Merle Haggard man"—I went to see Art Peabody at the Mockingbird Cafe.

The Mockingbird wasn't downtown by the other clubs, it was in a suburban shopping center across from a mall. People like Garth Brooks were discovered here. When I got there the front door was locked. Sir Tex had said four o'clock. I looked at my Timex. Four oh-five.

So I banged on the door. Eventually, I heard someone inside.

"We're closed," a muffled voice said from the other side.

"It's Webb Pritchard. I'm here to see Art Peabody."

"Hold on."

In a minute some keys rattled and the door opened. A big, bearded man in jeans, a too small T-shirt and sandals stood there. He looked down at me like he had no idea who I was.

"I'm Webb Pritchard," I said again, picking up my banjo case. "I have an appointment to see Mr. Peabody."

"You do?" the big guy said, glancing at the banjo case. "Who sent you?"

"Sir Tex."

"Who?"

"Uh, Tex. Tex Sandhurst. Reginald Sandhurst. They call him Tex."

"They do?"

Shit.

"He's a record producer. He called Art Peabody yesterday and I'm to understand Mr. Peabody's expecting me. I'm here to audition." The banjo was getting heavier by the second.

The big guy laughed. "Well, Mr. Pritchard, I'm Art Peabody and I never heard of this Tex dude, but since you're here and you've got your banjo, come on in. I'm kind of busy. I'll give you five minutes."

Sir Tex was dead meat. I would kill him as soon as I got my ass back to Telluride. Personally pin him up to his art-filled wall and throw darts at strategic body parts. Charge admission to come look at the bloody remains as performance art. The darts would be slightly barbed, and poison-tipped. They'd—

"Now who'd you say this Tex dude was?"

We had walked to the front of the place where the stage was. Peabody lowered his ample weight into a chair, turning it around so that his arms draped over the back. I unsnapped my banjo case and took out Lil Darlin'.

"Oh, I met him in Colorado. Telluride. That's where I've come from. He lives there; I'm just passing through, so to speak. Anyway, he told me he's a Nashville record producer and he sent me here. Said he had connections."

"Tex. Would he be a British dude, by any chance?"

"Yeah, that's him. So you do know him?"

Art Peabody chuckled and shook his great woolly head. "Oh,

man. Well, kind of. Yeah, he used to be around. Haven't seen him in at least five, six years. Guy kind of wore out his welcome in this town."

Great. I would definitely kill him when I got back. "Oh?"

"He burned a few people. Overextended himself financially, if you know what I mean. He left town owing money."

"He told me he ran TipTop."

"Used to. His partners kicked him out."

Maybe triple barbs on those poison darts.

"Well, I'm sorry my contact is so bogus," I said. "I didn't know."

He waved his hand in the air. "It's OK. Let's hear what you can do."

I tuned her up and ran through my new repertoire, the songs I had written, plus "Carry Me Back." I didn't play any of my old, usual stuff. The Scruggs and the rest.

When I was done, Peabody sat rocking thoughtfully back and forth in his chair.

"Hmmm," he said.

Was this good or bad?

"Tell you what, Pritchard," he finally said. "I'll be honest. I think you're a little raw for what we present here, and not mainstream enough. But you got some chops there, and your songs are good. What I'm gonna do is send you over to see Andy at the Station Inn. He might be able to help you."

"The Station Inn?"

"Bluegrass venue. They have open stages, lotsa good people in and out of there. You'd find some folks who I think could help you on your way."

He stood up. The audition was over. I packed up Lil Darlin' and thanked him. We shook hands and he walked me to the door.

"Your sound," he said, "is really different, and that's good. There's something about it, something timeless and . . . classic. You don't hear that much anymore. Where'd you pick that up?"

"Hank Williams," I said. "I've listened to a lot of Hank."

"No better teacher," said Art Peabody, and he let me out the door.

I went straight over to the Station Inn, which took some doing because it was so hard to find. It was down in a warehouse district on the edge of downtown, on a side street, and the place looked so unlikely I drove past it three times before I realized that was it. It was a saggy little white stone building with a faded old sign out front. Now

I remembered I'd read about this place somewhere. A real bluegrass mecca. Famous bands played here regularly. If nothing else happened, I figured at least I'd hear some good music.

They weren't really open, but the door was unlocked. Chairs were stacked up on the tables and the bar was closed. A vacuum cleaner stood on the stage. But a guy was there, so I walked up and introduced myself. Only this time, I didn't use Sir Tex's name.

"Hello. I'm looking for Andy. Art Peabody sent me over."

The guy was about fifty, balding, glasses, flannel shirt and jeans.

"You found him. I'm Andy Mullican."

Mullican?

"You related to Doc Mullican?" I asked.

"Sure. He's my dad."

22

You know him?" Andy Mullican asked.

"Uh, well, yeah," I stammered. "I met him a long time ago. I was just a kid."

The son chuckled. "Dad got around. He was quite the Nashville cat."

"Is he still alive?" God, if he were, he'd be older than dirt.

Andy Mullican sighed and shook his head. "Barely. He's in a nursing home. Sometimes he doesn't recognize the family."

"How old is he now?" I was curious. When he ran the Hayride, he was no young man.

"Uh, lemme think. He'd be ninety-seven now. Yeah. Hard to believe, isn't it?"

"Sure is. Hey, let me introduce myself." I stuck out my hand. "Webb Pritchard. Art Peabody sent me over."

Mullican shook hands and nodded. "What can I do for you?"

"I'm looking to get a start in the music business. I play banjo and sing. Somebody sent me over to the Mockingbird and Peabody felt I'd fit in better over here. I'd like to audition."

Mullican looked like he'd heard this line before. "Well, the Station Inn features bluegrass," he said. "That's basically what we're about. I'm not sure a solo act would work out."

"Wait'll you hear me."

He pursed his lips. "Tell you what, Pritchard. Come back tomorrow night about eight. We have an open mike. Sign up and I'll put you on. Will that do for you?"

"That'd be great," I said. "Thanks."

He went back to his work and I wandered around for a minute, looking at the posters of the famous that adorned the old plank walls. Everybody had played the Station Inn, from Bill Monroe to Emmylou Harris. There was bluegrass here almost every night of the week. Mullican and others like him were the keepers of the flame. Across town from where sueded hipsters ruled the Opry, the Station Inn opened its humble doors to a few hundred or a few dozen, or just a few, who wanted to hear it played the old way.

I knew what I wanted to do. I got into the big Lincoln Town Car— eat your heart out, Hank!—and went back to my hotel. I pulled out a phone book and turned to nursing homes. I hadn't wanted to press Andy Mullican for more information because A, it woulda seemed strange to him I wanted to track down his old man, and B, he might've wanted to come with me. I couldn't have that. If I was to see old Doc Mullican again, it had to be alone.

"Shady Acres."

"Yes, I'm looking for someone named"—Jesus, I suddenly realized I only knew him as Doc. That couldn't be his real first name—"Mullican."

"How do you spell that?"

I spelled it for her. Nope. Nobody there by that name.

"Nashville Rest Care, how may I direct your call?"

"I'm looking for someone named Mullican."

And on it went, down through eight or nine places. No Mullicans at any of them. I was about to give up when I had an idea. I turned to the white pages and found M. There were only two Mullicans: Andrew G. and Horace W. I dialed Horace W.'s number. An old lady answered.

"Hello, may I please speak with Mr. Mullican?"

She seemed flustered by the request. "I, I, well, he's not here. May I ask who's calling?"

"Yes," I said pleasantly, "This is Bob White. I'm an old friend of Doc's, and I just got into town. Worked with him on the Hayride many years ago. He may have spoken of me?"

She paused, searching her memory, trying to be polite. "I think I do remember the name, yes."

"How is Doc? I haven't talked with him in about, oh, five or six years."

"I'm afraid he's in a nursing home; he's not here at the house anymore," she said. "He's—not well."

"So sorry to hear that. Would this be Mrs. Mullican?"

"Yes."

"Well, I won't bother you, ma'am. May I send him a card?"

"Well, sure, I'll get you the address."

And she did, and in no time I was flying down the highway to nearby Hendersonville, headed for the Cumberland Care Center. I played out the scene every which way.

"Howdy, Doc! Remember me?"

"Hey there, Doc! Got any spare elixir?"

"Ho, Doc! No, I haven't aged a bit!"

But when I got down there I began having all these second thoughts. Christ, what was I doing? I couldn't run around contacting folks I'd known in the past. It just wasn't right. It might throw everything way out of whack. Plus, what if I gave the old geezer a heart attack or something? Aw, he wouldn't even remember me. He was probably a drooling old vegetable anyway.

I sat in the parking lot awhile, turning things over. Cumberland Care Center was set on a couple of acres of extremely green lawns. Almost a fake green. All edged neat and tidy, with flower beds bordering the sidewalks. Not a bad place, I supposed, to spend your last days on this earth. Shit, I hoped I never ended up like this.

My impulses got the better of me and I got out of the car. I just had to see him.

Horace W. Mullican lived in room twelve in the East Wing. He'd been here for about a year, they said. I walked down a long hall, passing rooms where ghostly old people sat propped up in their beds, hollow husks watching endless episodes of *Wheel of Fortune*. Waiting to die. Antiseptic smells. I came to the room. The door was open. I went in.

A very, very old man lay on his side in the hospital bed, shriveled and curled up in a fetal position. The covers were pulled up to his head. He took no note of me.

I pulled up a chair, deliberately scraping the floor with a loud noise, and just sat there for a minute, looking at him.

"Doc," I whispered. "Doc."

He stirred. His head, with its few wisps of colorless hair, rolled toward me. Now I could see his face. Was this Doc? Cripes, I couldn't even tell. All I saw was this shrunken apple of a face. You couldn't even tell if it was man or woman. Breathing through its toothless mouth.

"Doc."

He made a rasping noise in his throat and opened his eyes. They tried to focus my way.

"Doc, it's Webb. Webb Pritchard. From the Hayride."

He tried to say something. His lips were moving.

I leaned in real close. "What's that?"

"You're . . . fired."

I burst out laughing. "Why, you old coot. You remember me!"

Now a yellowed, clawlike hand emerged from beneath the covers and clutched at the air.

"Would you like to sit up? Can I make you more comfortable?"

I stood up and leaned over the bed and got my arms under him and tried to sort of get him into a sitting position. He didn't weigh anything at all. I thought of Doc as a robust man, heavyset. Now he was like a little old bird. I moved some pillows around and got him propped up. Now we were face to face, more or less. He looked at me with surprising sharpness.

"Well," I said. "It's been a long time, hasn't it?"

"Where did you go?" he asked in halting tones. He pointed a bony finger at me. "You ran off."

I nodded. "Had to, Doc. It's the way things were back then. Something just came up."

"Is Hank with you?" He peered past me with nearly sightless eyes.

"Hank? No, Hank's not around anymore, Doc. You know that."

He nodded. "Hank's gone." He appeared to doze momentarily.

"Doc?"

He raised his head.

"Do you happen to remember Nancy Taggart? Muley's girl?"

"Yep. Sure do."

One moment he was lucid and the next he wasn't.

"What happened to her? Can you tell me?"

"Hank's gone," he said.

I pulled up my chair a bit closer. "That's right, Hank's not here. But where's Nancy?"

"Nancy who?"

"Muley's girl. Nancy. You know. Real pretty, played the fiddle. Nancy."

"Oh. Nancy. Yep. Sure do."

"Do you know where she is? I've lost track over the years."

Doc turned his head and gazed out the window. He was lost again.

"Got married. She got married," he blurted out.

"Nancy got married? To who?"

His lips parted and clamped back together.

"Who'd Nancy marry, Doc?"

He looked confused. "David."

"David. David who?"

He looked at me but he didn't see me. I was losing him.

"Who'd Nancy Taggart marry?"

"Hank's gone, Webb. He ain't comin' back."

Shit, we were getting so close, too.

"I know. But who's David? Nancy's husband?"

Doc waved his hand in the air. "David Pelle— Pelle—"

"David Pella?"

"Eye-talian boy. Pellegrino. David Pellegrino."

Nancy had married somebody named David Pellegrino? Who the hell was he?

"Who's that, Doc? Does he play music?"

But he was gone, asleep in an instant. His mouth fell open and he burbled some spit down his whiskery chin. It was time to go. There was so much I wanted to ask him. I stood up, pushed the chair back where it had been and approached the bed. I reached out and touched his hand, lying weightlessly on top of the covers.

"Thanks, Doc," I said. "You were one hell of a boss. And you always hired me back."

I left the Cumberland Care Center and steered the Lincoln toward Nashville, humming old Carter Family tunes all the way.

The next night, the Station Inn was packed to the gills. I had to park two blocks away. I guess open mike night was pretty popular.

Actually, it was heartening to see so many people come out to hear bluegrass. After the way-too-hip-for-me Telluride scene, this was like a breath of fresh air. No spandex here. Nobody cranking up the amps to play "Don't This Road Look Rough and Rocky." Just folks like me in their stonewashed Target jeans and work boots, hankering to hear somebody play some Bill and Earl. Hell, Bill and Earl themselves might show up. Even Alison Krauss.

Mullican was at the door.

"Hello, Pritchard," he said, nodding cordially at me. "Glad you made it. You're on seventh. After the Hot Pluckers."

I worked my way through the crowd, noting that practically everybody had some kind of instrument case. We're all pickers here, I thought. Good. An appreciative audience. I set Lil Darlin' down toward the back. It was clear I'd have to stand.

The first group was better than I expected, I have to admit. At an open mike night, I was prepared to hear some rough picking and off-kilter harmonies, but these guys were hot. They sounded professional. I wondered if they were.

I got myself a beer and stood over near the bar. I was likely the only person in this place who didn't know a soul here. This had the flavor of a regular party, one I wanted to join.

A door to my right led to the bathrooms and also to a back room with a sign over the door: MUSICIANS ONLY. That's where people were warming up. After the fifth act finished, I headed in there.

I set my banjo case on a battered old sofa and nodded at the other pickers. They were all pretty friendly, but I was the stranger in town. I could see them stealing glances at Lil Darlin' and sizing me up. Who's the new dude?

As my time approached, I began to get nervous. Not my usual state. I mean, I'd been playing in front of sizable crowds night after night with Hank and the Hayride, and doing a solo spot. But this crowd was different. They'd know the licks and they'd know when I missed and covered up and when I was faking it. The hell with it. I didn't fake much. I was ready.

I went back out to the main room and stood off to the side in the shadows as the Hot Pluckers wrapped it up. They were a band that had women in it. That was a relatively new thing. Women in bluegrass had always been relegated to the back of the bus, so to speak. It was men's music. Back in the early days, you might have a guest female vocalist come up for one gospel tune or something like that. And there were always a few all-girl groups around, but they were sort of novelty acts. The stalwarts of bluegrass—your Jimmy Martins, your Osborne Brothers, your J. D. Crowes, your Stanley Brothers—never had women in 'em. Just didn't, that's all.

Now, though, it was different. Lots of groups had women members, and they were pickers, not just singers. Some women, like Alison Krauss, Laurie Lewis and Lynn Morris, fronted their own bands. Alison Brown was a hired-gun banjo player. So things were changing.

The Hot Pluckers came off and as the fiddle player passed me, she reached out and squeezed my arm. "Knock 'em dead," she said, and was gone.

Andy Mullican climbed up onto the small stage. "All right, folks, here comes a new face," he said. "He's not exactly bluegrass because he prefers to be high and lonesome when he plays that high, lonesome sound." The crowd laughed. "Well, maybe not high. Just lonesome. Let's welcome Webb Pritchard and his banjo!"

I got a nice hand as I stepped up. This was so different from the bar nights back in Tulsa so many years ago, where the music was a backdrop for beer bottle fights, or the cow palaces with the Hayride. I felt truly at home here.

"Good evening, ladies and gentlemen," I said, adjusting the mikes. "Thanks for having me. I'm not really alone up here, though. I've got Lil Darlin' with me and she's never let me down. She's as good a partner as a man could wish for. She's got a little magic in her, you might say.

"I come from Colorado by way of Oklahoma. But don't worry; I'm not gonna lay any John Denver on you."

The crowd cheered. "Rocky Mountain Low!" somebody yelled.

"No, I'm gonna do a couple tunes I wrote recently. Hope you like 'em."

I started with the instrumental "Slippery Creek," mainly to limber up and wash away any nervousness I had about singing. It was a good, fast tune, going in and out of a minor key a couple of places, and they seemed to really like it. I followed that up with "Balloon Ride," a vocal number, and then hit 'em with "True Gold." I know it sounds corny, but I gave it everything I had. I closed my eyes and pretended I was singing it to Marie. I could see her sitting there on her porch in Telluride, rocking in that white wicker chair.

I kept my eyes closed as I played the break, and I could feel the music deep in my bones. This song moved me every time I did it. It came from the heart. When I opened my eyes, I saw the whole room was with me. What a rush for a performer.

I finished with "Carry Me Back," and when I was done there was this moment of pure silence and then the crowd jumped to its feet. Cheering and stomping and clapping. God. I was just stunned. Somewhere in the back of my mind I could hear Hank saying, "Not bad, son. Not bad."

I didn't know what to do, so I just stood there and took some bows, right, left, center. To tell you the truth, I was about to cry. But Andy Mullican saved me from total embarrassment by jumping onstage and grabbing the mike.

"How about that?" he yelled, and the room got louder. "Webb Pritchard!"

"More!" somebody shouted, and then everybody started yelling it.

"Will you do one more for us?" Andy Mullican asked me. I nodded and the room eventually got quiet.

"Wow," I said softly into the mike. "Thank you. Thank you very much. I had no idea . . ."

I lit into "Ground Speed," my best Earl tune, and did it about as fast as I'd ever played it. It wasn't my own, but I was getting sort of shaky and didn't want to ruin a good thing. So I played it safe. Stuck to Earl's licks and didn't try to fancy 'em up. I finished and walked offstage in a hurry, holding up Lil Darlin' high in one hand, in tribute to the audience.

People surrounded me as I made my way back to the Musicians Only room.

"Way to go!"

"Best set all night."

"You were great."

"You in a band?"

"Who is that guy?"

Geez, if I'd known it'd be like this I would've fallen back in time long ago, come back and been a big star while I was still young enough to enjoy it. I was laughing to myself.

As I put Lil Darlin' away, I told people yes, I was solo, no, I wasn't playing the festival circuit—yet—and yes, I just might stick around Nashville.

That's when she came up to me. The Hot Pluckers fiddler.

She was about twenty-five, dark-haired, pretty. Not a bit shy.

"Hey, Webb," she said. "I told you to knock 'em dead but you annihilated 'em. You're one hell of a hot picker."

"Thank you. Your encouragement inspired me."

She stuck out her hand. "I'm Ann. And I think we have something in common. Besides music, I mean."

"We do?"

"Come on and I'll buy you a beer."

I couldn't refuse an offer like that, so I followed her out and we squeezed in at the bar. She sat, I stood. It was hard to talk because it was noisy and people kept coming up and slapping me on the back and saying nice things. I couldn't complain.

"Webb Pritchard." She said it like a statement. I just looked at her.

"My mom knew a man by that name."

Uh-oh.

"Who's your mom?" I asked, but I already knew. Had to be.

"Nancy Taggart. She was part of the Taggart Family. They played old-timey and toured around with the Hayride back in the forties and fifties."

Even though I'd seen it coming, it was still like a ton of bricks falling on my head. My breath caught in my throat.

"That woulda been my dad," I said, trying to appear calm. It was hard. "He was a musician. Dead now."

She looked at me. "She always said he was a big influence on her life. I think they had a romance before she met my dad."

"They might well have," I said. "I do remember my father mentioning her." I didn't want this girl to think old Webb had used her mom.

Trying like hell to be nonchalant, I said, "So. How is your mother?"

Ann's eyes fell to the floor. "She died. Two years ago. Cancer."

A great big lump welled up spontaneously in my chest. I pretended to drop some matches so I could reach down and blot the tears that had welled up in my eyes. Aw, Jesus. I was hoping against something like this. The day before, I had spent several hours on the phone and driving around, trying to find Nancy. None of the Pellegrinos in the phone book had panned out. I wondered if old Doc had been wrong. Probably. I got it together—sort of—and straightened back up.

"Sorry to hear that. Did she live in Nashville?"

"No, she and Dad moved to California in the mid-eighties, to raise horses. Me and my brothers stayed here and got into the music biz. It's in the genes."

"How many brothers?"

"Four. Three of 'em are in bands and Don's a producer at MCA."

We talked a while longer, Nancy's daughter and me, and then we parted with promises to stay in touch. Deep down, I wasn't sure I wanted to.

Andy Mullican came over and told me what a hit I was, and I thanked him.

"You're welcome at the Station Inn any time," he said.

On my way out the door, a guy stopped me. Said he was connected with a talent agency that handled bluegrass and acoustic acts.

"Let's talk," he said.

"Can I call you tomorrow?" I asked. I was in a hurry to get somewhere.

"You betcha," he said. He handed me his business card.

It took another five minutes to get past the people hanging around the parking lot. They all wanted to tell me how great I was. My smile began to hurt my face.

I finally got away from it all. Walked the couple blocks to my car. Climbed inside the big Lincoln and drove until I found a deserted overpass in a bad part of town.

I got out and stood by the railing, looking over the lights of Nashville. I wasn't sure if I could do this.

But it was easy. The hurt in my chest opened up and came out my mouth in a piercing scream, almost a woman's scream. I held on to the railing and cried. I cried for a long time, and then I left.

The guy's name was Keith Devereaux, and it turned out he owned the agency. He handled strictly bluegrass and acoustic acts, and he had some pretty big names. His offices were in an old house on Music Row, where all the record companies and such were located in Nashville.

I decided to be straight with him.

"I just got out of prison," I said, "and before that I played in bar bands. My heart wasn't in it. I've wanted to find my own sound and develop that, and go on the road with it. I'm forty years old. I'm no kid. But I'm ready to roll."

Devereaux listened and nodded, and we talked some more about what I might do.

"After hearing you last night, I think you'd go over well on the festival circuit," he said. "Smaller, more traditional festivals."

I told him about Telluride.

"You're not ready for that," he said, and added, "They're not ready for you," and we both laughed. He outlined a series of mom 'n' pop festivals around the country, mostly in the East, that he felt would be good for me. I'd travel in the RV. Make living expenses and not much more. At first, anyway. He'd take ten percent. I said that'd be fine. He said he'd make some calls. We shook hands on it, and he said we'd do the paperwork in a day or two.

I left Keith Devereaux's office and walked out into a fresh Nashville morning. After the paperwork was done, I had to get back to Colorado to wrap things up.

I had to talk to Marie.

23

A day and a half later, I was back in Telluride, with signed papers from Keith Devereaux saying I was booked into four upcoming festivals and he would get a percentage of my fee. What I hadn't made too clear to him was that beyond my six songs, all I really had were the standards everybody played, and I'd have to come up with some other tunes pretty quick. Six was enough to get started, but it wouldn't hold me for long. My first gig was exactly two weeks away.

In a funny way, I was glad the pressure was on. Without it, I think I might have just farted around some more in this mountain town. Now I had commitments. One of them was to Marie.

I had the airport shuttle driver drop me off right at her house. If need be, I could walk down to the Sluicebox later.

Everything looked the same as that first day I had pulled up to scope a parking space: faded lavender paint job, Carla's toys in the front yard. It now seemed like years ago. The front door was open. Somebody was home.

I walked up on the front porch and knocked lightly. No need to be barging in. Our last encounter hadn't been a real friendly one. I hoped to turn that around.

There was a shadowy movement within. Footsteps. Heavy ones.

A man came to the screen door. Big guy. A little younger than me. Chip-on-the-shoulder type. He had asshole written all over him. I knew it had to be the ex.

"Yeah?" he said.

"Is Marie home?"

"Who are you?"

"A friend. Name's Webb Pritchard."

"She's not here."

I knew she was.

"Are you sure?"

He gave me his best menacing look. I had a much better one waiting for him.

"I said she's not here. Now why don't you take your banjo"—he indicated the case at my feet—"and head on down the road, cowboy?"

"You know what?" I said, planting my boots and giving him my best menacing look, "I think you're her ex-husband, I think she's here, and for some reason you just don't want me to see her. But why don't we let her decide that?"

"Webb!"

Her voice came from somewhere within the house. That was it. I yanked open the screen door, breaking the latch, and pushed past the guy so fast he didn't have time to react. I ran into the kitchen. Marie was there, sitting huddled in a chair with her arms around Carla. I could see they were all right, but I could also see they were scared shitless.

"Marie!"

He hit me from behind and took me down. We crashed to the linoleum as the girls squealed and hightailed it out. I was littler and older than him but I was madder and smarter, so I knew this fight was gonna be very one-sided. I kicked him in the nuts with the toe of my boot and as he doubled over I flicked up my elbow and jammed it deep in his eye. That had a satisfactory effect. Finally, I wound up and hit him just as hard as I could right in the gut. He rolled over and lay there sucking air. I thought he might throw up. I got out of the way.

"When you get up, pal, get up slow," I said in my best Dirty Harry voice. But he didn't get up.

I stomped out of the kitchen and found Marie and Carla out in the front yard, looking like frightened deer, pressed up against the fence, ready to run if they had to.

"It's all right," I said, hoping like hell the bastard didn't come flying out the door with a butcher knife. Or worse.

"What's the deal?" I asked Marie, gently taking her by the shoulders. "He didn't hurt you, did he?"

"No," she said, her eyes flicking to the front door every few seconds. "He showed up late last night. Drunk. I let him sleep on the couch, and then this morning he just wouldn't leave. Said he's taking Carla. I wanted to call the sheriff but he wouldn't let me near the phone." She burst into tears.

I took her in my arms and held her tight, angling myself so I could see the door, too. Nothing yet. I must've hit him harder than I thought. Good.

"Go to the neighbor's," I told her. "Right now, both of you. Call the sheriff. I won't let him out of the house. Go!"

They rushed out the gate and ran next door. I watched until they got inside. Then I went back in.

He was such a wuss he was still sitting on the kitchen floor. Holding his gut. I could tell he was hung over.

"Fucking bitch," he said as I walked in. He looked up at me. "She's not worth it. I don't know why I even came down here."

"Why the hell *did* you come down here? I thought you guys're getting a divorce."

"We were. We are. I thought maybe Carla needed to see her dad."

"Oh, just a little weekend visit? Dad gets all drunk and mean and beats up on friends who come to call?"

"I'm sorry," he said, rising unsteadily to his feet. First person I'd ever hit who told me he was sorry. I tensed, ready to fight again.

But he stuck out his hand. "Mike Cook. I lost my temper."

We shook hands quick and tentative, like we didn't mean it.

"Well, Mike, as I was trying to tell you at the door, my name is Webb Pritchard and I'm a friend of Marie's. I've been out of town, and I was stopping by to say hello." I still wasn't entirely sure he wasn't gonna pop me again. I was itching to pop him again. "And though it's really none of your damn business, we're only friends, though I might like to get to know her better. At this point, it's up to her."

He nodded and sort of looked at the floor.

"I've been under a lot of stress lately," he said, running his hand over his unshaved jaw. For the first time, I suddenly noticed he smelled. "I own a small business up in Wyoming. Things aren't going too well."

"Sorry to hear that," I said, "but don't take it on the lady. Or your child. Or me."

He sighed. "Yeah."

"If I were you, I think I'd just head on back to Wyoming and arrange to see Carla some other time," I said. Christ, I sounded like Dr. Joyce Brothers or something. "What the hell," I said.

Right then the deputy sheriff walked in with his gun drawn. He pointed it at Mike Cook's head, then he saw me and started to point it my way.

"Hey, not me. Him," I said, backing away.

"Goddamn it, Pritchard, what the hell's going on here?" It was the same older guy who'd kept me locked up at the jail.

"Just a little domestic disturbance, Officer, no biggie," I said. "It's their deal, I just walked into the middle of it." Marie hovered at the door. "Ask her."

We got it sorted out eventually without anybody being arrested, or shot, and it ended with Mike Cook getting into his car and driving away. The sheriff stayed till he left.

"Why is it," he said to me as we all stood on the porch, "that you're always in the middle of shit in this town, Pritchard?"

"Don't worry," I told him, "I won't be here long. I'm leaving Telluride."

Marie looked at me. "What?"

"We need to talk," I said to her, and gave the sheriff a look.

So he left, and she put Carla to bed, and made us some lemonade, and sat in that wicker chair I had pictured her in so many times. And she cried for a while. I didn't say anything. She had a right to cry. It wasn't my place to interrupt.

Finally, eyes dry, many wadded Kleenexes at her feet, she said, "You're leaving?"

"I've got a job," I told her, leaning forward and taking her two hands in mine. "I know you think I'm a fly-by-night, and a nut case to boot, and I haven't shown you much since you met me. But things have happened. Some in the past, some in the present."

"In the past," she said, dropping her eyes. "I wanted to tell you—"

"Now listen," I said, interrupting. "Forget the past. This is the real deal. This is now. In two weeks, I start playing small bluegrass festivals back East. I met a man in Nashville—yes, I've been to Nashville—who signed me on. He's an agent. A talent booker. He heard me play at a club there and thought I could get a start."

I gently pulled her hands around and made her look me in the face. "I went over big, Marie. They loved me. I wrote some songs. I wrote one for you."

"You did?"

"Yes. It's the best one, too. Now listen. You don't have to decide now, but—"

"I can't go with you."

"Maybe not now, maybe not—"

"Webb. Get real. My home is here. My business. Carla's school. Her friends. We—"

"I love you, Marie."

She looked away real fast and I saw the tears welling up again. She bit her lip.

"I love you and I'm going to show you I'm not a dishwashing bum." I stood up and went to fetch Lil Darlin'. I thought, Everything will be all right if I can just sing her this song. That's how stupid I was.

I brought the banjo around and took her out of the case. Marie was looking, well, unreceptive. I put on my fingerpicks and moved over to the porch railing. There was a real pretty sunset just fading out behind me. If this didn't persuade her, nothing would.

> "Memories are silver, tarnished or bright,
>   The future, that story's untold.
>   Yesterday's dreams are tomorrow's dreams, too,
>   But times spent with you
>   Are true gold."

The last notes trailed off. It was as good as I'd ever done it. And why not?

"That's beautiful, Webb," she said softly. She had tucked her feet up under her and looked like a little girl. "You wrote that for me?"

"Sure did. It came to me on the wind."

Marie got out of the chair. She came over and put her arms around me and kissed me. It lasted a long time. She pulled back and ran her fingertips over my face.

"Nobody ever wrote me a song," she whispered.

I pulled her to me and we were hungry for each other, grabbing and gripping and pressing hard. She was squished into my banjo, the strings twanging dully against her clothing.

"Wait," I said, releasing her. I lifted Lil Darlin' over my head and set her down gently on the porch. Then I picked Marie up in my arms and carried her into the house. She felt lighter than the banjo. She nuzzled into my neck, not protesting a bit. Not sure where to go, I headed for a likely-looking door.

"Not there," she giggled. "Carla."

There was another door, ajar, and I took her in there. Laid her down on the big four-poster piled with quilts and pressed my body tenderly into hers. Her kisses were sweet and soft, her breathing quickened. Mine, too. We were in a hurry. In no time our clothes were gone, heaped in a pile on the floor, forgotten, useless. We burrowed under the covers, laughing like teenagers. We wanted to explore but there was no time. Not this time. Her sweet warmth took me in and filled me up, then drained it all away. I gave until there was nothing left. Just her body and mine, lying spoon-style as close as we could be.

"Good night, Marie," I whispered in the dark. Cuddled her close. Happy. My little bluegrass mama. We fell asleep.

In the morning, we tried to put off the inevitable through several cups of coffee, but finally we'd caffeined and danished ourselves into oblivion until there wasn't anything else to waste time with. We were sitting out there on the porch, her in her bathrobe and me just in my jeans, when she said she had something to show me.

"What's that?" I asked, getting a worried feeling in my gut.

"Just this," she said, reaching into the pocket of her bathrobe. She brought something out and tossed it over to me. It was a matchbook from the Plainsman Inn, Omaha, Nebraska. Circle-4865.

"You must have dropped that the last time you were here," she said, a small smile playing over her face. "You'd told me you'd been on the road with Hank Williams. In Omaha. I got curious. I called directory assistance and there is no such place. I called the Omaha Historical Society. They told me—"

"What?" I was on the edge of my chair.

"That it burned down in 1956."

I just looked at her, and her at me.

"You could've picked that up anywhere," she said, gazing into her coffee mug. "Antique store. Junk store. Whatever."

"I think I picked it up in the coffee shop," I said, "when Hank and me were having breakfast."

She nodded, pursing her lips. "You're scary sometimes."

I didn't say anything, and for several minutes we let that one ride. She finally took a deep breath and opened her mouth to say something, but I cut her off.

"I'll be leaving tomorrow," I said. "It's gonna take me a while to get all the way to Nashville in the whale. Then I have to get over to Winchester, Virginia, for this festival."

"Uh-huh."

"I'll sure miss that dishwashing job. But hey, it's something to fall back on."

"It sure is," she said, pushing a stray strand of hair out of her lovely face. "You have a skill you can carry the rest of your life."

"That's right. Absolutely."

I looked at her. "Marie—"

She shook her head violently. "Stop. We both know what the deal is. I can't just hop in that RV and go away. Not now, anyway. You go on out there and make a name for yourself. You can do it. Come back next summer and play Telluride."

"I'm not waiting until next summer to see you."

"Well. Good."

"Shit. I'm not sure what's gonna happen. I just know I love you, dammit, and now I have to go away and it sucks. Everything sucks."

"Everything does not suck. Have you told Red and Mattie?"

"Nope. I came straight here from the airport. I've got to go over there today. Somebody else I've got to see, too. A little unfinished business."

She stood up and stretched, her body showing through the thin robe. She turned me on. She saw me looking at her.

"Not now, hotshot. You're going to shower and get out of here and do whatever it is you need to do. I've got to get over to the store. I'll see you tonight."

"You mean I can finally shower here and not have to go to the campground?"

"Soap's extra."

"No prob."

Nothing more was said about the matchbook. She went back into the house and I thought, I'm the happiest man alive and my heart is breaking.

Red and Mattie first. I walked down to the bar, going in the front door this time. Red was on the phone. I didn't see Mattie or the boy. Red looked surprised to see me. He waved me to a bar stool.

"Back from Nashville already?" he said when he got off the phone.

"Yeah," I nodded, "and it looks like I'm out of here, Red. I'm gonna play some festivals back East."

"Ah, well, I expected something like that. You can't keep a good banjo picker down on the farm. Or a dishwasher. Sorry to lose you. Mattie and Mark'll miss you."

"You gave me a break when nobody else would," I said. "I appreciate that."

We heard the rear door slam. Mark came bounding into the bar. "Dad!"

Then he saw me and pulled up short. "Hey, Webb! You're back."

His mother came in behind him. "Well, look who's back."

"Hi, everybody," I said, reaching out to tousle Mark's hair. He looked embarrassed and jerked away. "Nashville turned out to be better than I expected. I'm gonna be leaving tomorrow; gonna be playing some festivals back East. I hate to go, but you know . . ."

Mattie laughed. "You just hate to leave this dishwashing job."

"That's right," I said. "Hard to leave the mighty Hobart for the bright lights of Music City. But that's how it is."

"You're having lunch with us," Mattie said firmly, and soon we were all at the front table by the big window, scarfing down burgers and fries. Mark inhaled his in about four seconds, a performance I'd seen before, and after he ran out Mattie took my hand in hers and squeezed it.

"Thank you, Webb."

"For what? I've been lousy kitchen help. And I've been blocking your alley for about three weeks."

"Mark. He looks up to you. Whatever you two talked about, he's, well, he's been better since you turned up. Can't you see?"

"Aw, he was just mixed up. I didn't do anything. Just told him you two loved him. Read him the riot act when he ran away."

Red swirled a fry in a puddle of ketchup. "Yeah, well, we thank you. But now that you're going . . ."

"Want a full-time job as a nanny?" Mattie joked.

"Tell you what," I said, "I'll take him on the road with me and return him to you after he makes it through adolescence. You ain't seen nuthin' yet."

"Deal," Red said, and we all laughed a little. I had to go. I gave Mattie a big hug, slapped Red on the shoulder and shook his hand, and looked around for Mark. But he was nowhere around.

"Tell him I said he's a good kid, and we'll meet again," I told them. Too bad he and I didn't really get to say good-bye. I somehow managed to get Orca out of the alley, after much delicate maneuvering and not-so-delicate language, and finally rolled her out onto Main Street. I felt free already.

In ten minutes I was in Sir Tex's driveway. There was his car. He must be home. I was eager to get rid of this platinum American Express card I hadn't earned. It was burning a hole in my wallet.

I rang the bell. No answer. Waited. Rang again. Nothing. Knocked. Knocked harder. Shit. I tried the doorknob, and to my surprise it turned easily. The heavy door swung open on silent hinges. I stepped into the foyer, my boots clattering on the marble floor.

"Tex?" My voice echoed through the house. I didn't hear a sound. That was strange. Where was the damn dog?

"Tex? It's Webb."

I walked into the house and went room to room. No sign of anybody. The kitchen looked untouched. So did the rest of the house. I hadn't checked the bedroom. It was upstairs, I guessed. I went up a spiral staircase and into a large white-carpeted suite. The king-size bed was mussed, slept in. So he had been here. I noticed a bathroom at the far end. The door was ajar.

I walked over and saw his feet before anything else. Bare.

"Holy Jesus!"

Sir Tex was lying on the bathroom floor, face down, next to the toilet. All he had on were some silk boxer shorts. I rolled him over. He wasn't breathing. His face was blue.

"Sir Tex! Tex! Can you hear me!"

Nothing. I ran for the phone.

24

One part of me was going, Oh shit, this is terrible, and another part was saying, Oh shit, I'm never gonna get out of this town. But I did what I had to do.

The paramedics came and loaded Sir Tex onto a stretcher and took him out of his big mountain house, helpless as a baby, with all kinds of tubes going in and out of everywhere. He wasn't dead yet, they said. Close. Downers and booze, most likely. The deputy sheriff showed up, too.

"Goddammit, Pritchard, I thought we were rid of you," he said, filling out his report in the kitchen. I gave him some coffee.

"Now, what exactly is your relationship to Mr. Sandhurst?" he asked, looking up from his clipboard, eyebrows raised.

"Not that," I said. And I told him why I had dropped by. On my way out of town. ON MY WAY OUT OF TOWN.

"Well, he has no relatives here, apparently they're all in England," the officer said. "We need somebody to take responsibility."

"Well, don't look at me."

"Can you stick around a day or so until he's out of the woods? If he dies, we need somebody to . . . handle things."

Shit. How could I go? I had planned on killing Sir Tex when I got back from Nashville, something about throwing poison darts at him, and now the sorry bastard had gone and nearly done the job himself.

If he didn't pull through, I'd still kill him. Did Telluride Hardware sell poison darts?

"The dog."

"What?" the sheriff asked.

"He's got a little dog. Horace. I don't know where he is."

The lawman brushed that off. "Oh. Well, listen, we've taken your friend down to the clinic, and if he's real bad they'll airlift him to the hospital in Montrose. We'll let you know."

"How? I live in my RV."

He looked exasperated. "OK. Be sure and come on by the clinic in the next couple hours. We need to stay in touch, Pritchard."

I sighed. He left. I ate some stale crackers I found in the cupboard. There wasn't anything to drink in the house except vodka and Bloody Mary mix, so I had some ice water and sat out on the deck for a while. Killing time. I fell asleep.

Something warm was in my hand. Something . . . yucky. I jerked awake. Horace was sitting there, licking my fingers.

"Now don't go thinkin' I'm your new boy," I said, pulling upright. "He's not dead yet."

The dog cocked his head and looked at me with his sad brown eyes. I hardened my jaw and put a mean glint in my eye.

"Don't pull that puppy shit," I said, staring him down. "You're not even cute. He's gonna be all right, OK? He's coming back." I reached down and stroked between his ears. He lay down at my feet and rested his head on my boot. Oh boy.

We stayed like that for a while longer and finally I stood up. "Horace," I said, "I'm going down to check on your master. I may not ever see you again. But it's been fun."

He followed me into the house and I made sure he had some water. There was a bag of Purina in the laundry room, so I gave him a bowl of that, too. Then I left, leaving the house unlocked. I'd have to tell the sheriff about that.

The doctor was down at the clinic. Today he had on a wetsuit. Must've been kayaking or something when they beeped him. His hair was still damp.

"Is he dead?" I asked. No point beating around the bush. I hadn't seen a morgue wagon outside.

"He'll make it," the doc said. "Barely. We pumped him out and got him stabilized. Looks like a massive dose of barbiturates mixed with

228

alcohol. A few more minutes and he would've died. Good thing you turned up when you did. Hey, how's the head?"

"Fine. Better. You have a way with a needle and thread, Doc. Can I see him?"

"Sure."

"Wait," I said, fishing out the American Express card.

"Oh, he has insurance."

"No, I want you to hang on to this and give it to him when he wakes up. It's his," I said.

He led me into a curtained cubicle down the hall. Sir Tex was lying there, still tethered to a million tubes running every which way. His color was normal, but frankly, he looked like shit.

"You look like shit," I whispered, leaning over him. "You've caused me a lot of trouble, too. When you get out of here I'm going to drop-kick you down the valley."

To my surprise, his eyes fluttered open. His parched lips tried to move.

"It's me. Webb," I said. "Look. You're gonna be OK. Why'd you go and do something stupid like that?"

He made a sort of bubbling noise. His eyelids raised to half-mast and gave up.

"Don't try to talk. Listen. I'm back from Nashville. I gave your American Express card to the doc for safekeeping. I put ten thousand on it. Just kidding. I got a gig, Tex. No thanks to you, as you well know, but I managed to play this club—not the Mockingbird—and this guy heard me and signed me up to play some bluegrass festivals. Back East. I'm leaving town. In fact, I was on my way out of town when I found you."

His eyes crinkled up. Was he trying to smile? Or was he about to puke?

"So that's the story. I went to Nashville on your dime, and I thank you for that. I'll pay you back when I'm rich and famous, like you said."

I reached out and squeezed his hand. "I fed Horace. He's OK. I've gotta go. I'll call you from . . . wherever."

It was after six. I drove over to Marie's. I found her in her living room, ironing in front of the TV.

"Oh my," she said, setting down the iron. "Look what I just did."

"What?"

"Look."

I came over. She pointed. Right there on the front of the blouse she'd been ironing was a little spider, squashed completely flat into the material, all his legs permanently pressed out in an eight-pointed starburst. Flat as a pancake.

"I ironed a spider!"

"You sure did. What do you think that signifies?"

"I don't know."

"Will he come out?"

We tried like hell to pry the little bugger off, but he wouldn't budge. He had become fused to the fabric.

"He didn't feel any pain," I volunteered. "That's what counts."

"This blouse is ruined," she said. "There's chicken for dinner."

The three of us, Marie, Carla and I, had a fine feast—almost as good as something Dot would cook, I thought—and then watched the Disney Channel until Carla went to bed. Then we switched to a cop show where people took their clothes off. They didn't let us watch anything like this in prison.

"This is about the most unrealistic show I've ever seen," I commented. We were sitting on the couch, holding hands. "But it's good."

Then came the news, then Letterman. We got through the monologue before Marie hit the remote and cut it off. We were both yawning.

"Bedtime for Bonzo," she said, standing up.

"I'm leaving first thing in the morning," I said, keeping our fingers entwined. "Do you know that?"

"Yes. I know that."

"Can I stay the night?"

"You may. Please."

We made love passionately. Afterward, we both cried a little.

"Marie, I'll be back," I said. "You can count on it."

She nuzzled closer.

"I love you," I whispered. We fell asleep.

The first shades of gray were just creeping into the dark room when I rose and dressed. Marie never stirred. She was a vision in that big four-poster, her hair spilling across the pillow and her arm like a shimmering brown waterfall. I felt like staying.

There was a doughnut in the fridge and I took it. Holding my boots in my hand, I tiptoed back into her room and looked at her one last time. I bent over her and brushed my lips against her forehead. She didn't move at all.

I knew I ought to just get the hell out of town before I had time to change my mind, but first I wanted to make one last visit to the spot in the woods. Where it all began. So I drove the RV down the hill and to the campground, parking on the edge as close as I could get. The western half of the sky still had stars. The eastern side was rapidly streaking to pink and gold. It was going to be a real pretty day.

I found the fire ring and the big log. I just stood there awhile, breathing in the fresh morning air and listening to the birds. Nothing like daybreak in the woods.

The sun broke over the edge of the trees and its hot fingers hit the back of my neck. A zillion new sunbeams sliced through the leaves like lasers. I turned around and its brilliance caught me full in the face. I reached up to shade my eyes.

Man, it was bright. Almost too bright. The sunrise burst in its full glory and filled the sky, filling me. A sunbeam seemed to pick me up and sweep me away. I was powerless. The light held steady, holding me firm, and set me down again. Then it cut off like somebody had hit a switch.

"What's your hurry, son?" Hank said. "I ain't through with you yet."

We were back in our room at the St. Regis Hotel in Nashville. Christ, I was still wearing the fancy duds I'd worn down to audition at the Ryman. The ones I'd had on at Castle Recording Studios. God, they were rank now. How many days had it been? I started stripping them off. I popped the snaps on the shirt and balled it up in my hand. I threw it out the window. Pulled off my pants and pitched 'em in a corner. I hated them now.

"You riled?" Hank asked. He was leaning against the bathroom doorjamb. Mr. Casual.

"Goddammit, Hank," I said. "Goddammit."

"Don't 'goddamn' me, boy. I'm helpin' ya."

"I'm sick of this shit," I said. "One second I'm enjoying the sunrise, feeling like a new man, and the next I'm yanked back here into the same old bullshit with you. When does it end?"

Hank smiled. "You'll get it."

"Get what?"

"Come on," he said. "We're goin' out on the town."

"You go. I'm staying here."

"I'm the one oughta be mad," he said, taking a stroll around the tiny room. "Here I am, showin' you the ropes, and you go off and try to get ahead of things and join the Opry. Ditch me when you think I'm not lookin'."

He stopped and stared me down with his feverish eyes. "I'm always lookin'. You don't be needin' to be lookin' over your shoulder, either, 'cause I'm right here," he said, tapping his temple. "Inside your head, Webb."

I hated him because he was absolutely right.

"I'm not going out with you."

"Suit yourself, then," Hank said, and walked out.

I was so pissed off that right then and there, I gathered up my things and checked out of the St. Regis. I guess I was leaving the Hayride. I wasn't sure. I knew I was leaving Hank. I just had to get out of there.

But after walking around downtown, I found out the only place I could afford was right down the block at the Drake, an even worse flophouse. Just my luck. Cripes. Too embarrassed to go back to the St. Regis, I paid the man four dollars and climbed the dark, dank stairwell to the second floor. It all smelled like piss and cigars. As I walked into my room, I could hear two people yelling at each other next door. Great.

"You never give me the money!" she hollered.

"And I ain't ever givin' it to ya, ya bitch!" he hollered back.

My life was shit.

I took a bath, which helped. At least now I didn't smell. It was a start. I put on fresh clothes and decided my new place was so depressing I had to go out. So I went out. I didn't even know what day it was, so I looked at a newspaper. Thursday. Two days after the Ryman? I'd been gone two days? Jesus, no wonder those clothes had reeked so bad.

I found myself in a little hole-in-the-wall bar called Babe's. Country on the jukebox. Lotta Hank, unfortunately. Everybody's favorite. Couldn't get away from the guy. I ordered a beer and drained it in two gulps. Asked for another. Sucked that right down and was halfway through my third when somebody slid onto the bar stool next to me and said, "Slow down, child. What's the rush?"

"Lula Mae!"

"The one and only."

"God, you're a sight for sore eyes."

She ordered herself a Coke, of all things, and looked me up and down.

"What the hell's the matter with you? You disappear for a couple days. Nobody could find you. You're not at the hotel. You're blowing this Hayride thing, Webb. Doc's fit to be tied. You on a bender or something?"

"No. I just had to get away for a while."

"Well, get back in the game. We've got trouble."

"It's not my problem." I finished the beer and was trying to signal the bartender for a fourth when Lula Mae grabbed my hand and slammed it down on the bar.

"Ouch."

"Listen. It's Nancy."

I sat up straight. "What?"

"She showed up tonight at the hotel, crying. Hub Jenkins tried to rape her."

"Oh my God." I started to get up.

"Sit down. She went out to his house for a rehearsal and he made her stay after the others had gone. Then he—"

"I'll kill him." Now I did get up. I threw some money down on the bar. Lula Mae grabbed on to my arm.

"Hold on. Don't be foolish. Nancy ran out and somehow got to a neighbor's. Hub lives way out in the country. She got into a corn patch and hid until Hub gave up. Then she called her pa and he came and got her."

"Muley didn't kill him?"

"I don't think she's told him the whole story. Gave him some blarney about not being ready to join Hub's band. But she told me."

"I'm going out there."

"How?"

"We'll . . . steal Hank's car."

"We? I'm not along for this escapade. Hub Jenkins keeps guns. He knows how to use 'em. Uh-uh."

"I need you to show me where he lives. I'm not afraid of that old man. Come on."

"I haven't got the sense God gave a headless chicken," she said, following me out of the bar.

We snuck around the back of the St. Regis. Hank had parked the Caddy in a real good spot for stealing it: the darkest corner of the lot. It only took me a couple of minutes to break in and hotwire it. I didn't spend four years behind bars for nothing.

"Where'd you learn to do that?" Lula Mae whispered as the engine coughed to life.

"Harvard," I replied, and rolled the big machine out into traffic. I prayed we wouldn't see Hank strolling along the sidewalk. That'd tear it. But we didn't. We somehow got out of the Nashville city limits in that boat without anybody spotting us. Lula Mae directed me onto a rural highway heading south, and I gunned it to eighty-five. The night air felt great whipping in the windows.

"Hey," I said, "let's forget Hub Jenkins and just keep goin'. You and me. We'll come up with an act. We'll live in Hank's car."

"How many beers did you have?"

We drove for twenty miles. I was having such a great time I almost forgot why I was out here. Until Lula Mae reminded me.

"She said Hub grabbed her and wouldn't let go. He bruised her arm. You oughta see it. Black and blue and yellow. Told her if she didn't do what he said she'd never make it in Nashville."

For some reason, I thought about the crip who came to steal my tools. I'm not really a violent man. At least, I don't think of myself that way. But what that guy did was wrong and he deserved to have his fucking kneecap blown away. I still wasn't sorry I did it. And I wasn't going to be sorry for whatever I was going to do to Mr. Hub Jenkins tonight.

"There." Lula Mae pointed at a county road sign coming up in the headlights. We were way out in the country now. "Turn right. Go about two miles. His place is on the left."

When we'd gone a little over a mile, I cut the lights and slowed to a crawl. The big Caddy purred along. Thank God she wasn't a rattletrap. It was awful quiet out here. Just crickets.

We saw the house. Lights were on. I pulled off the road and tried to wedge the Caddy behind some bushes in case a sheriff or somebody happened along and got suspicious. I popped the trunk and took out the tire iron. Lula Mae looked worried.

"You stay here," I said. "If I'm not back in a half hour, uh—I don't know. Lemme think."

"Bullshit!" she whispered. "If you think I'm staying out here while you go have all the fun, you're crazy. Let's go."

There was no stopping Lula Mae when she had an idea in her head. We tried to lay low and creep along through the field toward the house. There were muddy patches and we were both getting our shoes wet. Good, I thought. I hope he has white carpeting.

It wasn't hard getting up to the house. We skirted some gravel and stuck to the wet grass. I stepped in some dog shit and almost yelled a curse, but stopped myself in the nick of time. Oh man, if there's a dog around . . . But we didn't see or hear one. There was only one car in the driveway, an older Ford. We could hear a radio playing inside. Country music. With Lula Mae right behind me, I got under a window and as slowly as I could, raised up and peeked in through the white lace curtains.

Hub Jenkins was sitting in an easy chair, his back to us. He was drinking a bottle of beer, reading the newspaper and listening to the radio. Quite an idyllic little home scene. You bastard.

I motioned for Lula Mae to take a look. She did, and quickly bent back down. "What now?" she mouthed at me. I tapped the end of the tire iron in my palm and grinned. She frowned and shook her head.

That's when the dog barked.

"What is it, Lucy?" Hub said. Not breathing, I peeked again. The world's oldest, fattest dog had struggled to her feet and was starting to shuffle over to the window where I was. Holy shit.

"Hear something, girl?"

Now Hub turned in his chair. I ducked back down, fast.

I took Lula Mae's hand and we ran around to the other side of the house. Now the dog was barking to beat the band. Big, throaty, angry barks.

"What is it? Who's there?" Hub called. "Go find 'em, girl!"

We heard the front screen door open and the dog's toenails rattle on the porch. I wondered if we could outrun her. I didn't think so. We circled back around where we'd been, then came up near the porch again. Too late. Lucy was upon us. Barking, growling, snarling, the big black Lab had done her job. I turned around, raised up the tire iron and made a move toward her.

"I wouldn't do that, friend," Hub's voice said behind me on the

235

porch. "She may be old, but she's got you between a rock and a hard place. A very hard place, if you ask me."

I heard the sound of a shotgun shell being loaded.

"Turn around," Hub said. I did.

"Now drop that tire iron." I did.

"Put your hands up." I did.

"What the hell are you doing on my property, Pritchard? Who's that with you? Come on out of those shadows."

Lula Mae stepped out.

"What the— Lula Mae? Lula Mae Loudermilk?"

"Howdy, Hub."

"What in the hell is going on here?"

Neither of us said anything. The dog kept barking, circling. Hub seemed to have a handle on me being there, but Lula Mae's presence had thrown him. He kept looking at her, confused.

"If you put down that shotgun, we could talk," I finally said.

"We got nothing to talk about," Hub said. "You didn't pass the audition but that's no reason to come out to a man's house brandishing a tire iron. What were you gonna do? Kill me?"

"Let's talk," I said.

"Hub, put that gun down right now," Lula Mae said, taking a step toward him. "If you don't, I'm coming up there and taking it away from you."

"Lula Mae—"

"Right now, Hub. Put it down. And call off your dog."

He looked at me hard. Kept the gun leveled right at my gut. Lula Mae started toward the porch steps.

"Lula Mae—" he said. His eyes faltered.

The gun lowered.

"Put it down, Hub," she said firmly. She kept moving toward him. She reached the bottom step. He bent over and set it down.

I moved quick as a snake. I sprinted up the steps past Lula Mae, grabbed up the shotgun and pointed it right at Hub Jenkins' head.

"Now we'll talk," I said.

I moved him back into the living room and made him sit in his chair. Old Lucy, tired of barking, wandered in and plopped at his feet. Lula Mae stood with me.

"Will somebody please tell me what in tarnation this is about?" Hub asked. "Lula Mae, have you lost your mind?"

"Nobody's crazy here," I said. "I'll be more than happy to tell you what this is about. It's about Nancy Taggart."

His eyes flickered. "What about her?"

"You tried to rape her, you old dirtbag. They hang people for that," I said. "Capital punishment."

"That's not true."

"What? That you did it or that they hang people? Pick one."

"I never touched her."

"You're lying!" Lula Mae exclaimed. "I saw her bruises, Hub. You ought to be ashamed. I thought I knew you. I'm sorry I called you. An innocent girl like that. If I'd known—"

"We know what you did," I butted in. "Or what you tried to pull. It won't happen again. Will it?"

Hub looked miserable. He sure the hell should've. "No," he said.

"It doesn't end here," I said. "You don't think you're off the hook, do you?"

"I don't know what the hell you want," Hub said.

"Here's what the hell I want." I spelled it out for him.

"I can't do that!" Hub started to get up but I backed him down with the shotgun.

"Sure you can. If you don't"—I walked forward and pressed both barrels against Hub Jenkins' sweating forehead—"we'll make sure Nancy presses charges. Attempted rape. Assault. The Opry won't stand for that. Your career's in the toilet, pal." I laughed. "Course, that's if you live through what her dad'll do to you when he finds out. You ever met Muley Taggart?"

Hub Jenkins sat in his easy chair, getting smaller and smaller. Lula Mae and I began backing out of the room. I never took the gun off him.

"Nine o'clock. We'll be there," I said as we left the room.

Out in the yard, I fired the shotgun into the air. The blast was deafening.

"Come on!" I grabbed Lula Mae by the hand.

We started running. I pitched the shotgun into the cornfield. We didn't stop running until we got to the car.

25

Hank noticed the mud and straw stuck to his car, and the near-empty gas tank, and the missing tire iron. But he never said a word about it. He just walked around the Cadillac, chewing on a toothpick, working it around his mouth in that way he had, finally flicking it away and turning his back. I got the message.

Saturday night in Nashville in the fifties—a hot time in the old town tonight. Everything was open, and everything was hopping. Pretty girls everywhere you looked, dressed to kill. Big skirts and high heels and higher hairdos. Loud music pouring from every honky-tonk and bar. Streets full of people having a good time.

The Hayride was supposed to leave Monday for a swing through northern Alabama. I had stuck close to my room at the fabulous Drake, avoiding Doc in case he fired me. I was scheming to slip into the caravan with Hank and hope Doc didn't notice I was along until it was too late to kick my ass out.

But tonight I had plans. Nancy met me at eight o'clock at Babe's, the bar where Lula Mae had found me. We could hardly get in the door, the place was so packed.

"You ready?" I asked her. She looked great in a pale blue dress. No clodhoppers tonight.

"Yep."

I leaned over and hugged her, but she didn't know the real reason. I hugged her so tight she squealed.

"Stop it! You're messing up my hair."

"I can't help it."

I was thinking about her daughter, forty-three years later at the Station Inn. Telling me about Nancy's cancer.

"Nancy," I whispered in her ear, "I want you to know that I love you, and that I will never forget you. You're the best."

"What are you talking about?" She pulled away, laughing. I touched her hand. So soft.

"I mean it." I raised my voice above the din. "You're an angel."

A big lump was coming up my throat, but she started jitterbugging right there in the crowd and I had to laugh. I started jitterbugging, too, until I bumped a crewcut in an army uniform who gave me a dirty look. I settled down.

"You nervous?" I asked her.

"Yes. No. Yes."

"Don't be. It's gonna be great."

"Shouldn't we be leaving soon?" she asked.

I checked my watch, the heavy Benrus stemwinder that turned up on my wrist instead of my battery-powered Timex whenever I was back in the past. Eight-thirty.

"Let's go," I said.

We figured Hank would be at The Barrel, his favorite bar in Nashville. Sure enough, there he was, getting an early start on things, a girl on each arm and a big silly grin on his face. A scotch in front of him.

"Hey, Webb!" he shouted when he saw us come in the door. "C'mon over here and meet my friends."

"He's in fine shape," Nancy whispered.

"Don't worry," I said. "If anybody can do it, he can."

"Howdy, Hank," I slapped him on the back. "Hello, girls. I'm Webb, this is Nancy."

"Give this man a drink!" Hank brayed at the bartender. "The lady, too!"

"No thanks," I said, "we've gotta be somewhere. And so do you. Come quietly and there won't be any trouble," I added darkly.

"Whaddaya mean? I'm not going anywhere," Hank said, getting a tighter grip on each girl. "We just got here. Party's just startin'."

I leaned over and whispered in his ear. As I spoke, his mouth opened and his eyes got wide. Finally he shut his trap and released the girls. He scraped his skinny butt off the stool and slapped a ten-dollar bill on the bar.

"Gals, the man's right," he said. They both looked mad. "I'm awful sorry. I'll be back. Wait for me."

Out on the sidewalk, I checked my watch again. We had less than ten minutes.

"Come on," I said, breaking into a trot. Hank and Nancy followed.

We turned onto Fifth and ran into a solid wall of people. Saturday night at the Ryman was a total zoo, thousands of folks trying to pack into the auditorium for the Grand Ole Opry. The show had started over an hour ago, but the scene outside was still pandemonium.

"This way!" Hank shouted, and we ran around to the rear, to the stage door at the side where he and I had gone in before. Only this time, there were all kinds of people milling around, performers and stagehands and hangers-on. Everybody recognized Hank.

"Is that Hank Williams?"

"Look, it's Hank Williams!"

"Hey, it's Hank!"

"No. Where?"

The people parted like the Red Sea to let us through. Nancy and I sort of got lost in the crush, but we followed Hank's white cowboy hat bobbing along up ahead. We made it to the arched doorway and started up the steps. A man stopped us.

"Sorry," he said. "Performers only."

"We're with Hank Williams," I said. "He just went in."

"Sure you are," the guy said. "Everybody's with Hank Williams."

"Really," Nancy pleaded. "We were right behind him and we got pushed back."

It was clear the guy wasn't going to budge when the door banged open and Hank stuck his head out.

"Y'all comin'?"

I gave the guy a wink and we rushed up the steps. It was about two minutes to nine. We'd barely made it.

Backstage, people looked startled to see Hank. He wasn't welcome here; they'd kicked him off the year before. But all of a sudden here he was, and the performers all loved him, even if the management didn't. He was instantly swallowed up in a mass of well-wishers.

I felt a tap at my elbow. Lula Mae was there, holding out Nancy's fiddle in one hand and Hank's guitar in the other. Next to her, Dinger Purdy was holding out Lil Darlin'.

"Here ya go, Mr. Webb," the Opry janitor said with a grin. "Sure is good to see you and Hank again."

"Thanks, Dinger," I said. "Glad we could make it."

I kissed Lula Mae on the cheek. "Go give it to him."

She marched up to Hank, stuck the guitar out and said, "Knock 'em dead, hillbilly."

On stage, Hub Jenkins' segment was just beginning. He was decked out in a spangled sort of suit, wearing heavy pancake makeup and a toupee. I'd never bought any of his records and couldn't remember any songs he'd done. Whatever he was here, he'd faded right out during my lifetime. Just what he deserved.

He was finishing his big number when a very serious-looking man in a business suit, obviously not a performer, rushed up to Hank and began speaking in an agitated manner. I moved closer to hear better.

"Mr. Williams, I must ask you and your party to leave immediately," he said, looking askance at the mob of people who had glommed onto Hank. "You understand."

Hank just looked at him.

"Really, Mr. Williams, I cannot allow you to be here. You're no longer with the Opry. You understand."

Hank just looked at him.

Beads of sweat popped out on the guy's forehead. "Please, Mr. Williams. You understand. Don't you?"

I was hoping to stick around for the fireworks, but at that moment Hub Jenkins was saying out front, "Here's two young people I think you're going to like, let's give 'em a big hand, Webb and Nancy!"

Suddenly Nancy was beside me. Somebody, probably Lula Mae, nudged me and I found myself walking up to the microphone center stage at the Grand Ole Opry on a Saturday night. There were thousands of people at the Ryman, filling the balcony, packing the pews. The Holy Grail. I had made it.

I gave Nancy one reassuring nod. We only had one shot, so we did "True Gold." Her voice never sounded sweeter. My banjo never sounded truer. We chased each other around the harmonies and she lifted her fiddle line high into the clouds before dropping it back down low to glide under my drone string. We each took breaks, mine fast and furious and hers more fluid, letting the melody carry us to the top of the house. We sang the last chorus and closed out with a nice flourish. Nancy did her little two-step at the end and we were done.

God, maybe I should stay here, I thought as the crowd went wild, stamping their feet and whooping it up. This I could get used to. Millions had just heard us on the radio. The Hayride suddenly seemed very small.

Out of the corner of my eye I saw Hub Jenkins approaching, but I wasn't about to give up this microphone.

"Ladies and gentlemen," I said directly into the mike, "thank you very, very much. We sure do appreciate that nice welcome." Hub stopped in his tracks. "You're very kind. What a wonderful honor it is to be a guest on the Grand Ole Opry. Believe me, you have no idea."

The audience clapped. Hub musta been steaming but I just kept going.

"But right now, I want to introduce a very special guest. An old friend, you might say. Somebody who's been away for a long time. You all know him—Hank Williams!"

The place went berserk.

I had no idea if Hank was going to walk out onstage. For all I knew, the guy in the business suit had had him thrown out. I turned, and didn't see him. The noise in the Ryman threatened to blow the roof off. The crowd was on its feet, sounding like a hurricane at full bore. Nancy looked at me and raised her eyebrows.

Come on, Hank. Come on.

The stage was trembling from the racket. I was trembling, too. I looked out past the footlights and tried not to panic. This was bigger than the Super Bowl.

Like a primal force, a roar rumbled up from the center of the audience as Hank strolled out, casual as hell, nodding and smiling ever so slightly. He came up to us, doffed his hat to Nancy, shook my hand, and stood there as the old Ryman just went nuts.

I took Nancy's hand, we took a bow and ran off. This wasn't our moment.

Well, it took a good two minutes for things to calm down enough for him to say anything or play anything.

"Thank you, thank you," he finally said. All the lights went down except for a single spotlight on Hank. "Nice to be back," he said. "I missed y'all."

Pandemonium again. Another minute went by.

"Here's 'Jambalaya.' " He did that one, with Hub's band jumping in and backing him, and then he did "Lovesick Blues," which always rocked the house. I saw women weeping in the front row.

When he finished, he waited for the applause to die down, and said, "I owe somebody a debt here tonight. Without him, I wouldn't be here. Webb, come on back! Nancy, you too!"

We ran out, pulled into Hank's golden orbit, oblivious of whatever trouble we might be in later. Trouble would have to wait this time.

"How about 'Amazing Grace'?" he said to us.

Perfect.

Hank stood in the middle, Nancy and I on either side, the three of us joining hands.

The audience began to sing along. Thousands of them, standing and swaying in time to the music, communing in a moment of pure joy.

> "Amazing grace, how sweet the sound
> That saved a wretch like me
> I once was lost, but now am found,
> Was blind but now I see."

I could feel the energy pouring off the people out front as the entire Opry cast moved onstage to join us. Lula Mae came up beside me and took my free hand.

Hank leaned over to whisper something in my ear.

"You done fine, son. Good luck."

> "Through many dangers, toils and snares,
> I have already come.
> 'Tis grace hath brought me safe thus far
> And grace will lead me home."

I felt the spotlight growing hotter and hotter, blinding me, blotting out the audience and everything around me. Hank's hand was suddenly gone. Lula Mae was gone. Nancy was gone. My body was weightless. My feet lifted off the stage and I rose up to the top of the Ryman, the music falling away, fading, fading.

> "And grace will lead me home . . ."

243

Quiet. The brightness returned, my feet felt solid earth. I reached up to shield my eyes.

Sunrise.

I was back in the woods. Only a moment had passed. A single bird chirped. Then all his buddies chimed in. The sun broke over the tops of the trees and spread its glorious light. It was time to go.

I walked back to the RV and got in, arranging the things I'd need. Kleenex, Cokes, sunglasses, wet wipes, cough drops, tapes. Nashville was a long way away. I pulled Orca out of the campground and swung her onto the main highway. It only took a minute or two to get through metropolitan downtown Telluride. I didn't even look at the place as I passed through. Kept my blinders on, staring dead ahead.

Maybe I could stop at Dot's for lunch. She'd have something good. I could count on it.

The RV chugged up the valley, the town dropping out of sight in my rearview mirror. I dug around till I found the right tape. There it was. I popped it in. Adjusted the volume. Sang along at the top of my lungs.

> "Take me back to the place
> Where I first saw the light,
> To the sunny sweet south, take me home.
> Where the mockingbirds sang me to sleep in the night
> Oh why was I tempted to roam?"

Epilogue

Two years later, I happened to be in Nashville and decided to go revisit the Ryman. See if any of that magic hillbilly dust, as Emmylou Harris has called it, still floated in the air.

The place had been restored as a shrine and museum. Sometimes it was still booked for shows, but they were special events now, not regular affairs. I bought a ticket and went in, roaming around with tourists off the bus. There were plaques and old photos and stage costumes under glass. One of Hank's suits was there.

I went down and sat in a pew and looked at the stage. Remembering. Thinking how loud it was that night at the Opry. Ungodly loud.

A man got up and gave a talk on the history of the Ryman, his voice bouncing around the nearly empty auditorium. It was dark and cool and air-conditioned, not at all like the hot, sweaty nights Hank had known.

After the talk, the man said we could wander around, so I did. When nobody was looking, I snuck backstage. Things had changed. They'd redone the bathrooms and dressing rooms and opened it up some. Put in tons of electronics. I guess it was better now. I'd have to bring Marie here one day and try to tell her how it was. But you really had to be there to know.

The old stage door hadn't changed. It was still the same, the stone steps curving down to the alley under that gothic archway.

I heard the sweep of a broom. An old man came down the hallway, working methodically, swish swish, swish swish. He wore overalls. He must've been close to eighty.

"Dinger?"

He looked up. His eyes were sharp.

"What?"

"Dinger Purdy? My God, is that you?"

He leaned on his broom and gave me a good look.

"Webb! Good God Almighty, it's Webb Pritchard! Why, you haven't aged a day!"

I reached out and squeezed his bony old shoulder. "How are you, Dinger?"

"Well, I'm still here, ain't I?"

"That you are. You look well."

"My arthritis acts up, and my gout . . . Wait. I've got something for you."

"What's that?"

"Come here."

He put down his broom and shuffled off into some dark recess. He went down some beat-up stairs you'd never know were there. They hadn't done any renovating back here. We were somewhere off under the stage. The ceiling was so low I had to stoop. He yanked on a chain overhead and a light bulb snapped on.

"Look here," the old man said. He reached up and tapped a loose brick. Sprinkles of mortar sifted down.

"What is it, Dinger?"

"See for yourself."

I touched the brick. It was so loose it moved under the lightest touch. I grabbed hold of its rough edges and began working it out. It only took a minute. I held the brick in my hand.

"So?" I said.

"Look in there. See what you find."

My hand poked into the hole. My fingers felt around in the dust. There was a piece of paper. I pulled it out.

It was yellowed and crumbling with age. I unfolded it carefully.

"See? He left it for you," Dinger said. "I never knew if you'd come back to get it, but he said you would."

On the paper in a familiar hand was written, "Dear Webb, I always though 'True Gold' was as good as 'Carry Me Back.' Hell, it was better. Hank."

I had to laugh. He was right, as usual.